A Touch Too Much

by

Alexandria May Ausman

Book cover illustration by Alexandria May Ausman
Editor: Jon M. Ausman

Library of Congress Control Number: 2025916433

ISBN: 978-1-963335-51-4 (ebook)
ISBN: 978-1-963335-49-1 (paperback)

Published By:
Ausman & Cousins LLC
1700 North Monroe Street
Suite 11, Box 284
Tallahassee, Florida 32303-0501

For author interviews: ausman@embarqmail.com

Das Kaiser Haus Series

The Rise of the Priceless (Chapters 1 to 10)
Metal Illness (Chapters 11 to 19)
Jonas the Vampire (Chapters 20 to 29)
Prince of the Elders (Chapters 30 to 40)
Leo's Lamb (Chapters 41 to 50)
Mastermind Malfred (Chapters 51 to 58)
Priceless Lost (Chapters 59 to 67)
Broken Silver (Chapters 68 to 74)

The Collar King Series

Return to Das Kaiser Haus (Chapters 1 to 7)
Felicity's Child (Chapters 8 to 14)
Tears of the Violin (Chapters 15 to 22)
The Golden Collar (Chapters 23 to 30)
Rise of the Mortar King (Chapters 31 to 38)
Prisoner of the Stone Palace (Chapters 39 to 46)
Mortar Transformation (Chapters 47 to 54)
Taube Returns (Chapters 55 to 62)
Chocolate Dreams (Chapters 63 to 70)
Pocket Soup (Chapters 71 to 78)
Lucus's Revenge (Chapters 79 to 86)
Night of the Stasi (Chapter 87 to 94)
Revenge of the Mortar King (Chapter 95 to 102)

The Most Brutal Man in Europe Series

Claus's Revelations (Chapters 1 to 8)
Priceless Changes (Chapters 9 to 16)
Silver Well (Chapters 17 to 24)
Book Four (Coming soon)

The Psycho Series

Cemetery Kid Redux (Chapters 1 to 20)
Stop Calling Me Psycho (Chapters 21 to 33)
Motor-Psycho (Chapters 34 to 44)
Delusion of the Collar and the Key (Chapters 45 to 53)
Brutality's Prisoner (Chapters 54 to 64)
Aesthetic Akathisia (Chapters 65 to 74)
Metallic Burden (Chapters 75 to 83)

27 Masters Series

Anita the Benevolent (Chapters 1 to 7)
The Beast and the Witch (Chapters 8 to 16)
High Priestess of Schizophrenia (Chapters 17 to 24)

Stand Alone Books

Book Eight Characters: A Touch Too Much

Angie: a former Master
Betty: spouse of Charlie
Boyd: a deputy sheriff
Carla: spouse of Dennis
Cathy: a deputy sheriff, dispatcher
Charlie: a law officer in next county over
Christian Axel: secret husband of Psycho/Rachel, trainer and original Master
Christine: the second Mistress, a sadistic beast
Christy: a friend of Stacey
Cindy Slater: a town slut
CJ: college LGBT leader
Debbie: Psycho's psychopathic and sadistic mother
DeGrove, Doctor: a misogynist college department chair
Dennis: the county sheriff
Diana: CJ's partner
Dude: a command hallucination, an aggressive anger shard of Psycho
Eva: Cindy's mother
Fisher: a child rapist
Frankie: a DCFS caseworker
Ginger: a FemDom, Mistress Ten
Gothic Barbie: a vengeful, sexually sadist Dominant shard
James: an abandoned, neglected child
Jane: DCFS employee under Ruth
Javier: an alleged repeat offender
Johnny: Nikki's foster child
Jon Ausman: the current Keyholder

Johnathan Porter: an accidental friend, a former underwear model

Joseph: a foster parent

Julie: a previous sadistic Mistress who fled the law

Keith: a deputy sheriff, jailer

Kick Start: a high school classmate and friend of Psycho

Kirstin: Linda's new lover

Linda: a deputy sheriff

Livevil: a shard of Psycho

Looper: a disembodied voice, Psycho's narrative hallucination

Maddy: a child who was raped and murdered, Angie's best friend

Margaret: a counselor

Mark: a deputy sheriff

Matthew: a deceased submissive

Mickey: Connie's deceased former boyfriend

Mitchell: Timmy's cousin

Nikki Pool: a neglectful mother

Nora: a DHS employee

Paul: Maddy's older brother

Psycho: a schizophrenic trying to survive

Psycho Tron: a shard of Psycho

Rachel: Psycho's birth name, Simon is Rachel

Randall: a deputy sheriff, a bull

Sarah: Nikki's foster child

Schmitz: a crooked law officer

Seine: a fire dog

Sheryl: a DCFS manager, the 17th Master

Simon Brag: a command hallucination shard of Psycho, her lost inner self

Smith, Doctor: a college President
Suzy: Maddy's sister
Tammy: Master Eight, an interim
The Chose One: a shard of Psycho
Theresa Sorrall: a foster mother
Timmy: Psycho's spouse
Trenton: a deputy sheriff
Wilkinson, Preacher: a local minister
Will: a deputy sheriff

Preface

Finally the World Goth Queen has been born. This early version of the insane Matron of Gothdom is not quite the same gothic model you all came to know and love. However, this is where the delusion first began. Oh, you did not know she was a symptom of schizophrenia created by intense stress and rape? Well, aren't you all so lucky you stuck with this story. A secret is about to be revealed about this most enigmatic shard of a shattered mind.

Psycho Tron, and The Chosen One have taken on a heavy load. Together they have managed the unmanageable. Yet, even with the two working days and nights, still more is required of the demonic duo.

PC and Fax have offered the ailing schizophrenic some comfort from the stresses of pent up emotions. Simon offers sound advice, even if we cannot take it. This offset helps to keep Psycho from falling in the abyss of pure insanity or to push her right in faster.

Finding an outlet is paramount to survival in these challenging times. From the depths of our darkest places will rise a shard that is older than all the rest. She is beautiful, seductive, and ready to make even your most fearful nightmares come true. The blue-eyed devil will love you, fool you, blind you, capture you and enjoy your screams. Her affections come with a price so high, she could not even afford it.

So, ready to tie up those loose ends, errrr, get on with our story? Go ahead and grab that black bag to your left. Don't worry about what is inside. We will show you soon enough. You will feel the gory, errr, glory of justice in this book. Don't worry we have this beaten, errr, under control. Just sing it with me. I am a Barbie girl, in a Barbie world. Life is fantastic, wrapped in plastic. Come on Barbie, Let's Go Party.

Chapter 58: The Gothic Barbie; a Criss-Cross Delusion
Master Boyd and Interim Master Sheryl

"You see Master, I am only loving you. Isn't that what you wanted? Me to love you? This is how I was taught to love. My love for you is so deep. No need for tears. However, I do appreciate them. Turns me on. Now, tell me you love me like you mean it."
--The Gothic Barbie to Master Boyd, May 1998

Master Boyd held me tightly while I vomited till only air came forth. I leaned back into his chest feeling faint after the visceral exercise.

He looked at Master Sheryl angrily. "See what you are doing. Psycho is sick. Her weight is unacceptable. She is stressed to the gills over this shit job you are forcing her to do. You should be ashamed of yourself. I am taking her home. If you get in my way, I will have your ass under the jail," he growled.

Master Sheryl put her hands on her hips appearing just as angry. "You touch her I will call you in for kidnapping. Psycho doesn't want to go with you creep. I know who you are. You may fool everyone else, but I see right through you."

Master Boyd laughed smugly. "Oh? Who am I, Sheryl? This girl is my fiancé and my ward. Go ahead and call in a kidnapping. You are the kidnapper here. Psycho baby, just calm down. I will look after you." He lifted me like a child from the chair carrying me towards the door of the office.

Master Sheryl yelled out from behind us. "You stop right there. I swear I will fucking have your balls for this asshole. Put her down. I am calling the cops." She picked up the phone to make her call.

Master Boyd pushed open the door with his foot chuckling. "Stupid bitch. I am the cops."

I just whimpered more confused and afraid than ever. Simon said to trust Master Boyd. He said we are very sick, but we hate this man. He is dangerous. The world outside blazed into my eyes forcing them closed. My brother the sun punished me for hiding with my father darkness too long from his loving smile.

Master Boyd pushed my unit into the passenger's seat belting me in very gently. He spoke calmly assuring me all would be fine. I swooned and felt nauseous. The child was coming. I felt the labor contractions beginning in my abdomen. This was not possible. I was sterilized, and robotic. On top of that I had just given birth to The Chosen One only a week before. How could there be another full-term pregnancy so close to the other one? Maybe Psycho Tron was different. Machines can move and think faster than humans. Maybe they can create new life faster too?

I sat there in total psychotic confusion trying to justify the feeling of birthing a baby. I knew I could feel it. It couldn't be real. Yet, it was happening. The rhythmic pain of creation moved to my head as it had before. I noticed the contractions were now regular and growing closer in time.

The time was coming. I was about to become a mother once again and Master Boyd was the father.

He got into the vehicle looking at me appearing afraid. "Psycho, baby can you hear me? Honey you are not moving again. I think you are going catatonic. I will take you to the ER and the doctors at home will fix this. Just hang in there for me. I know you are scared, but I won't leave your side. I won't let anyone hurt you."

I sat there in my trance hearing his words. I could feel them like small stones hitting my force shield while the motor of his car whirled to a start. The movement of our travel to Wheatly lulled me into comfort. I needed to relax. Giving birth is very tiring for a mother to be. I would need to save my strength to cut the cord and free the child from the unit.

We had only gone a few miles when a squad car pulled us over. A police officer walked to the window appearing upset. Master Boyd knew the man. My Master was still in his uniform from his shift that night. It was a strange sight to watch a cop pull over a cop. They both laughed at the oddness of this situation.

They chatted about my Master's right to take possession of my unit from Master Sheryl. He showed the officer papers that said he owned me. The police officer chuckled as Master Boyd and he discussed how histrionic Master Sheryl tended to be. I couldn't say anything. My throat was paralyzed.

I heard the man congratulate Master Boyd in 'capturing one fine looking woman' for his pleasures. I wanted to scream for help, beg for mercy, but all I could do is watch the cop while he stared at me.

I recognized that look he was giving me. Master Boyd had that same expression before he took sexual advantage of my unit. It frightened me a great deal. My eyes darted nervously to Master Boyd relieved he was there for once. I knew if I had been alone, this creature would do more than gaze with lust.

The police officer allowed Master Boyd free passage out of his county into his own only five miles away. He went back to his car while we got back on the road. Master Sheryl had been unsuccessful in stopping me from being taken by force back to my Master's home base.

I shuddered realizing Master Boyd had always been the more powerful of the two. Simon had been right. My Master could do whatever he wanted when he wanted. He had merely been allowing me to stay with Master Sheryl. My blood ran cold with this most frightening discovery. I believed I was no longer safe from his unholy touch no matter how far I fled.

Master Boyd rushed me to the ER in Wheatly. He apparently expected the attending doctors would take me into custody. He even offered to sign papers to have me committed, until they informed him there were no bed available. I would have to be taken the sixty miles and placed in the Snake Pit if he wanted me to receive inpatient treatment. This caused my Master to back off the idea of hospitalization. He feared the Pit as much as I did. He too knew the reputation. The idea his prize would be handed off to some other sexual predator rather than himself chilled him to the bone.

Instead, I was shot up with Lorazepam and another heavy sedative. This calmed my catatonic behavior within about twenty minutes. I was able to move and respond, but now I was higher than a kite. Master Boyd took me to 'our home' after only a few short hours in the care of the physicians. Once again, my serious psychotic symptoms had been ignored and swept under the rug. This time, just as in times past, the result would be devastating. At least for my Master…

Master Boyd aided me through the door of the house. I had to lean on him to walk because of the sedatives. He took me straight to his bed where he laid me down. My clothing was removed but I was hardly aware of it. I could hear him telling me to rest but his was voice coming from far away. The world was rapidly dissolving into a void of peace. I felt like I was floating away, but then again, something seemed to be pinning me to the spot.

I opened my eyes to see Master Boyd's face looking into mine. He was sweating and panting. Confusion to this odd vision caused me to try to get up. I thought he was wanting my attention for service. It was only then that I realized he was taking his service already. My Master pushed my overmedicated unit back onto the pillow without much effort.

I whimpered in fear as he continued to take advantage of my helpless state without mercy. His excitement was evident. Master Boyd was rapidly increasing the harshness in his thrusting with a cruel disregard for my comfort or interest. I could do nothing to stop him but lay there and take it.

As he violently engaged my unit with carnal congress, I recalled his initial forced attack. His partaking of my sexual service was very similar. It was with great horror I understood My Master was turned on to frenzy status when I was unable to fight back. It was lost on me why he had stopped assaulting me like this over the last few weeks – he had become a bit gentler about it – but one thing was clear; the kinder Master Boyd would never last. The look of extreme pleasure on his face told me this was what he desired most. Rape was his aphrodisiac.

I was in a great deal of pain as he began to reach his apex of brutality. I couldn't help but feel very lost. I assumed he thought me too fucked up to be aware of his foul betrayal. However, just like when catatonic, the sedation could not prevent my experience of indignity and terror as his helpless victim.

I closed my eyes as he climaxed trying to block off the experience of his spasm of lust. It took all I had to fight back the undertow of despair when I was unsuccessful. Nothing could stop my nerve endings from reporting the physical sensations of his rape. My mind, which had settled down after the shots from the ER, started to ache once more.

The delusions of birthing shards were no doubt being fueled by my knowledge of Master Boyd's sexual predator nature. Master Boyd's obsessive love for me was only a cover to excuse his need to exert complete power over one too weak to stop him.

My perception that the pieces of my personality were children, conceived by my Master's cruel rapes, was a defense mechanism out of control. I was, as usual, telling myself lies to hide the truth of this soul crushing exploitation from my consciousness. The betrayal by Boyd, at one time my long trusted friend and savior (and his monstrous secret), was simply too much for me to bear. The agony of knowing the truth of his intent the entire time was literally tearing me apart.

I watched him get off my unit. He gently pulled the covers up over me then kiss me on the forehead softly. My Master appeared adoring and loving even brushing some of my wig hair from my eyes. One would never guess he had just used such brutality in his non-consensual attack. I was bleeding onto his sheets.

The thought that I was nothing more than his toy crossed my mind. Master Boyd would use me for his enjoyment while not caring if his play was too rough. He was possessive of his doll and he would not allow anyone else to even look at it. He wanted me to do as I was told by him. My Master told me I was not allowed to speak until told to or to open my mouth unless it was to take in his lustful advances.

I had followed his directives to the letter, becoming the Psycho Tron. Unfeeling, uncaring, robotic and compliant. Yet still he insisted on forcing damage on my unit during sex when it was not necessary. I had failed to meet his needs or this behavior would have ceased. The Psycho Tron was just not the right expression. I had to find one more compatible with his extreme wantonness.

My mind recalled Johnathan's statement that Barbie was his first love, the perfect woman. She is made of plastic, fake smile, big boobs, tiny waist, and completely there for your command. Johnathan told me Barbie is every boy's dream come true. You can cut and dye her hair, keep her naked or dress her how you want. Even raping or ripping off her arms never seem to dash her happy expression. Barbie is there to make your fantasies real. She is always pleased to serve you. Barbie is the symbol of feminine sexuality and seduction.

Johnathan called me his Gothic Barbie. Master Boyd was jealous of my ex-model lover. He wanted what he had enjoyed with me. I suddenly realized this was the answer to my puzzle. Barbie would please Master Boyd so completely, he would never feel the need to injure me again.

I felt the contractions in my head growing closer still as the Barbie shard prepared for her entry into the world. I took short, shallow breaths trying to control the aching. Then the trance set in just as it had with the creation of the Chosen One. I saw the Gothic Barbie walk out of the static, ready to seduce our Master without mercy. She was ready to serve his every dark desire and make his dreams of our twisted love come true.

Gothic Barbie was composed of all that was left of the original us. She was the core from which all of us were born. This was our reflection that was shattered when Debbie fed us the poisoned oatmeal. This delusional shard was passionate, seductive, and creative.

However wonderful she may appear to be, she was dangerous. When her adoration was mistreated, she could be cold, brutal and sadistic beyond imagination. This chaotic duel nature came from the long history of training as a sexual sadist. The strong loving heart of the Gothic Barbie had refused to embrace this fate. Her denial of Master Debbie's commands had resulted in a punishment so extreme. She had been broken into a thousand pieces and our Simon had been exiled for life.

Now, after lying dormant for many years, deep within I felt her mysterious presence rising. I gasped at the pain while she forced her way to my consciousness. My nose began to bleed from the trauma of her birthing. I sat up in the bed while the blanket was stained with the crimson flow. My mind split into two when the mother of us all burst forth into the world of the real.

Despite my intense fear of her I understood she was called forward to aid our unit of measurement. Gothic Barbie was just the weapon we required in the battle for our survival among all this environmental chaos. Master Boyd's inhuman treatment had awoken the sleeping demoness. She would give him what he wanted. In time, he would realize one should be careful what they wish for.

The Gothic Barbie looked about the room with eyes that had been closed for many years. The colors were brighter; the sounds louder than she had recalled them to be. A mirrored dresser reflected the image of a thin, black haired, blue eyed schizophrenic with a nosebleed. She smiled at it. It smiled back with a look of satisfaction. She had left the world being driven within after losing her battle with Master Debbie. This time, she determined she would be the victor. Master Boyd the novice sexual sadist stood no chance against the seasoned Master sexually sadistic Gothic Barbie.

Gothic Barbie chuckled. "Let the games begin," she said out loud to Simon who had just entered the room.

His eyes went wide in shock. "Holy shit. This is not happening. You go back to sleep. This will never do."

The Gothic Barbie looked at him with disgust. "Ah, there you are Rachel. What? No loving welcome for your old self, hmm? Didn't you miss me? I sure as hell missed you. We all have. Come here and give us a hug. I want to feel us together as one. Remember how wonderful that used to be?"

Simon backed away. "Keep your fucking hands off me. I am not called Rachel anymore and you know it. I never liked you and you hated me. Why are you here? We have this handled. We don't need you."

She laughed wickedly. "Do you have it under control? Are you Rachel? I think not. Seems to me, this unit is shattering fast. This is your fault and you know it. You didn't take control. As usual you are useless. I will fix this problem. Now, stay out of my way or so help me, I will make you sorry for it," the Gothic Barbie growled.

Simon backed away further from us. "Please go back to sleep. You will only make this worse. If you do what I know you are planning then he will kill the unit. Then you will die too, you know, not just me and everyone else."

Gothic Barbie hissed, "Shut up pussy. No one is going to die unless I let you keep up our useless pandering to this worthless Master. He needs to be taught a lesson about pain. You are not the one to do that. You can't even get back inside fool. I am still in here. Get out of my sight Rachel, you are pissing me off and cramping my style. I need a shower, then I will get to my job. Equal service for equal service. Isn't that the game we are supposed to be playing? Well I am here to level out this playground bitch." She got out of the bed headed for the bathroom pushing Simon out of her way.

"Fucking bitch. You are going to get us killed. Fuck me," Simon yelled after the Gothic Barbie.

She turned looking back at the frightened Simon. "Ah, don't you wish someone could fuck you little Rachel. But alas, you are stuck forever watching but never getting to play. Run along now and attend your trains. Isn't that what you do now? You're a drunken railroad man? What a joke." Gothic Barbie closed the bathroom door on Simon cackling demonically at her cruel statement.

Master Boyd heard the water of my shower. He came running worried someone else had somehow got into the house.

"Psycho? Is that you baby? You're taking a shower?" He stood there looking at me through the shower curtain appearing stunned.

I smiled then pulled back the translucent barrier. "Why yes, it is me. You want to join me? You can come help me get squeaky clean, I mean moaning clean. Why don't you shuck off those clothes and bring your sexy self over here? I can wash your back, while you scrub mine," I cooed while I winked motioning him to join me.

His mouth nearly hit the floor in surprise at my offer to voluntarily engage in a sexually charged activity. "Uhm, okay? Are you feeling alright baby?" He began pulling off his clothing as he prepared to enter the bathtub as I had requested.

I smiled seductively. "Oh, I am feeling amazing lover. Don't take my word for it. Come feel for yourself," I moaned out.

Master Boyd smiled appearing thrilled at his sudden change in luck. It seemed, the woman he had sexually desired so much it had driven him to rape, desired him back. My Master could barely contain his excitement at this unexpected invitation to engage me as a willing and interested partner. He jumped into the shower still throwing off articles of his police uniform. Half of his garb now laid wet sprawled across the bathroom furnishings. He tossed then without thought of anything but of what was waiting for him behind the rubberized curtain.

As he climbed into the shower, I reached around his waist kissing him wantonly pulling him close. He yelped in shock of my affection's aggressiveness. I moved my kissing to his chest biting lightly as I felt him shudder in passion. He moaned out in pure pleasure when I reached down and began to manually stimulate his already very ready manhood. I ignored the rivets of water pouring down on my head while I dropped to my knees without being command to do so.

Immediately, I began to employ my services of oral sex using techniques he had never been privy to before. I was very experienced in this art but had refused to grant the full extent of my talents to him before. This was due to his chronic cruelty towards my person. This time, I held nothing back.

Alternatively using my tongue and velvet throat I took him to the brink several times. I could feel his unit tense while he fought back the urge to grab my head in interference. Each time he started to try to get involved, I would caution him to allow me to proceed unhampered. I would then go back to the task. This reminded him I was well versed in stimulating his drives.

Playfully I pulled him back and forth like a puppet on my string. I kept my awareness of his closeness to completion. When I felt him ready to go, I would change my stroke to prevent him to reach his apex. I continued to keep him a prisoner of my foreplay until he was begging for release like a whining child. At first, I ignored his pleas. I patiently worked on him till he was near madness with desire to climax. Only then did I end my sensual torture still holding him captive in my embrace.

I stood up slowly nipping his unit until I reached his chest once more. Then I pulled his face to mine him kissing him deeply.

Now sure he was ready I whispered in his ear, "I want you to take me Master. I beg you to find your release the way a man is supposed to have a lover." He quivered in pure fervor as I turned around offering him his opportunity to mount.

My Master didn't waste any time. He took ahold of my shoulders and entered me from behind thrusting wildly. He had become nearly insane with sexual frustration from my tormenting blow job. I moaned and yelled out passionately calling his name loudly. This nearly sent him over the edge.

I could feel his manhood vibrate ready to crest. I realized his performance would end before it barely began if I did nothing to stop my over stimulated Master. I pulled away from his thrust while demanding he hold his passion back and await my own.

My sudden controlling behavior cooled his appetite as I was now aware it would. My Master feared controlling women and this fact thwarted his rapid release. He began to back off his mount seeming confused by my giving him orders instead of the other way around. That made me giggle to myself. He didn't like it when he was told what to do. That was too bad for him. I knew him much better than he had bothered to get to know me. I was aware of how to get him back on track.

I prevented his withdrawal from the mating by moving backward with him. Just as he was about to complain of my nearly crossing his line of telling him no, I distracted him by moaning loudly that his very presence was making me hot and that I needed him to fuck me harder. I pushed into his still engaged unit demanding he do it now.

His interest grew strong upon hearing those words come spontaneously without his having to force them from me as he always had to. He re-engaged. This time his attention was much more vigorous than before.

In only moments, my Master completely forgot what had upset him. Briefly, it had occurred to him who was really in command this time during the sexual engagement, but now he had lost his head to unbridled thrusting. The Gothic Barbie was literally testing her ability to Master this Master. She found his weak spots without even trying.

Master Boyd was swept away by the waves of pure bliss. He was helpless to stop following my commands both from my continued encouragement of his prowess and by the sensation of what he perceived was an extremely interested partner. His moaning became descriptions of his affections for my unit. I responded to him with crude reports of my desires for his lust.

Our lovemaking rapidly went into a fevered pitch. It didn't take long for it to explode into orgasm in unison. We both cried out loudly in pleasure of our shared zenith. Master Boyd groaned out how much he loved me while releasing. His climax was strongly encouraged by the contracting of my vaginal walls.

My Master gasped holding still as he enjoyed the sensation of my rapture. There was no longer any doubt in his mind he had achieved my sexual interest in him at last. My internal spasms indicated he had pleased me well. This time, I had not treated the act like merely a service. I had offered it appearing to want to be with him intimately.

He fell forward panting and spent. I held his weight purring that I enjoyed his congress a great deal. My Master slowly disengaged my unit. He grabbed my right upper arm spinning me to face him. He then pulled me close to kiss my mouth with gentle affection. He ran his hands across my breasts, then fondled my backside pulling me closer still.

Master Boyd looked at me his eyes glazed with satisfaction. "That was, it was just everything I ever dreamed of. You do want me. That means you do love me. I never thought you ever would, but you do, don't you?" He was searching my soul for his answer.

I smiled seductively. "I do want and love you Master just like you asked me to. You now belong to me, just as you believe I belong to you."

He closed his eyes letting out his breath in pure relief. "Ah, I have waited so long to hear you say those words to me. I do love you Psycho. You are right. I only ever wanted you to truly love me the way I love you. I can't live without you. You have made me so happy. You can't even imagine. I just thought I had ruined it by, oh, it doesn't matter anymore. I have your love at last and you will always have me forever." He stroked my cheek looking at me with tears of gratitude welling in his eyes.

I chuckled wickedly. "Oh, that is correct Master. I do have you. Now, let me finish your bath service. I am sure you are hungry. I will cook for you, then I will feed your other needs until I am ready to go back to work."

Master Boyd frowned. "Go back to work? Psycho, baby, you need to give up that job and Sheryl too. You are sick, very sick. You need to be in the hospital, but I won't let them take you to the pit. Stay with me and I will take care of you until this cycle passes. I will protect you from yourself and the people like Sheryl who will rob from you. I love you. I want to take care of you, good or bad, for the rest of our lives. I swear it to you on my life. I will never let anyone hurt you again." He held me tightly in a hug.

I snickered. "Oh? Then I have your promise you will never hurt me yourself again, Master?" I soaped up his chest looking at him mischievously.

He pulled back in surprise. "I would never hurt you Psycho, I promise."

I smiled diabolically. "I will remember you said that. I would keep that promise if I were you. You see I believe in equal service for equal service, Master. I always make sure debts are paid in full when someone takes more than they earn. I will give you exactly what you asked me for. I will love you the way you love me." I continued my bathing service to him while he stood there appearing confused by my strange statement.

After our shower, I made him his favorite meal without his command. He was served and I took my place at his feet kneeling also without being ordered. His newfound affection was evident when he asked me to join him at the table and eat something myself. My Master watched me take in my lunch appearing dreamy and full of adoration. The sudden appearance of free-willed worship of his person led him to believe I did in fact have loving feelings for him as he did for me.

This illusion of amour for his person was sending him to cloud nine. He finally had his very own true lover despite his many faults and unacceptable forcing of my submission. Had Master Boyd behaved himself by accepting my last-ditch attempt to provide what he had requested of me then my story would end here. Sadly, for him, he didn't head Gothic Barbie's warning. But we are getting ahead of ourselves.

NOTE: *Obviously, he did not appreciate his last chance to obtain what he had said he wanted the most. The trouble was, Master Boyd is mentally ill, just like me. His sickness is soul deep. There is no cure for what ails him like there is no way to fix schizophrenia.*

In time, it would become apparent this relationship was never going to work no matter what delusional thoughts or attempts I made to meet his demands. Our love affair would become fodder for rumors likely still whispered from time to time in those small towns. It was a seven-year battle of epic and volatile fights and makeups not unlike that of many other famously poor matches throughout history.

The problem was very simple: Master Boyd and I were never meant to be together in the first place. No matter how much he wants to believe that false. His taking me against my will, and his serious mental sickness, had doomed this possibility from the very start. Not to mention that I never viewed him as a potential lover to boot. While he was offered many chances to redeem his foul deed, he could never banish the very demon that had created my hatred for him in the first place. I did try, and so did he to be honest, to make this unholy union work. It was impossible to ever makes something beautiful (love) from something so ugly (rape).

Once he was full and the dishes washed, I returned to his bedroom with him. My Master and I slept cuddled in the loving arms of the other just as true lovers would. He fell asleep immediately feeling confident his many years of chasing the uncatchable had finally come to an end.

I too feel deep into slumber with a headache threatening to blow my head off my shoulders. My psychological health was now deteriorating at an alarming rate. I was too many people at the same time, catering to too many people all at once. There was no doubt my center would not hold for much longer.

My Master was awakened to his alarm going off. It was time for him to dress and get ready for his shift. I stirred to his kissing my sleeping unit. I opened my eyes returning his smile. Without a word I pushed him back onto his pillow. Quietly I pawed and groped him appearing eager to engage once again in carnal congress with him.

Master Boyd attempted to protest my aggressive sexual behavior. I ignored his commands that I stop. Despite his voiced desire I cease my foolishness he was overcome by his drives when I crawled on top. Before he could escape, I forced his entry into me again appearing to volunteer for the romp. He had tried to roll me over several times, but I would thrust downward harshly. My Master would become immobilized by the surge of pleasure each time which knocked him back down to his submissive spot.

I yelled out loudly calling him Master nearly driving him insane with passion. I scratched and nipped him causing him to yell out for more. I rode him to orgasm keeping him on his back while I maintained control of the act in my top position the entire time. He cried out my name overwhelmed by yet another strong climax, that was immediately followed by a pounding on the front door.

"Boyd, damn it. It is Dennis. Open this fucking door," Dennis's voice echoed into the bedroom.

I giggled realizing Dennis had heard our very loud lovemaking. Master Boyd's eyes went wide in terror at the same realization.

"Coming Dennis," he yelled while narrowing his eyes at me in warning to be quiet. Too late for that.

I got off his unit quickly. I then aided him to rapidly cover himself with a robe and slippers. He ran from the room closing the door behind him.

I began to dress myself trying not to laugh as I listened to the exchange between my Master and Dennis in the next room.

"Boy, I knocked on that door for five minutes. You could hear your yelling for miles. What the hell is going on? I thought maybe someone was killing you," I heard Dennis say.

Master Boyd began to stutter, "Uhm, well, it well." I walked out of the bedroom smiling sweetly fully dressed but obviously sweating.

"Hello Dennis, can I get you something to drink? I have to get to work myself shortly, but I have a few minutes to attend to company. Right Boyd?" I shot a wicked smile at my now stunned Master.

Dennis turned bright red. "Oh, Psycho, I didn't know. Your car isn't here. I suppose, uhm yeah, I could use a Coke if you have one around. Thank you, sweetie." He shot an embarrassed smile now realizing he had interrupted his officer's interrogation of his fiancé.

I moved rapidly to retrieve the requested drink for the cop still chuckling to myself at the discomfort my presence was causing them both.

My Master looked at the floor sheepishly. "Yeah, so Psycho has been sort of living with me. She had a spill at work today. I was uhm, just, well you know how it is," he trailed off unsure what to say to his being caught with his hand in the cookie jar so to speak.

Dennis cleared his throat and hitched up his pants. "Well, my apologies Boyd for interrupting. I mean for not being more sensitive. It is hard to believe you are an engaged man now."

"Well he is very engaged as you heard Dennis. Aren't you Boyd," I said as I kissed my Master's lips lightly enjoying a great deal his place of helplessness in front of his commanding officer.

Master Boyd just nodded appearing surprise by my brash willingness to answer. Dennis blushed again and looked at the door while I moved in on my Master seductively wrapping my arms around his waist.

"Honey, I will need to borrow your car to get to work tonight unless you can find a way to drop me off at the office in Cumberland. I am going to be late. Can you help me out?" I batted my eyes innocently.

My Master's eyes began to darken with storm clouds of anger. "I thought we decided you would quit that job," he said through gritted teeth.

I giggled. "Oh baby. Now you know I am a working girl. Dennis, could you and Boyd drop me off at the Cumberland County line? I have to make a phone call, but I can get a ride to my car from there." I looked at Dennis who stood there unaware of my knight's move right around Master Boyd's attempts to keep me hostage in his house.

Dennis smiled. "Of course, Psycho. It would be a pleasure. I hear you are doing fine things there in Cumberland County. Tale is you are making one fine investigator. You know it really is too bad you and Boyd can never have children. The babies would have beautiful blue eyes and a pedigree for fine social service to boot." He chuckled taking a drink of his Coke.

I smiled while releasing my fuming Master. "Ah, perhaps we will adopt Dennis. If you boys will excuse me. I have a call to make." I winked at Master Boyd as I went to call Master Sheryl. Got you, Boyd. Remember to just lay there and take it big boy, like you expect me to do.

Master Sheryl answered her phone on the second ring:

"Psycho, are you okay honey? I have been worried to death. I assumed that asshole had you locked up in some damned cell while perverts, oh never mind. Are you okay," she asked.

I chuckled feeling very strangely. "Oh I am better than okay. I ready to get back to work now. Can you pick me up at the county line on highway 80 in about two hours? I am catching a ride with the cops here in Wheatly."

She paused. "Sure thing. I will be there. See you in a couple of hours." She hung up.

I felt dizzy suddenly. The world began to spin with codes popping up all around the kitchen wall next to Master Boyd's phone. I realized Psycho Tron was trying to take control of the unit. I pushed her down. It was not time, not yet.

I walked back out to find Dennis alone sitting on the couch. "Where is Boyd?"

He motioned toward the bedroom. "Getting dressed. We need to leave right away if we are to drop you off before we then clock in on time."

I nodded while smiling. "Oh, what did you need Dennis? You stopped by for some reason, right?"

Dennis almost spit out his liquid. "Shit. That's right. I came by early to invite Boyd to Sunday supper with Carla and me. She wanted to privately celebrate his engagement to you. I suppose it would only be right to invite you as well. Since you are living here. Psycho, you know it ain't right your being here and still married. I mean it is not my business, but it does look bad."

Master Boyd walked out of his room. His uniform was still damp from our little tryst in the shower earlier. "Psycho filed Dennis. The rat bastard evaded the server. She is applying again in a couple months right, baby?" He looked at me still furious at my escaping his hold for the night.

I nodded with a huge fake smile on my face. "Don't worry honey, I will get him next time. Dennis, I respect your honesty. If you think it wrong for me to live with Boyd before marriage, I will move out right away. I would never do anything to compromise Boyd's stellar reputation."

Master Boyd had enough of my now obvious thumbing my nose at him. "Uhm, Dennis, this is kind of sensitive, but Psycho is currently homeless. She is here because I don't want her out of the streets again with her, you know, the (clears throat) problem." He threw a glare at me that dared me to say another word against him.

I smiled sweetly at my Master. "Well, he is right. Thank you for caring so much Boyd. You are too good to me you know." I winked playfully at my angry Master.

Dennis snorted. "Okay, tell you what Boyd. My lips are sealed about Psycho staying here with you. But let me warn you both, get that damned divorce and get hitched as fast as you can. The town will start flapping their lips soon enough. I will not have them calling either of you adulterers. Got me you two?" He shot a warning look at us both.

Master Boyd and I nodded that we understood his order. I internally reminded myself to call Mitchell the second my Master attempted to file in my stead again. For now, I had not escaped his clutches, but I had found a weakness in his plan to make me his prisoner.

All I had to do was talk Timmy into tap dancing around until rumors of my residence with Master Boyd erupted through the towns. If I could avoid divorce long enough, it would set Dennis on a path of righteousness regarding living in sin. I could then manipulate my Master's boss into ordering he release me. Ah, the plan was perfect and a lucky break for a change.

The officers walked out of Master Boyd's house with me following close behind. We walked to the squad car. Dennis opened the back door and looked at me a bit pensively.

"Uhm, sorry about this Psycho, but you will have to ride in the back. I have shot gun and well Boyd does the driving. Hope that is okay. I am sure you have many unpleasant memories of this, and I admit this is damned weird. Never thought I'd see the day where our Psycho would be riding with us willingly, nor be engaged to my boy." He smiled while looking at Master Boyd proudly.

I got into the backseat with many unpleasant memories flowing like rivers of lava through my shattered mind. However, the worst were not of my numerous arrests, but of my Master's cruel raping of my unit after he forced my submission to his collar. I winced from the sound of door shutting me in. Fear filled my veins as my own pleas for mercy erupted in my ears. I did my best not to start wailing in agony from the torture of seeing those two nights replaying in my mind while Master Boyd and Dennis got into the front seat.

"Hey, the county line please. Remember, not the jail this time," I said stifling a sniff from the tears threatening to erupt from my eyes.

Dennis chuckled. "You got it Psycho. No jail tonight. Boyd just head that way. I don't think we need to tell Cathy all our business. What do you think?"

Master Boyd shot me a threatening look in the rearview mirror. "I think none of this happened Dennis. I didn't see you and you didn't see Psycho and me."

Dennis chuckled. "Wish I didn't hear you either. Gosh boy, save some of that for your wedding night, will you? Psycho, what the hell do you do to my officers?"

I shook my head bitterly while staring back defiantly at Master Boyd's reflection in his mirror. "Not anything more than they did to me, Dennis."

The rest of the ride was uneventful. Dennis prattled on about his kinfolk. Master Boyd, in typical fashion, quietly nodded or shook his head in response to the discussion. I sat in the backseat allowing Psycho Tron to finally come forward to take possession of the unit. The Gothic Barbie was not needed for our next role as Investigator and submissive to Master Sheryl. The pass off occurred both physically and psychologically.

Master Sheryl's blue green Taurus was waiting parked by the sign for the county line. Master Boyd pulled over while Dennis got out to open my locked door. Psycho Tron stepped out without emotional affect regarding her release from the rapist's possession. She began walking toward her awaiting ride.

"Psycho wait, come here," yelled out Master Boyd while rolling down his window.

She turned and returned to her Master's door. "May I be of service," she said in a monotone voice.

Master Boyd smiled at her. "You are leaving me without a kiss goodbye? Now tell me you love me like you mean it." He leaned out for his kiss.

Psycho Tron leaned down and received her adoration from the Master without affection. "I love you," she replied without inflection or adoration.

Master Boyd raised an eyebrow. "You feeling okay, baby?"

I flashed a fake smile recalled from our programming. "I feel fine. Be safe. See you this weekend. Have a nice night. Goodbye now." I turned quickly got into the car with Master Sheryl leaving Master Boyd still unsure of the change in me he was sensing.

The squad car turned around heading back to Wheatly, while the Taurus headed back to Cumberland. I was now free of Master Boyd for another few days.

Master Sheryl immediately began a flurry of questions nearly overloading my circuits seeking information.

"So, did he hurt you? What happened? Where have you been? What was that kissing shit all about? I mean do you actually plan to marry that asshole. Charley told me he stopped the two of you. He said you were not fighting to get

30

free. What the fuck is going on? I want answers now Psycho," Master Sheryl rambled out in a rapid-fire fashion.

I shook my head. "Negative Master. I do not plan to merge with his unit for the duration of my usefulness. We are not compatible programs. My data was in error, but the malfunction has been corrected. No viruses detected. The upgrade was successful. There is negative reason for your concern. His hard drive shall be obsolete soon enough like all the others. I would like to get back to the filing now in progress. Thank you very much and have a nice night," I said flatly.

Master Sheryl shot a look of concern at me. "Really? You tore the fuck out of Jane's office, were kidnapped by a cop, and returned in the middle of the fucking night by that same cop. Psycho, this is beyond crazy. Now you want to go back to work right now. Your fucking insane you know that?"

I nodded my head. "Affirmative Master. However, that is of negative interest to you. I am ready for data entry. You have commanded the program to become Area Manager and continue running without system failure. You may drop my unit at the office for continuation of this process."

She let out a sigh. "Well you do have a mess to clean up. I suppose your chores at home can wait till tomorrow night. Okay, I am taking you to the office but let me warn you that any more tearing shit up that I am not sure I can hide it next time. They will arrest you for busting up government property."

I looked at her without blinking. "I had a Grand Mal seizure of my internal functions Master. This shall not happen again. The error has been deleted."

Master Sheryl took me to the office and dropped me off. She offered a few more warnings and commanded I do work only. She left after watching me successfully enter the building. I walked to PC then to Fax turning them onto the power grid.

PC whirled to life yawning. "Ah Psycho Tron, great to see you. Wait, that bitchy you isn't lurking around, is she?" He strained his electronic eyes looking for Simon.

"Yes, he is," said Simon causing both PC and I to jump with a start.

I looked at Simon unblinking as if in a trance, "You have negative reasons to be in our energy field. We have a directive to follow. Your commands are not compatible with Master Sheryl's programming."

Simon sat down on the edge of Jane's desk eyeing PC. "I didn't come to interfere with your work. I came to offer a warning."

PC snorted. "What would that be? Never leave home without taking a Midol?"

Simon glared at PC. "You know your humor is getting on my last nerve, asshole. Shut up."

I looked at Simon. "State your warning. We shall check it for errors and viruses," I said without emotion.

Simon shook his head chuckling. "This is a fucking madhouse. Hell, no one needs to lock us up because the gang is all here. Psycho, if you are in there somewhere then listen to me. This sharding has to stop. The cracks are getting so big it will damage our connection. Do you hear that? It will break me from the unit. Do you remember what happens if I get cut off for good?"

PC giggled. "You get bitchier? Right? That is the answer. No one likes to go without sex for long."

Simon fumed at that. "Oh Judas Priest. Is that all anyone thinks about anymore? Sex!"

I started at him blankly. "This does not compute Simon. I am checking the memory storage now as you requested. Thank you, have a nice day."

Simon dropped his head in his hands. "My fucking head hurts. God damn, we are fucking insane. Someone please help. I need someone to put an end to this bullshit. I really need a reset."

PC looked at the wailing Simon appearing very serious suddenly. "You are so right bitchy Psycho Tron. Tell you what. Let me tell you something that will help you unwind. So, I met this girl in a bar. After a while she said, 'would you like me to show you a good time?' I couldn't turn that down, so we went outside. She took off her coat and ran 100 meters in 9.8 seconds. Best fucking time, I had ever heard of." He began laughing wildly at what he thought was a very clever joke.

Simon fell to his knees screaming, "Make it stop. I can't take this shit. Help! Help me please!"

I looked at my very upset inner self. "Enough Simon. This will not be tolerated. You set the program. We follow your commands. We cannot delete our pathways, and neither can you. There is memory in the drives indicating you are not always correct. My sensors indicate you are threatening termination in a false capacity. Now you must allow the data to be entered before our deadline arrives. Thank you and have a nice day. Goodbye." I pulled my chair to the desk now ignoring Simon's weeping while I began blindly opening the CHRIS programs in PC's hard drive.

The entire night Simon moaned and groaned non-stop. He continued predicting our current path of multiple shard delusion would ultimately lead to serious impairment. The disturbed railroad man would not shut up despite my refusal to listen to him. PC split his time between insulting Simon to cracking dark humor jokes. Psycho Tron mindlessly entered hard file records into the new electronic database appearing undisturbed by either of their attempts to interrupt her task. Fax spit out several announcements about super deals on last minute cruises, and time-sharing deals too good to be true. None of the three of us believed a fucking word of that bullshit gossip.

As my brother the sun began his morning climb to the apex of the world, I suddenly realized there was a way to make everyone happy. This whole mess was caused by a short circuit in the mainframe. This serious malfunction was causing our Simon and defunct shards to get out of control.

Ah, now I could recall there was a way to repair the damage. All I had to do was get extra wire, electrical tape, and a knife. Once I had located the loose or broken wiring, it could be replaced or secured whichever was required.

I looked up from PC's keyboard. "PC, is there an automotive store close to this building in town?"

PC smiled "Auto Zone is about a block away. Hey Psycho Tron, I know what you are thinking. Smart. Yes, fix the wire. Want me to run a scan to locate the problem?"

Simon looked up suddenly startled by my appearing to notice PC once again. He was sitting cross legged with his head in his hands at my feet after attempting to get me to focus on him for hours.

"Hey Psycho, wait. No, you are not allowed to damage the unit. Master Boyd said no scars damn it. That was a directive." Simon stood up appearing very scared after reading our mind.

PC sneered. "Oh grow up bitchy Psycho Tron, I can run that scan now if you want nice Psycho Tron." He smiled at me.

I shook my head. "Negative PC. Keep your sensors to yourself pervert. You are attempting to use your position as my co-worker in a negative fashion. You will terminate this request immediately or I shall remove your power source."

PC laughed hard. "Oh Psycho Tron Baby, you are turning me on now. Come on, just let me tell you one more thing before you turn me down. How does a computer fuck a robot? He nuts then bolts baby." His laugher was so loud even Simon had to cover his ears over it.

"That is it PC, I am shutting you down. Your hard drive has gotten overheated." I flipped his power switch while PC told me he was only joking.

Simon sat there staring at the now empty screen. "Now that was fucked up Psycho. We really need better medication."

Psycho Tron turned toward my brakeman. "As for you Simon. For the last time understand you set this program by allowing Master Boyd to interfere with our pathways. His presence in the line of Masters was not part of this plan. If you wish to threaten this unit you will need to take a number and wait your turn. Until we have the time to grant you proper audience, I would suggest you shut the fuck up."

Simon's eyes went wide. "Are we seriously telling me to shut up. None of you have the fucking authority to do so. I am the Master here. We do what I say."

I smiled with my teeth sharp as a shark suddenly turning shards. "Bring it on railroad man. I dare you. You are a pussy when you are barking orders but never taking the abuse over them. You get in my way I will throw your ass from the train. You can't scare me. As for you being Master, uhm, hate to tell you this baby but we already have two of those. That makes you third in line. As it is, we are starting to think we don't need you at all. There are plenty of assholes just like you clamoring to tell us what to do or where to go. So you best watch out. Or do you want to push me? I think not," the Chosen One growled.

Simon backed away. "Holy shit this is really bad, really bad. Okay, look call Master Boyd tell him to send us to the Pit if necessary. We are not going to survive this. We need help."

I stood up popping my neck. "That is why I am here Simon. to help. Now, I have creeps waiting for my attention. Including one who calls herself my Master. Hmmm, kind of like your sorry ass. Ah, you know what they say, too many Masters in the kitchen." I pushed past the stunned Simon slamming the door hard behind me.

I walked to Master Sheryl's house and went inside. She was granted wake up and breakfast service by the Chosen One herself. My Master was somewhat startled by my sudden change in verbal usage and tempo.

"Psycho, you said they told you that your disease is Schizophrenia, right," aske Master Sheryl as she watched me change my outfit preparing for my field work.

I nodded. "Yeah, so what? Who gives a flying fuck? I told you that shit when you collared me remember, Master." I snorted.

She shook her head appearing stunned. "Well, it is just, you seem different sometimes. Like a different person different. You ever been told maybe you have a Multiple Personality Disorder?"

I started to laugh hard. "Seriously? Ah, you laypeople really need to stop listening to pop psychology, Master. That disorder has been debunked. Such a thing has been proven to not exist. It is now called Dissociative Identity Disorder and no, I do not have it. They checked hoping that it was that." I put on my long black coat.

She narrowed her eyes. "Why would they hope that?"

I glared at her. "Because that disorder has a cure Master. Schizophrenia doesn't. They wanted an easy fix to their fuck up. Instead they swept me under the rug like trash. So, thanks to that I must forever bow down to assholes who treat me no better than that garbage everyone thinks I am. Now I must get going to keep you people from fucking up more kids with your mishandling and coddling of these riff raff parents. Later, Master." I took off leaving the confused Master Sheryl behind to ponder my obvious insult toward her and her agency.

I looked at my schedule. A chronically neglectful mother named Nikki Pool was my first case that day. She was a diagnosed psychopath with two children under the age of ten. The children's father was the local drug dealer but had no association with his offspring. Miss Pool's case was a cause of constant headaches for the local DCFS. She never abused the children or neglected them enough to warrant taking them into custody. Nikki did, however, push the borders with a long history of ignoring the medical, educational and environmental needs of her children. That morning a new report had come over the wire on her once again. The neighbor reported she was not feeding the children, and both appeared poor in weight. I snorted at the caller's report.

"Look out Nikki, I am on my way to kick your ass if those kids are not fat little piggy's." I tore out of Master Sheryl's driveway throwing rubber while laughing wildly ready to kick ass and forget the names.

Oops, I wouldn't want to be a child abuser around the Chosen One, or Simon around any of the shards at this moment, and maybe not Master Boyd either. I wonder about that Gothic Barbie. She seems pretty damned interested in our serial rapist Master. Wonder what her game is? Simon sure was scared of her.

Now I have published a photo that has a backstory you may not enjoy. It is an actual photo taken the day Master Boyd caught me at Darlin with Simon's key and my collar. It was taken in the very spot the forced submission you read about occurred which was only moments after the photo was snapped in fact. You will notice a red ring around my throat from being dragged by the throat by the cop the final few feet to that spot. I didn't write about it because I didn't think it necessary to discuss it with so much other brutality already there to talk about.

However, that force is noticeable in the photo. What is also noticeable is the look of fear in my eyes, and the fact my arms are in cuffs though he was careful not to show only my upper unit. I found this photo at Master Boyd's home in 2004, but that will be told in a future story. Just know I have held on to it all this time trying to decide if I would post it or hold it due to its reminding me of gunpoint submission and the rapes right after it was taken.

On the original photo before it was scanned into a thumb drive Boyd had written on the back *"Psycho before MY COLLAR"* in Master Boyd's hand. I realized he wanted to document what he thought were my last moments not wearing his collar or anyone else for that matter. So, another lucky or unlucky chance photo to show you a blast from a dark past. There are others that I will decide to share or not when their times come in future tales. I decided to post this one after much soul searching only so you can have an idea of what I looked like at this time, just as I have done my best to show you a good vision of all these other people as I remember them.

Chapter 59: To Live in the Mirror is Evil; The Backward Delusion
Master Boyd and Interim Master Sheryl

Are we having a bunch of fun yet? It is like a funhouse inside our head. The reflections are chaotic, distorted and becoming quite numerous. How the holy hell did this get so out of control? We would ask Simon, but he is just as confused by all of this as we are. Now, out of the depths of our darkest recesses comes yet another shard. Oh, my Goth. When will this ever end?

Gothic Barbie has arrived to give Master Boyd exactly what he wants. Her charms are working wonders on the rapist's heart. Soon he will be captivated by her seductive caress, and devil may care attitude. He has no idea that all services he provides to us will be returned in fair proportions. Our debt to be paid to him is mounting up. We are not worried. Our cruel doll is trained in the art of twisted love. She will give our Master everything he has asked for and maybe a bit extra to cover the interest.

Psycho Tron, PC and Fax are ground zero for the entry of data to fulfill their complex commands. Together they toil to meet the demands of everyone around Psycho. Despite their quick wit and artificial intelligence still more is required daily. Simon has appealed to the emotionless Robot begging for mercy. This is something that is not in the program. Too bad such a kindness simply does not compute.

The Chosen One is ripping apart the foul abusers of the land. She is without fear, cares or empathy. She too believes in an eye for an eye justice. Ah, but what happens when the eyes were blind? This hero of the downtrodden is unable to navigate the slippery slope of barely bad nor the borderline salvageable. When the crime is balanced, and punishment already granted this shard will have no clue how to settle a zero score. An answer to this riddle must be found or all is lost in her bid to raise Master Sheryl to Area Manager.

From the static one will rise that will speak the language of the blessed and the damned. She will be neither good nor bad but capable of both. She is a perfect backward image of what she perceives. Her nature is not written in ink but in quicksilver. This shard will be whatever you want it to be. Go ahead and show her your true reflection. You define her. She will obey your desires but can see your lies. Just remember, nothing is for free. You must pay her price. If you want to find her, then look deep into the mirror and say her name three times: Livevil, Livevil, Livevil.

Off we go to journey into the most disturbed mind. This time keep that black bag we told you about. Don't look inside. You will ruin the fun. Oh, and grab that looking glass, you know. the shattered one next to the Robot and Barbie doll. Tell the Fax to stop spouting lies, and whatever you do don't turn on your PC. Simon is waiting next to that broken-down train. He is working day and night to get it back on the tracks. We may have to walk this time. Hope you have a strong back because we have a shit ton of baggage to carry. We will give it a little more time, then it is off on our own we go. Simon will just have to try to catch up.

"I just love your shoes. Where the hell did you get those? I used to have beautiful shoes. Then I became a mother, and then a foster mother too. Shoes were a luxury I had to give up. If I can get on a pair of slippers, I am pretty   *happy."*

Cheryl's first meeting with Livevil, April 1998

The Chosen One looked up in the sky. The darkening western horizon threatened the first of the spring storms. The breeze picked up whisking an abandoned twinkie wrapper across her platform clad feet. Her long black jacket flapped helpless against the rushing air. She smiled with teeth sharp as a shark looking up the hill at the trailer. The mailbox number matched. This was the place of description. She had parked Sheryl's Taurus off the side of the road at the bottom of the washed-out driveway that led to the home.

As the Chosen One began the long climb up, she pulled up her coat collar chuckling in glee, "Time to pay for your crimes, sinner," she hissed under her breath.

I knocked on the door. A woman answered. She was in her mid-twenties with greasy ash-blond, long hair. Her face was round with a budding double chin. Her eyes were small and looked like green marbles against her pasty pallor. The young woman was already frumpy with slumped shoulders and wide hips. She smiled at me appearing pleased to open the door to this most unexpected visitor.

"Holy shit, now this is fucking awesome. Are you lost? Oh, who gives a fuck. Come in any way," said Nikki with

43

impulsivity and lack of natural fear only seen in a true psychopathic personality.

I smiled back. "I am from DCFS. I have received a complaint of neglect. I will ask to see your children, Miss Pool. Still want me to come inside?" I raised an eyebrow appearing humored.

Nikki rolled her eyes chuckling. "A complaint? Again? Oh well, shit. Nothing new there. Sure, come in. I got nothing to hide. Johnny and Sarah are in the back of the trailer playing. Come in."

I stepped into the single wide manufactured home immediately looking about for any anyone waiting in ambush. I saw nothing but old green shag carpet, shitty furniture, and a bit of useless clutter in the dimly lit living room. To my right was a small kitchen with a large window and no curtains. If it had any the entire area would be dark as pitch. All the living room windows were blacked out with house paint. I saw a crappy metal table with yellow chairs. On the table was a coffee cup and three plates. The smell of food from the meal wafted in the air.

Nikki stood there still smiling in amazement looking me up and down. "Now this is just beyond, well fuck just cool as hell. Johnny, Sarah, get your asses in here now" she shrieked causing me to cover my ears.

Two children came running. Neither child was frail or thin as reported. The boy was toe headed with bright blue eyes and of average size for a child his age of seven. The girl sported darker locks and marble eyes like her mother. She was actually a bit overweight for her stated age of five. Sarah smiled at me and Johnny stopped dead in his tracks appearing stunned.

"Holy shit, Mom. Do you see what I see?" He put his hands up to his cheeks in a dramatic look of shock.

Nikki snorted while she laughed at Johnny's behavior. "Oh hell yeah I do. Isn't she beautiful? Oh my God, can we get a photo with you. Uhm, what was your name again?"

She began pawing through the clutter on her coffee table next to a small old-fashioned TV looking for her camera. Johnny and Sarah joined their mother all yapping at once trying to decide where this missing item was last seen.

I stood there unsure what to do. This mother clearly was not neglecting her children nor were they being starved. I looked about trying to find something wrong with this picture other than foul language used by an underaged child.

Nothing stood out. She gently moved her daughter to look under the baby for the camera while the boy child laughed and dug in another pile of crap on another table. School was out for spring break, so educational needs were not being neglected either. For a psychopath Nikki was showing a great deal of attendance to these kids. They clearly were not beaten, frightened or shy.

My head began to ache once again. Another child was coming. The Chosen One was baffled. Only Psycho Tron could give birth. She was the one sleeping with Master Boyd. Wait, there was that one time on accident. I sat down on the raggedy couch feeling faint. The child was coming fast this time. Each birth was getting easier as they usually do. My mind was no longer green having already creating life three times. I felt the trance coming on as the Pool family continued their scavenger hunt seeking out the polaroid machine.

In the static I saw the scales of good and bad. They were balanced and I was unable to determine which was more and which was less. The confusion created the color of grey in my visual field. The Chosen One was lost in the fog of it. I looked in the mirror of my mind. The reflection staring back was the same but like a shadow of the real. The right was left and the words of my case file unintelligible. I saw the proportion of right and wrong tip with each glace. The movement was minor but visible only in the reflector tool. The reverse image reached out her hand. I took it and pulled her out of the silver backed glass. She smiled and said live spelled backward is evil. I nodded while she pushed her way out of the cracks in my psyche to take control of a situation where there was not a pure sinner, but not one even close to a saint either.

Johnny yelled out, "Mom, look. That lady is bleeding out of her nose. Quick, get some paper towels. Gross."

Sarah yelled out, "Bloody boogers. Bloody boogers," while clapping her hands.

My trance broken I reached up to pinch my nostrils trying to stem the flow of birth. "I am sorry about your furniture Miss Pool. I seem to have busted a leak."

Nikki looked up from her digging horrified at the sight of my minor emergency. "Oh, let me get you something to clean that up. Wow! That is a real gully washer. Damn, did you do coke? My old man used to do coke and he would get some fucking powerful nose bleeds." She continued to ramble on about her children's father's drug habit and side effects of heavy usage of it.

She returned with several handfuls of dime store paper napkins. I blocked the now ebbing flow of crimson. Feeling fatigued by my entry into the real but not in need of a nap.

I looked at Nikki smiling sweetly. "Well darling, do you have a cup of coffee you would be willing to share with me so we can chat?" I looked at her kitchen.

Nikki smiled excitedly. "Fucking right on. Sure thing. Do you take cream or sugar?"

I got up and followed Miss Pool to her small kitchen with the children tagging behind. "Just creamer darling if you have any that is. Otherwise black will do."

I sat down in one of her shitty chairs and began my interview with her. She didn't appear to mind the questions nor seem angry about the complaint. Next, I asked her to leave the room while each child was briefly spoken to and observed. The complaint was obviously false. While there was no doubt this mother needed the open case they already had on this home, no new charges were being committed, at least for now.

I was grateful that only an unfounded finding sheet would need to be filed. The case was already active. So, my job was done in record time. My nose had stopped bleeding and her coffee sucked. I was ready to be on my merry way.

"Well, Miss Pool, thank you so much for your compliance with DCFS today. I see that this was obviously a mistake. However, I would remind you to follow all your caseworker's suggestions so that you can finally be struck off the books with the agency and get on with your life. I would think by now you are tied of weekly visits and microscopic living." I chuckled at that knowing deep down Nikki didn't give a flying fuck about much of anything but Nikki.

Nikki smiled bitterly. "Well, uhm, what did you say your name was again? I know it was my kid's daddy's mom. She is always stirring shit. I ain't never going to get the DCFS fuckers off my jock, you know?" She was looking me up and down again appearing in awe.

I nodded. "Maybe not till the kids are grown, Miss Pool. I have read your records. Very impressive list of findings there. I realize being a parent is a difficult job, but you must take it seriously or the state will take it from you," I cautioned while still smiling.

Nikki chuckled. "I wish. Those hellions, no one wants them. They've got my own fire blood in them. I feel damned sorry for any asshole who thinks they can do better. Shit, Johnny would burn the God damned trailer up if I don't watch out, and Sarah would steal the cane from a blind man."

She looked toward the living room where the two children were rough housing in play.

I looked at her sternly. "That may be Miss Pool, but they come take those kids while you go to jail. You understand that I bet."

Nikki's eyes went wide. "Ah, there is the old DCFS I was waiting for. You are something else you know? You look bad, but you aren't really, are you? Not really. Is this some kind of new thing they are pulling to scare me straight? Sending someone who looks like they come from hell but actually is working for the so-called Saints who never do wrong?" She narrowed her marble eyes suspiciously at me.

I laughed hard. "Nope. You are wrong there darling. They don't have a plan at all. I can see your problem if you think those assholes at the office are saints. But probably I am being evil. Maybe even more than you are. Now you have a lovely day, Miss Pool. Don't take offense to this but never let me meet you again. Next time, I won't be so nice." I stood up to leave.

Nikki chuckled. "You are fucking cool as shit. You can arrest me anytime, chick. You never told me your name. You know what? I am going to call you Purgatory. I like that name. See you around Purgatory."

I turned back startled. "Excuse me Miss Pool? Purgatory?"

She laughed hard. "Yeah, Purgatory. Cause you ain't good enough for Heaven, but you sure don't seem bad enough for Hell either. Hey, call me Nikki. Come by for coffee anytime, Purgy. I think you are a badass."

I just shook my head. "Sure thing. Have a wonderful day Nikki."

We left her trailer feeling odd. Nikki was without a doubt more Sinner than Saint but at the moment was right smack in the middle. Livevil had reflected a person of gentle kindness and patience with a flair for caution. That could only mean Nikki was harsh, cruel, impatient and struck without warning. I expected she and I would see each other again soon.

The rest of the day was a constant spin of shards from The Chosen One to Livevil with dizziness in between. By eight that night when I finally arrived at the office to file my paperwork, my head was pounding with one hellish headache. I used my key and entered Jane's office to turn on PC and Fax. I had a mountain of work to finish before my shift at the funeral home began in only a few hours. The Chosen One opened the door but Psycho Tron closed it behind us.

PC whirled to life appearing full of humor at my shutting him down over his indecent remark early that morning. "Psycho Tron, hey, I have one for you."

I shifted my springs while sitting down. "Negative PC. We have data to enter. The script is running too long. It is sure to stall the program. Clear the history please. Thank you, have a nice day."

PC snorted. "All work and no funny make Psycho Tron number two a grouchy buddy."

"I resent that," said Simon sourly as he entered the office catching PC's insult against him.

PC rolled his electrical eyes. "Ah fuck. Can't you stay home just for one damned night? Since your bitchy ass started hanging out with us, Psycho Tron is never fun anymore."

Simon glowered at PC. "Okay, you know what? How about this asshole. I got one for you. So, this guy says to another guy, 'Every day the same bicycle tries to run me down." The second guys says, 'Wow, man sounds like one vicious cycle.' Now, which one is the nice Psycho Tron, PC?"

PC's eyes went wide. "Holy shit, did you just tell a joke? It totally sucked, but WOW. Totally appreciate the effort Bitchy Psycho Tron," he snickered.

Simon grabbed his forehead. "Fuck you. Your gigs suck and your mega hurts my head."

PC's laughter shook the walls. "Now that was clever. Ah, you are fucking fabulous, Psycho Tron." His electrical grid whined loudly.

I sat there staring blankly at them both. "Syntax error. Malfunctioning within the mainframe will result in a termination of the program. Simon you must switch off for re-boot."

Simon growled, "I don't need a fucking re-boot. I just figured if I started speaking your God damned language you would finally listen to me. There is another motherfucking shard out now. Have you seen this monster? Psycho, it must stop, now. We go back to Master Boyd tomorrow night. Gothic Barbie, shit Psycho, listen, please stop the sharing. Give up the job. Shit can Master Sheryl and embrace our fate or we will be destroyed."

The phone began to ring. I looked at it unsure what to do. PC informed me the time was too late for office hours. Simon said to let it go to the answering machine. I felt dizzy as I realized the only person calling this late would be the rapist Master himself.

Gothic Barbie answered, "Hello, Department of Human Services and all that bullshit. Can I help you Master," she cooed into the receiver.

There was silence for a moment. "Psycho? Hey baby, how did you know it was me," said Master Boyd appearing surprised.

I smiled. "Ah, I was just sitting here thinking dirty thoughts about you Master. I think I may need a shower."

Master Boyd cleared his throat. "Uhm, yeah, that would be very nice. Why don't you come home and I will be happy to assist you."

I knew he was at the jail based on the racket in the background. He was likely with others around him unable to speak his mind freely. Gothic Barbie felt the spark of joy at his helplessness to her taunting him.

"Oh, what I wouldn't give to have you with me right now Master. I am so hot I don't think I can even make it back to Wheatly. I need it right now. There is no one around. Maybe I will take matters into my own hands. Perhaps something in my black bag will help me scratch my itch. It is really deep, hmmm. Yeah, I need to find assistance right now. Can we hurry this up? I am about to explode just hearing your voice lover," I purred.

He cleared his throat appearing nervous. "Uh, black bag? Psycho, baby, you feeling alright?"

I moaned out faking sexual ecstasy, "Oh I feel wonderful. You really should know. Haven't you felt me Master? You have never seen my black bag or what I can do with it. Don't worry lover, you will soon enough. Ah, I really need to go or cum." I breathed out then, hung up the phone laughing my ass off.

Simon and PC stood there eyes wide in total shock.

"Wow! I think I just busted a nut myself. Who the fuck was that lucky asshole," yelled out PC still in shock.

Simon threw a worried look at PC. "Shut up. That is your mother, dummy. She was just leaving. You must stop this game. Take that black bag back to hell where you belong."

I looked at Simon. "Aw, little Rachel, are you still tagging along? Big baby. You couldn't tell our eyelids to

53

blink. Powerless, useless, worthless, ugly and stupid. You have always been a pussy. Go back to the cemetery and hide in your outhouse schizophrenic, and let the real Master do her job," Gothic Barbie snarled at him.

PC looked at Simon. "Rachel? I thought your name was Psycho Tron. Oh shit, I think I am having a fucking melt down over here. Will someone please tell me what is going on?"

Gothic Barbie looked at PC. "Calm down baby. I got this in my hot, loving hands. You just tell your dirty jokes and take everything I give you like the bitch you are. I will show you no mercy, but baby you'll thank me in the morning," I hissed at him.

PC just stared. "Okay, Rachel, Psycho Tron two, whoever the fuck you are. Leave now, I think I am in love here. You are cramping my style. Get out. Let her give it to me without mercy. I want to be her bitch."

Simon pushed PC hard. "Shut up. Shut up! God help me, everyone just shut the fuck up."

The phone rang again. Gothic Barbie smiled wickedly.

"Hi, sorry the answering machine tongue is broken. This is the vibrator filling in for that unsatisfying bastard. You may leave your name and message after the moan, ahh," Gothic Barbie said moaning out loudly.

"Psycho, what is going on. I mean it. I am coming to get you if you don't stop this right now," yelled Master Boyd through the phone.

I snickered. "Oh? You're coming right now? Ah, so am I Master. Oh yeah, harder baby, harder. Sorry I have to go; it is a multiple. I am going to need both hands for this." I hung up the phone laughing even harder this time.

PC was beyond turned on at this point. Sparks began to shoot from his control panel.

"Uhm, Psycho Tron Two, Rachel, whoever you are please flip my switch. I can't take this anymore." Simon reached out and turned him off glaring at Gothic Barbie angrily.

"Alright. That is enough. You have Master Boyd beyond angry and upset now. If you plan to torture him fine. But you are going to get the unit battered at this rate. He is likely on his way now with his ass on fire over your little game," Simon said sternly while eyeing me with fury.

I smiled knowingly. "He can't come running Rachel and you know it. He used up all his sick leave chasing us around. Boyd can fume all he likes. He is stuck. And soon I plan to stick him even more." I started to laugh loudly enjoying my tormenting of Master Boyd's need to control my every move.

Simon shook his head and sat down on Jane's desk. "It is a dangerous game you are playing. We must go back tomorrow. He will still be angry."

I whirled about in my chair to face Simon. "And what about our anger, Rachel. Shall I ignore that? I think no, no, no. Oh, how I love that word no. Hey, Rachel, let me tell you a good one. Do you know how to save a man from drowning?"

Simon shook his head. "Jump in and pull him out of the water?"

Gothic Barbie laughed diabolically, "Ah, no. You take your foot off his head."

The phone rang again. Gothic Barbie raised an eyebrow looking at Simon.

"Persistent cuss, isn't he?" She smiled evilly while she picked up the phone.

"Psycho? Psycho? I can hear you breathing. Answer the fucking phone," screamed Master Boyd.

I smiled realizing he was still at the jail with an audience of co-workers watching his temper tantrum. "Uhm, yes Master. What can I do for you," I said sounding innocent.

He snorted angrily. "You can start by telling me what the fuck is going on. Are you there alone? Who is there with you."

I looked around the room appearing confused. "Define alone, Master."

I could almost hear his blood pressure rising. "I mean is there another human being in the office with you. You know fucking well what I mean, God damn it."

I stifled my chuckling as I heard Keith saying in the background, "Holy shit. Check out Boyd. I have never seen him so mad."

My plan had worked. Every officer within those jailhouse walls was now privy to my Master's hair trigger temper. No more bullshit belief he was just a shy, kindly, calm, good old boy.

"Oh. Well then yes, I am alone Master. Just me, oh, and Simon," I said appearing unaffected by his anger.

Master Boyd took a deep breath. "Now tell me what the fuck is going on. You are behaving strangely. Where is Sheryl?" He was calming down while in the background I heard other officers chuckling at his predicament.

I smiled. "I guess she is at home, Master. I haven't seen her. I was just doing some reports then heading to work at the funeral home. Are you feeling alright? You seem a bit tense." I held the phone to my thigh snickering at my baiting him.

Master Boyd growled, "Yeah, you could say I am tense. My fucking fiancé is behaving like a loon."

I sniffed feigning crying. "What? Master, why? I don't understand. Why would you call me a loon? Don't you love me? I love you. Now you call me at work and insult me for no reason. You don't love me at all. I was fooled. Oh, I can't take this. My heart is broken. What will I do without your love? I may have to jump off the bridge now that all is lost." I hung up the phone again.

Gothic Barbie nearly fell out of the office chair with laughter. Simon crossed his arms shaking his head.

"What the fuck are you doing? Do you know what that guy can do to us? He is a fucking cop." Simon stared at me hard.

I smiled knowingly. "Yes Rachel, he is a police officer, with a nasty little secret hmm? You know what is wrong with all of you? You only think about what these insects can do to us. You forget what we can do to them. He is a man. A man has weakness. More than that Rachel, he needs us but we do not need him. He will never kill the goose that will tolerate his golden eggs. Stop being afraid you fucking toad. You have been on your fucking knees so long you have forgotten how to stand up. Well, I am here to remind you and Boyd who is the one holding all the cards. Now watch, he is about to call back. You will see me own this man."

The phone rang nearly sending Simon sprawling from the suddenness of it.

I picked up the phone holding it making weeping sounds.

"Psycho, Psycho, baby, honey I am sorry. I sometimes forget you are sick. Look, forget I got angry okay. I do love you. You have to believe me," said Master Boyd appearing ashamed of his behavior.

I sniffed loudly. "Really Master? You mean it? I don't think I could go on without you. I love you so much it hurts.

I need to hear you say you love me, like you mean it." I smiled wickedly.

I heard him clear his throat. "Psycho I have never loved another. I love you more than anything. I would do anything for you. You must believe me. Please don't hurt yourself, in fact that is a directive. You will be home tomorrow night. I can prove I love you then."

I pretended to calm my grief. "Okay Master. I will try to hold on. If you are willing to prove it, I am willing to believe it. I guess I am just really missing you. Do you miss me? I can hardly wait to see you. It is driving me crazy." I repeated his own words back to him that he had tortured me with for months almost daily.

Master Boyd coughed. "Uhm, I am, you are, uhm I am almost ready to quit my job and come get you. It is uhm." He hesitated.

I smiled knowingly. "Turning you on, Master. Ah, well wait till you see what I have planned for us this weekend. Now I must go to work. Tell me you love me, like you mean it, and hang up the phone before Dennis catches you."

He paused. "I, uhm, I love you. See you tomorrow baby." He hung the phone up just as directed appearing to understand on some level I had just turned the tables on him but unable to stop himself.

Simon sat there staring in disbelief. "That actually worked? God damn, it worked. You had him eating out of our hands. How, just what the fuck?" He looked at me confused.

My head began to spin as the codes ran up the walls like reverse waterfalls. "We do not have access to this information. Please remove yourself from our sensors. The program must be running or this data will be lost as well. Thank you have a nice day."

Simon sighed. "Okay, I give up. I suppose this shit is working. Just promise me no more shards?"

Psycho Tron flipped on PC's switch. "Negative. Duplicate files will be copied, as necessary. Thank you have a nice day."

PC lit up yawning. "Okay so Psycho Tron get this one: I saw six men kicking and punching the mother-in-law. My neighbor said, 'Are you going to help?' I said 'No, six should be enough.'"

Simon laughed. "Is there some way to switch him to tell good jokes?"

PC frowned. "Hey, at least I am serving a function. What exactly is it that you do?"

Simon looked at me then back to PC. "I used to know how to answer that question PC, but now, I think I am becoming obsolete."

The rest of the night was uneventful. The next day I drove down to the courthouse in Wheatly to await the arrival of Stacey to switch off cars and ride to class. I had not slept in two full days. My fatigue was so deep I fell asleep while waiting the thirty minutes parked in my car. A banging on my window startled me into consciousness.

Master Boyd was standing be my door looking in at me. I was groggy but rolled down the glass.

"Hey baby. Just checking on you. Making sure you made it home okay. Did you bring your stuff home for the weekend?" He was eyeing my seats for signs of my luggage.

I nodded while wiping my eyes. "Yes Master. I was just catching a few winks before class. Are you off shift?" I looked for the squad car before spotting the black vehicle of my nightmares parked two spots down.

He opened my door, "Uhm hum, now come here and let me hold you a minute. I will be sleeping all day and dreaming about having you all to myself again." He reached in pulling me out roughly forcing me into his embrace.

I stood there not struggling feeling dizzy. "Thank you Master for checking on me. Stacey will be here soon." I looked around feeling trapped and anxious suddenly.

My Master hugged me tightly to his unit. I felt his excitement stir making me nauseous as usual. He began to squeeze harder making it hard for me to breath.

"Master, you are hurting me. Please, your hugging is too tight," I plead nearly breathless into his ear.

He smiled and put more pressure around my ribcage. "I don't know what you were up to last night, but I didn't like it. I also don't like the bullshit you pulled in front of Dennis. Do you hear me," he squeezed even tighter.

I felt I would faint. "Yes Master, please." I couldn't speak as my lung worked uselessly.

He leaned down kissing my neck close to my ear still smiling in case anyone was watching. "You fuck with me and I will make you sorry. You don't tell me no. You don't talk back. You don't hang up on me, and you don't play games. If you do, you know what? I think you need a reminder of what I could do if I really wanted to. Tonight, when you get home, I will have something special waiting for you. Now tell me you love me, like you mean it." He loosened his grip.

I felt the tears starting. "Master please, I beg mercy. I don't know what I have done to offend you, mercy."

Master Boyd smiled with thunderclouds in his gaze. "I said tell me you love me like you mean it. I won't tell you again." He began crushing once more.

I gasped, "I love you Master, please no more." My ribs started to feel like they may snap.

He chuckled while rubbing his face into my wig. "I hate this color on you. I will get a blond one again. If you try hard, I might forgive you for making me angry. We will see."

I sniffed feeling very helpless. "Please Master, what can I do to make you forgive me?"

Master Boyd laughed. "Ah, I think we both know. I will see you tonight. Have a great day in class." He let me go and took off getting in his car driving off suddenly.

I started coughing almost hitting the ground just as Stacey pulled up behind my car. I realized he had seen her coming first. I grabbed my backpack and jumped in her passenger's seat telling her to move it.

The entire way to class I fretted over his threats. Stacey must have noticed my agitation. She looked at me appearing concerned.

"So, Psycho, we are going to graduate in like two weeks. It is beyond amazing, but it is really happening. I wanted to wait but since it is going to be crazy with finals and all going on, well I am taking you out to breakfast this morning on me. Surprise!" She looked at me smiling proudly.

I nodded bitterly. "Okay. Whatever you say. I am not really hungry Stacey, but it is very kind of you anyway."

She frowned. "I thought you'd be thrilled. I mean that time the guy, who was that guy, the tall good looking one you used to date. What was his name? Oh, never mind, that time we went with him you loved it."

I felt tears welling again. "Matthew, Stacey. His name was Matthew."

She smiled. "Oh yeah. He was hot. Hey, why did you two break it off? I mean he even dressed like you. You guys were perfect for each other. I mean I thought for sure you'd marry him. Now, this whole business with Boyd. Wow, who'd seen that coming," she said mindlessly.

My tears began to fall at the thought of how far I had indeed dropped from happiness. "I think it would be smart to shut your yap up now Stacey. If you want to go to fucking breakfast fine. Do it quietly." I looked out the window trying to remember my brother's beautiful face wondering if he missed me at all in his land of forever summer.

Stacey pulled into a local restaurant that had an old railroad theme like the dying town did. I got out recalling this place when still living with Mistress Ginger and Matthew. We had pulled the 'stop looking at that redhead' game right in the front booth. It felt like millions of years though it had only been a few. I felt despair in my heart when we walked by the now empty tables. The ghosts of my past were haunting me already and I had only just turned twenty-six.

She ordered a huge breakfast. I ordered only coffee. I was still feeling sick to my stomach. Everything was going wrong. I couldn't seem to find my grounding. My moment of graduation from college was finally approaching. I had worked for years to obtain that sheepskin. It was supposed to save me from a world of subjugation. Instead, I found myself so horridly entangled in my dark world of exploitation there didn't appear to be a way out. Like quicksand, the more I struggled, the deeper I got.

I barely noticed Stacey was yammering on about her kids and my kids growing up together. I looked up trying to catch up with her non-stop conversation. My own thoughts were simply too depressing to entertain.

"Yeah, so it is great. DHS hired me to do Medicaid. I got the call yesterday. You and I will be working together. Well, we will see each other I mean from time to time." She smiled while cramming eggs into her gaping maw.

I blinked trying to clear my focus. "What? What did you say?"

She rolled her eyes. "Damn you never listen. I said Sheryl got me this job with DHS. I will be working with you."

I shook my head. "That is not possible, Stacey. I don't work for DHS. I work for DCFS out of Cumberland, not Wheatly." I was quite upset Stacey even mentioned Sheryl's name.

Stacey chuckled. "Oh I know, but your catchment is also in Wheatly Sheryl said. I was sure glad I knew you. It is because I said I knew you I got the job. Now, we can stay friends forever. Our kids can grow up together. We can have a BBQ and have Sunday dinners. You and Boyd can come over anytime."

I looked at the table unable to believe my ears. "You used my name to get a job with Sheryl without asking me? Really?"

Stacey stopped eating looking confused. "Why sure. I mean we are friends and all. I figured you wouldn't mind. Sheryl sure thinks the world of you. She said you are the best worker DCFS has ever seen. I figured that is why you are with Boyd now. You are both cops. Well you are kind of a cop just like him."

I slapped the table growling in anger. "You fucking pinheaded, twit. I am not your fucking friend and never fucking have been. I hate you. I have always hated you. You are a worthless bag of air, Stacey. You spread narrow minded drivel like the slim from a slug everywhere you go. You are only slightly brighter than a fucking refrigerator light. You're a bully, Stacey. You always have been, and you always will be. You know one of my biggest regrets in life is that I didn't chase you down that day back in high school and wail the piss out of you. If you somehow got the impression I thought better of you, now you know what I think of you." I got up and slammed out of the dining area pacing by her car ready to blow a gasket in anger.

I assumed I would be walking home from school. However, Stacey came out of the diner, got into the car and we finished our last ride together in silence. When she dropped me off at my Intrepid, she told me she'd see me at graduation and drove away. I never saw her again to this day.

Not because she didn't try to catch me out, call my many residences or even see me when I worked for DCFS. It was because I always saw her first, and side stepped the WASP bully who never should have been a part of my story.

NOTE: *When I first became the Goth Queen, she attempted to contact me once again, even getting her old buddy Christy to help. I blocked and banned them both* *immediately. I saw both their profiles. To this day, they are the same old holier than thou windbag pushy bitches they have always been. Good riddance to them both. I do have stories about Stacey and Christy I could have told but I didn't bother.*

These assholes didn't deserve to be mentioned any more than I had to for this story to be accurate. Like Kick Start, Matthew, and Angie before her, at some point I may tell stories of my interactions with this human pig but to be honest, I would rather forget she existed. Sorry, just being honest. I meant it when I said I hated this bitch.

One of my biggest problems with Stacey was her interference with my relationship with CJ and Diana her partner and the LBGT. Her continued bad behavior caused me to lose touch with these two very influential people in my life at a time when their support would have been very helpful. I had been instrumental in helping CJ gain her charter for their organization. The three of us had opened many doors and got changes pushed through. Those changes stopped the random campus rapes, bullying, and beatings of those who lived alternative lifestyles in a time when that was not accepted.

Many of you recall CJ identified himself as a Trans-man. He ended his life not long after leaving college due to intense pressure from those hateful little towns. It is not likely I could have done much to stop him. I had learned after the death of Matthew that when someone has truly decided to commit suicide there is not a lot you can do. That said, I do wish I had been able to at least have given it a shot. I never forgave Stacey for her cruel statements, and purposeful insults. To be fair, CJ and Diane should not have held me accountable for her immature behavior either. It was just a bad scene in both directions.

I stood looking at the purple car wondering if maybe I should try to make a run for it. I tried to calculate how far I could go without income. Sheryl was still taking my income and Master Boyd controlled the government check for my care. I just felt I couldn't handle dealing with whatever cruel punishment Master Boyd had planned for me. I sighed realizing there was nothing I could do. If I ran back to Master Sheryl, I would make it worse.

Plus, I had not visited my children or Seine all week. I missed them terribly. Master Boyd would always take me to visit them for most of the weekend if I stayed compliant. If I denied him, he could not only chase me down using his badge, but he would also have me put away into the Snake Pit for as long as they wanted to hold me.

I was so broken by his crushing commands, lack of giving me choices, and foulness in taking his special services of the collar. He never consulted me on anything. A Master is there to aid me in my struggle, not to create one. Master Boyd didn't seem to understand I am not a slave, nor really a submissive at all. I provide service in return for service, but that didn't give him the right to treat me like his property. His constant abuse of the already very impressive gifts granted by Simon's Key were appalling and beyond my understanding. I would have been happy to grant him all his desires without being forced to while being harmed in the process. He need never worry that I would leave him or betray him. My loyalty to my Master is always unwavering. His brand was uncalled for, rape unnecessary and engagement unwanted.

He would punish my enacting my right to say no by forcing the very act I had denied him in the first place. No matter how much Simon wanted us to kneel to Master Boyd's authority, our Master had done everything possible to prevent it. We could not trust he would not accidently harm or even kill us in some fit of rage. Or worse keep us away from our family for their entire lives.

I got into the Intrepid taking a deep breath. The world began to spin around as if I were caught in a vortex. I started the motor feeling a trance coming on. I felt very odd, as if I were falling inside of my own unit. Each mile closer to Master Boyd's house I got further inside myself till finally I was completely contained within.

Yet, my arms, legs and head were still moving. I wondered if I were being moved by remote control. Nothing was making any sense. I pulled into his driveway fearful of what was on my mind, revenge. This bullshit abuse had to stop. I suddenly realized I had become the very shard that was required to teach a lesson in empathy for pain. Gothic Barbie was now in full command. At last a real Master had arrived to set this mess straight.

Gothic Barbie walked to the door and tried the knob. It opened right up. Master Boyd was still sleeping. She walked into his room taking off her clothing stifling a giggle. Fully undressed she walked to the dresser and removed the handcuffs laying with my Master's badge and keys. She turned and crawled up on top of the dreaming Master dragging the cuffs along the side of his unit.

Master Boyd opened his eyes to see my face above his smiling wickedly. "Good morning Master. I have come to provide the services you have earned. All of them."

I reached down and grabbed the groggy officer's wrists. He began to sit up, but I leaned down engaging him in a deep kiss, probing his mouth with my tongue. I lifted his arms above his head without breaking our game of tonsil hockey. Before the drowsy cop could fully become aware of his 'fiancé's' real presence in the room, she had cuffed his hands together behind the metal bar in the headboard. Master Boyd was now my prisoner.

His eyes came open wide when he heard the click and felt the metal around his wrists. What? What are you doing." He tried to sit up but was held in place with his arms above his head.

I smiled at him dreamily. "Oh, why Master I am loving you the way you love me. Isn't that what you wanted?" I tried to re-engage the kiss, but he pulled away angrily.

"You fucking let me out of these cuffs right now or I will…" I reared back and backhanded the fuck out of his mouth busting his lip open with my ring.

"Or you will what? Bleed?" I started laughing wildly.

Master Boyd's eyes went wide and I could see the sudden terror as he realized his serious situation. "Psycho! Psycho, stop this. You will get into so much trouble. I can have you put away. I can have you arrested for assaulting an officer."

I purred. "Awe, now lover, you could do all those things. I will give you that chance. But first you owe me services and you broke your promise to me. You promised never to hurt me. Shame, shame. Ah, that is okay. I will forgive you. Once we have equaled out the score. Then I will let you go. You can do with me as you like. Beware though, you will never find another one like me. If you end me, who will fuck you." I ran my fingernails into his chest ripping it open, scratching deeply bringing blood.

He yelled out, "God damn it, Psycho, let me go now and I will forget everything."

I laughed. "But I won't. You stay right there lover. I will be right back. I brought you a surprise. Oh, what was yours for me? I want to make sure we didn't get the same thing for each other. Ah, I bet we did. You know what they say, mirrored minds think alike." I kissed his now sweaty forehead then hopped off his bed headed to my car.

The spring winds lapped at my naked unit bringing chill bumps to the skin suit. I giggled as it played with my wig. I smiled into the sky at my brother the sun who laid his warm hands on me in a hug. I took a deep breath of the damp air, listening to the birds call out to roost for the night. It was a beautiful dusk coming. Ah, how I love that unholy hour.

Oops, I almost forgot, my better half was waiting on me to adore him. All I needed was my black bag.

I opened the trunk and grabbed the black duffle bag that Gothic Barbie had packed. Inside were all the tools of her trade. The instruments of pain and pleasure when used by trained hands. Luckily, Gothic Barbie had almost a decade of intense immersion in the cult of the sexual sadist. She had forgotten more than most would ever know about the dark art. There was no need for Master Boyd to be worried. It is like riding a bicycle, once you know how, you never forget.

I could hear my Master yelling and demanding I let him out of his restraints long before I entered the house. The idea that Dennis may interrupt crossed my mind. Ah, we would need to make sure my Master didn't lose any return of his services due to the kindly officer with good intentions. I walked into find Master Boyd twisting with all his might trying to break his headboard to free himself.

I chuckled at that. "Well, since you are so frisky this afternoon, let's see if we can find better use for all the energy."

Master Boyd looked at me his eyes wide recognizing that he had said that very sentence before he sodomized me the first time he brought me to his house.

"Psycho, baby, you need to stop this. Stop now that is a directive," Master Boyd yelled almost frantic now trying to get free as he noticed my black bag.

I threw the bag down and unzipped it. Thudding tools, sexual torture devices of every kind and rope spilled out into the floor. Master Boyd let out a yelp and began jerking hard on his headboard. The heavy wood groaned but held him tight. The metal bar didn't budge. He was sweating and cussing while I dug through my 'tools' looking for, ah there it is. My ball gag.

I took out two long pieces of nylon rope. Master Boyd kicked at me while I stood at the foot of bed waiting patiently. Finally, he wore out a bit. I grabbed one ankle and worked quickly tying it rapidly in a square knot while he pounded me with his other free leg. I took the blows chuckling at his now very cruel threats of shooting me and making the evidence disappear. I warned him to watch his mouth when it seemed to me that I was the one with access to his gun and he was the one tied up now.

That cooled his temper when he finally realized I was indeed the one who controlled this scene. I then quickly bonded his other leg to the other post nearly spread eagle. When he was complexly secured, I straddled the now whimpering Master Boyd again holding the ball gag.

I smiled at him evilly. "Now, while it turns me on to hear you scream, I need you to shut that beautiful mouth of yours. Oh unless I want it to open for my pleasures." I put the ball gag in his mouth and tightened it to a near unpleasant level on his head.

His eyes were wild with terror as he stared at what should never have been. The Gothic Barbie who is the Master sexual sadist.

I slapped his thigh hard. "Let the games begin. Ah, I have waited so long to enjoy you, lover. You are a man of my own heart. You do things without understanding how they feel to your partner. I am here to teach you about pain and pleasure and how to know the fucking difference, you rapist." Master Boyd's eyes went wide as he watched me jump off his unit and head for his phone.

I picked it up and dialed Dennis's house. Lucky for me Dennis answered on the second ring.

"Ah, hey Dennis, it's Psycho. I was just talking to Boyd and he thinks we can make it to Sunday dinner just fine since as I am staying the whole weekend. Unless you think that, is too, uhm, obvious? I am filing against Timmy next month. I have a line on where the bastard is this time," I chirped happily.

Dennis chuckled. "Damn Psycho, I never thought I'd be yapping on the phone to you from Boyd's number. How is my boy? We had a long week you know."

I snickered. "Oh he is in the shower Dennis. I told him to get a nap. I plan to give him a rougher weekend."

Dennis cleared his throat. "Oh my goodness. Okay, well you two stay out of trouble. See you Sunday."

I laughed hard. "Dennis, I can assure you Boyd won't have the strength to cause trouble when I am done working him over."

Dennis blew out his breath. "Ah uhm, what in the hell is it that you do to my officers Psycho," he snorted.

I stopped laughing then said coldly. "It is all in the records Dennis. See you Sunday." I hung up now sure that Dennis would want no part in interrupting his boy's weekend romp with his fiancé.

I returned to Master Boyd who was now near tears having heard me end his last chance to be saved. I smiled at his extreme distress at being held helpless unable to defend himself. I crawled back on top of him grinding my sexual organ into his stomach moaning while looking into his frightened eyes.

"Ah you have to just lay there and take it don't you? Doesn't that just make you feel sexy? It makes me feel so hot. I could do whatever I want and you can't stop me or say no. You know what, I don't like that word. So, from now on, I better never hear you say it. Now, I am going to fuck you. I am going to thud you. Then when I have tortured you to near madness, I am going to sodomize you dry just like you have been doing to me. I am getting wet just thinking about it. Oh, I may do everything twice. Then when that is all done, I am going to mark you Boyd. Because once I have done all that and you are filled in every way with me, you will belong to me."

Master Boyd began to shake his head no with his eyes filling up with tears. I reached down and kissed his wet forehead. "Now, you could make me stop. All you must do is give me Simon's Key. I will take it as payment in full for what you have taken from me. Otherwise, I will take out each service you owe in fair trade. Equal service for equal service. Your choice. If you say no, well, do I need to tell you again what happens when you say no? I don't want to have to hurt you to get you to mind, but I will." I cackled enjoying my return of his horrible words.

I removed the ball gag so he could decide his fate. "Psycho, look, I don't have Simon's Key here. I put it away in a bank vault. The banks are shut down for the weekend. Untie me, undo these cuffs and on Monday we can go together and get it. There is no need for all this." He started to breath hard as I looked deep into his eyes.

He wasn't lying about the key being in a vault. Oh well, too bad for him. I wasn't waiting till Monday to get my paybacks.

I smiled. "Aw, well looks like you are in for a long weekend honey bunny. I will start taking my fair share immediately. Let me show you one of my favorite tools. Ah, you are going to just love it." I jumped off the bed headed for my bag.

Master Boyd screamed out, "Psycho please, look, I will give you the key Monday I swear it."

I turned around with fire in my eyes. "Oh? Like when you swore you would never hurt me? You are a liar. When I hurt you tonight and when I rape you, I want you to take it like a man. After all, I am just a little female, and you made me take it. Didn't you my lover, my Master, my husband? I am going show you everything you and all these other morons in these towns find so fucking fascinating about my history. After tonight, we will be mirror images. Both of us victims of sexual sadism. Now, do scream please. It turns me on when you scream."

I grabbed my leather tawse from the bag and began my thudding without mercy starting with his thighs. Taking my time, we moved to my canes then to my leather strap. When I was finished welting every inch of his safe zones on the front of his unit, Master Boyd was a crying mess. His screams were indeed satisfying and downright sexy.

I found him suddenly much more interesting as a sexual partner. Well, as an unwilling, non-consenting victim to be exact. Master Boyd was certainly not enjoying the play near as much as I had been. I crawled upon his now raw, bruised, welted, angry thighs he hissed and winced while I nipped at his sore areas.

Then I began employing oral stimulation until he was finally unable to keep down his lust. When I was sure he was almost there I manually tortured his scrotum sending his interest right back to its rightful place in my fucking presence. I told him every time he achieved erection; I would torture his soft parts just as cruelly. I was his Mistress. How dare he get a hard on. He was my bitch, not the other way around. Gothic Barbie smiled and laughed.

Then chuckling I informed him I understood he could not be trusted. I pulled out my Kali's Teeth cock ring and collared Master Boyd.

"Now, we understand each other rapist. If you get hard, Kali here will bite it off for you." I winked then kissed his now weeping face.

I used the rope from his bonded right ankle to force him over to his face. I switched his feet but kept his spread-eagle position. Master Boyd was now feeling very freaked out. I imagined he was near insane from chronic thudding, terror of what was coming next and downright humiliated. Welcome to my world asshole.

After allowing him a drink of water and bringing him a bottle to piss in (he refused, oh well, too bad for him) I began my thudding on his backside and back of his thighs. Just as before, I took my time torturing him. The hours passed as I took breaks from my hard but pleasurable labors. I even took time to let him rest for my next promise.

I made sure to show him one of my very favorite devices. I explained to the horrified Master Boyd, this one was completely new, never been used. It was only right that a virgin be used to break in a virgin. I explained it was a perfect empathy teacher for a male who didn't seem able to keep his hands to himself when told no by a young lady.

His begging became fevered at this point as he watched me lace on my very own rape mechanism. My Master promised me all sorts of things, all lies of course. I laughed at his pathetic attempts to keep me from sodomizing him as he had me. Nothing he could give me would make up for what he did. Other than returning the favor.

I looked at my sobbing Master. "Cry all you like, Master. You see I could show mercy and make this less painful by lubing it up. However, you didn't show any mercy, did you? You didn't hear my pleas, my cries of agony or begging you to stop. Yeah, I seem to recall you didn't give a fig. So now I will return the favor. I told you I was going to rape you. The good news is all you have left after that is my mark and we are even, your debt paid. Until you owe me again, which for your sake you'd better hope you don't." I climbed up on the bed and without hesitation pegged Master Boyd till he was near catatonic from my cruel, dry thrusting.

I raped him well, forcing him to call me Mistress. I still don't feel a damned bit bad about it. Not too many of us who have been forced into sexual congress get the chance to pay back the favor. You have just met one of them. Master Boyd learned a lesson about unnatural practices without consent, lubrication, or mercy that night.

Once I was satisfied, he was horridly humiliated, bleeding hard enough, in pain and ready to just die. I finally stopped sodomizing the idiot. I then flipped his big ass over bonding him on his back once again. I removed my cock collar, got him erect and forced him to lay there while I took my own pleasure. He wept the entire time. Likely because despite the despicable acts I had forced on him, his unit still responded to my most experienced techniques at lovemaking. My Master learned what it feels like to be forced into orgasm by your rapist during a rape.

He was beyond worn out and this time was happy to use the bottle to eliminate his urine. I guess I did fuck the piss out of him. I gave him another drink of water while I retrieved my wire. He watched in horror as I fashioned the letter P and heated up the wire. I put my mark on his upper left bruised thigh. I told him so every time he went to try to rape me again, he had to remember my name. His yelling in agony was the most beautiful music I had ever heard.

Once I had finished my final assault on his unit, I packed away all my tools. I walked them back to my car to haul off to the dump the second I left his house. I would no longer require them. Master Boyd had either learned his lesson or next time I would murder the bastard. I still wore his fucking collar and killing a cop was not a smart move. Not for a schizophrenic, mother of two who allegedly was engaged to the fool.

I returned to the shaking, blubbering Master Boyd. I untied his feet but left him cuffed for now. With great gentleness I treated his wounds and his burn. I even aided him in all his sensitive spots by providing secret healing salves exclusively for torn and ripped mucus membranes. Then very kindly I kissed him. I even praised his bravery and courage at having endured his first session of sexual torture.

He seemed confused by my loving after care. I explained to him that I had not attacked him because I wanted to hurt him. I had done it to teach him empathy for what his behaviors were doing to me. Then I spent the next hour explaining his role as my Master, why giving a choice was necessary, and made it clear I would no longer allow him to treat me like a slave or rape victim. I asked him if he enjoyed being my plaything.

"No, I suppose you are right. I did have that coming. I should have thought, I just didn't." He sniffed now calmly.

I looked at him harshly. "You thought like everyone else that I didn't matter, didn't have feelings, didn't you? You assumed I don't know who I am, so you could do what you wanted."

He looked at the ceiling. "Well, I am still cuffed up, so you won't believe me no matter what I say. But you are right, I guess. I really didn't think at all. I just wanted you. So when you said no, I took you anyway. Your life was so horrible. You always showed up beat up, or kidnapped or worse. I thought I was doing a good thing. I guess I got all caught up in it. I realize now I was wrong."

I shook my head chuckling. "You are almost there. You took what you wanted thinking no one would stop you. When I told you no, you tried to beat me down. You are selfish, cruel, and you raped me because it made you feel powerful. That is the truth. You are as sick as I am Master."

Master Boyd looked at me. "I won't deny any of it. So, now what? Will you kill me?"

I laid back next to him. "Ah, no I will let you go. And likely you will kill me or hurt me again. I am not afraid of you. Sooner or later if you let me live I will get you while you sleep. One of us will die or…" I hesitated.

He turned his head appearing curious. "Or what?"

I sat up on one elbow. "I will let you go, and we start over. I will mind your collar, and you will do your fucking job properly. Right this minute I consider us even. I will forget what you did if you forget what I did. We can do this right. I want to love you Boyd, but you must try to be worthy of it. The way I see it you have sexual needs no normal will tolerate. I have problems no normal wants to deal with. You and I are similar in many ways. We are both monsters in our own fucked up worlds. I will willingly submit to you this time, if you will willingly submit to my requests for freedom of choice."

Master Boyd sighed. "I won't stand for my fucking collar to tell me no. Kill me right now if you want to but that is never going to happen, Psycho."

I chuckled. "Boyd, listen to me. You must allow me to accept punishment instead of just taking what you want. I won't ever deny you if you are reasonable. No matter what you ask. Just be reasonable and allow me to ask for punishment. Then use something other than what I said no to for it. I need that freedom or, well, you need to return that Key to me. I will fight you till you kill me or I will kill you."

He closed his eyes. "Okay, okay. You are right. I know you are right. I will never find another you. I need you or I will be alone. I will give you choice of punishment if you use any other word but no. As for this mess tonight, I swear if you uncuff me I won't punish you or otherwise retaliate. It never happened and you never breath a word of it. I keep the Key and you submit to me willingly and I will stop taking without asking."

82

I nodded. "I agree to your terms, Master Boyd. Now I am going to uncuff you. Remember your vows and I will never neglect my own. If you are lying, just make sure to make the death quick please. I am very tired. I would like to get some sleep anyway I can. Death looks pretty fucking good to me right now." I got up and got the cuff key. Within moments Master Boyd was free to keep his promises or to end my life.

He sat up wincing while he rubbed his now cut and bloody wrists. "Wow, I look like you did during the Julie days."

I stood at a distance ready to run. "Yeah, I was trained, she wasn't. I promise nothing is broken. You will heal up without any scars. Save the brand." I waited for his fury.

Instead he smiled at me appearing tired. "Well come to bed baby. I suppose tomorrow we will be taking it easy. I am beat." He chuckled at his accidental pun while looking at his welts.

I snorted. "Yeah, you look it." I crawled into the bed while he wrapped his arms around me engaging me in a loving kiss.

I pulled free. "You aren't angry at all?" I eyed him suspiciously expecting he would throttle me in my sleep.

He laughed. "Oh I am super pissed, but I told you I had it coming. I hated myself for what I did. I do love you Psycho. More than you can know. I just can't stop myself. At least now I can stop feeling so fucking guilty about it. We agreed, we are even. Nothing between us to prevent you from loving me the way I love you right?" He stroked my cheek looking very sincere.

I laughed at that. "Just be careful how you love me, I always return the service." Master Boyd joined me in laugher as we laid back in each other's arms slowly drifting into the sweet release of slumber.

Wait, what? He didn't get up and kill me? I didn't force Simon's Key? What is this happy bullshit? Well, if you want to know why I didn't shit can this rapist and he didn't strangle me right away you must keep reading. I promise a lot more fun is coming. I always keep my promise.

Chapter 60: The High Price of Twisted Love
Master Boyd and Interim Master Sheryl

I hope everyone is staying safe out there in that cold, brutal world we all call home. Now, let's get back to the distraction of a time, long ago, and far away. This part of our journey had so many lessons to teach. It was chalked full of betrayal, violence, loss, revenge, redemption and finally love. Wait what? Love? Well, that depends on how you define that most enigmatic word. Twisted feelings can get all mixed up. Master Boyd is the King of the misunderstanding of emotions and motives. To this very day it is unclear if he was ever truly a Master in the line of twenty-seven others. In all our life, we shall never meet another so confused, complex or perpetually fucked up individual, other than perhaps ourselves.

Gothic Barbie has set the record straight. She cleared away the dead from an epic battle of loss, degradation and hostility. Through her most cruel and loving touch Master Boyd has learned the lesson of empathy for his collar. It is now up to the deranged cop to employ his hard-earned knowledge to save his place as holder of Simon's Key. New understandings will create a delusion that will pull the Psycho and the Policeman into a dance of consensual violent love. This dance macabre will become the fuel for many dark imaginations.

The sexually sadistic shard is far from done with her task. There is another Master of Neglect left lying around waiting for her turn. The Gothic Barbie has not forgotten that this situation has become a storm from the bitter power hungry Master's continual disregard for her needs. While the male needed lessons in pain, this Master requires schooling in boundaries. Taking without giving is theft. The Gothic Barbie simply will not tolerate a criminal holding her ring of silver. Equal service for equal service. It is time to pay back all that Master Sheryl has stolen.

Oh, aren't you just all hot and bothered to get on with this amazing journey into our sorted past? We knew you would be. Stop looking around for that black bag you naughty ones. We threw that away. This time grab that ticket book, the one over by the Barbie Doll. Get ready to throw off your black clothing and exchange it for that white jacket. We know just how to scare someone straight. Even if she has no soul, even the Devil fears something.

"Oh Sheryl. What are you doing here? I didn't know you knew Psycho. Can I get you a plate, I guess?"
--**Officer Charlie to Master Sheryl, August 1998**

I awoke to the sound of Master Boyd's alarm. He had forgotten to shut it off for the weekend. I snickered realizing it had slipped his mind thanks to my distracting him the night before. I rolled over. My Master was stirring. His sharp jaw was grinding while he moaned out in pain.

"Aw, what's the matter Master? Sore?" Gothic Barbie giggled while wrapping her arm around his chest.

"Christ, I can't even move. What have you done to me," yelled out Master Boyd with his eyes still closed while he winced from my touch.

I laid my head on him listening to his heartbeat. "I loved you Master, don't you remember? Just like you asked me to."

Master Boyd slowly lifted his bruised arm to rub his face. "Oh Psycho, this is horrible. I want to just die. Shoot me and put me out of my misery. That is a directive." He groaned.

I chuckled. "Now, now Master. You expected me to serve you after loving me all night and day the same way. I only gave you twelve hours of love. You will get up and you will attend your services to me. Just as I attend them to you. No excuses. Service for service lover. You and I need a shower. Plus, I have your wounds to attend. We wouldn't want your big bad self to be brought down by infections, now would we?" I rubbed his shoulder lightly.

"I can't get up Psycho. Even my eyelids hurt. Just leave me, save yourself." He chuckled then moaned again in pain. "Oh my God, I can't even laugh without pulling something." Master Boyd suddenly expelled a loud fart as he tried to sit up.

"Oh, my God. What the fuck. Shit, that just slipped. I am so sorry, baby. Christ, I can't control it." He looked at me terrified as he continued to cut the cheese in rapid succession.

I stifled my giggles at his horrible discovery of forced sodomy side effects. "You are just so romantic, lover boy. It does seriously suck, doesn't it? You see when you force a dry fuck up the ass it tears up the sphincter muscle, Boyd.

87

That is why it bleeds, fool. It will take a few days before you re-gain complete control of your more personal functions. I wanted to share with you the pleasure you gave to me. Oh, you are going to have so much fun you lucky boy. Just think of all the fun still in store for your ass, literally. Days of burning when you get calls from nature, embarrassing uncontrollable gas, oh, and the itching when it heals. You should be totally looking forward to that. I thought you would appreciate knowing exactly how that feels. Not just the act but the days of pain and humiliation after. What a rush huh? Don't you just love it? Doesn't that just turn you on, lover boy?" I glared at him hatefully while crossing my arms.

Master Boyd's eyes went wide. "You ruined me? I am going to be stuck like this? What am I going to do? Oh my God."

I shook my head while rolling my eyes. "Quit being a baby. It will heal up, just like the rest of you will. In a few days you'll be right as rain but you won't soon be forgetting our little special backdoor lovemaking moment my darling. I will warn you just this once. If you ever dry fuck me like that again, I will cut you a new asshole instead of just return the favor next time. You understand me?"

He nodded appearing ashamed of himself. "Yeah, I hear you. I didn't realize how bad it was. This is terrible. It was beyond a nightmare."

Gothic Barbie smiled. "You are turning me on, Master. I think we can warm up those stiff muscles and make you forget your discomfort with a little fun. Then a shower." I quickly straddled him despite his loud protests of discomfort.

I engaged him in a lover's kiss. It became so wanton his busted lip began to bleed again. Master Boyd tried to push me off, but I would not let up. Despite his best efforts, his manhood began to give in to his rising temperature of passion.

My unit was grinding into his eagerly. He closed his red, swollen eyes begging me to let him rest.

"Please Psycho, I don't have the strength for this today. Give me a few days to heal up, then I will fuck you silly," he whined.

I grabbed his wrists holding them to his chest. "You didn't give me days to heal. I want you right now. So, you will lie there and take it like I did. Remember, you did this to yourself." I snickered at my returning his own words to him.

Master Boyd just nodded. "I suppose you are right. I didn't think about how you felt. This is hell. I should have been more understanding." He looked at me appearing sincerely sorry for his past cruelties.

"But you didn't think. So, you are about to learn it the hard way. Cry if you want, but I am going to have you." I began kissing his neck while he shuddered, and goose bumps rose all over his skin.

I forced his entry and began a slow methodical thrust which made him yell out in torment. His now viciously bruised upper thighs and raised blister brand were rubbed by the friction of my mount. His erection didn't fail while I maintained the position of power, likely to his surprise. I took my pleasure from him forcing his submission to my lust. He needed to learn to find interest when he was not the one in control. After his initial misgivings he was swept away by his carnal sensations. Just as in the shower days before we found our climaxes in unison. Master Boyd's call outs of orgasm were very loud this time and tinged with curses for his many injuries.

Though I tried to stifle it, I giggled at his complaining. "See, wasn't that nice? Time to get up. You need a shower and medication."

Master Boyd looked at me appearing afraid. "I told you I can't, God damn it. I can barely move."

I slapped his sore thigh making him yelp. "Bullshit. You can and you will. Get up. Laying here will only make it worse. I am going to get you some Ibuprofen to help, but you are getting up now." I hopped off his unit headed for his kitchen to get the mild pain reducer.

When I returned, he had only managed to sit up a bit. He had his eyes closed, still groaning loudly. I stood there holding his Coke and pills shaking my head.

"Well, look at what we have here? The big badass cop who was going to shoot me just last night can't even get up to take a piss. Get up Master. Stop being a baby." I snorted with disdain.

He turned and looked at me. "Okay, I am getting up. I need help, I think. I am not sure I can even walk. How the fuck did you do it all those times? I saw you beaten like this and still doing what I told you or fighting with Dennis and me." He looked at me in awe.

I growled, "You'd be surprised what you can do when you have to Master. Get your lazy, pussy ass up now. If you don't, I may be turned on just enough to go get my black bag again. I hate to waste the opportunity to punish the weak. It is a real turn on for me. You know like it is for you. Mirrored minds think alike."

His eyes went wide. "Seriously? That is what you think is my turn on?"

I leaned back my head laughing loudly. "Think? Master, I know it. You are a dark one indeed. I can see right through you. I have become you, Master. I told you this last night. Your sitting there helplessly is making my motors run. I am warning you, better get up before I hurt you more than I already have."

Master Boyd looked at the floor. "I won't accept that is what I really am, Psycho. You have me all wrong. I don't get turned on by hurting the weak. That would make me a..." he trailed off suddenly appearing to realize I was right.

"A rapist? A bully? A criminal? A twisted fuck? Am I getting warmer, Master?" I glared hatefully at him.

My Master gritted his teeth as he pushed his legs to the floor taking a brief rest on the edge of his bed. "How can you ever love me now that you know that about me? There is no way you could ever love me, admit it. I am finished. You will eventually leave me and I will be all alone. I don't think I can handle that. I waited all my life for you. Now that I have had you, I can't bear to let you go, not ever. I also can't stand the idea you won't love me even if I hold you hostage. I am doomed to you always hating me for what you think I am." He seemed to become overwhelmed by his sudden insight to his cruel nature.

I sighed. "Look Master, you are one sick bastard. You can lie to yourself if you want but I know better. If you were a decent human being, I would not be here in your house with your orgasm inside my unit and your mark on my arm, now would I? You and I both know you had no business fucking with me in the first place, against my will or with consent, which you didn't have. You were supposed to be protecting me from rapists and exploiters. Instead, you became one yourself. That is done. You can't undo what you did, nor will I allow you to sit there denying that is exactly what you really are. That is not relevant to me. I am not able to be picky. I need someone who will care for me and help me stay as independent as possible. I can't help being schizophrenic any more than you can help your sexual perversion of total control of the helpless. I don't have to love you or even like you to give you what you want in return for what I need. It would be nice if I could love you for real. It is always possible you could change my mind about you. After all, you already did change it once. I did love you before you took advantage of me like you did. Because of that, I hate you more than you could ever know. However, you have this one chance to start over. Maybe if you are fair, caring and treat me right, it could happen again, who knows? Stranger things have happened in my life and in yours too."

He nodded his head still looking at the floor. "You are right. I could change your mind. I am a perverted freak. I never realized it but yeah raping you was amazing. I think about it all the time. I admit it makes me crazy wanting to do it again but if I ever did that to any other woman, I would go to prison. So, I had to have you for myself. You are the only woman that I could do that to and get away with it. I want you to know, for what it is worth, I really do love you. Even if I could just take any woman I wanted without punishment, I would still only want you. That is what is killing me inside. I love you so much, but I have to hurt you to feel aroused. It is just so fucked up. I don't understand it. I would do anything to make it stop." He began to sniff as if tearing up at his confession.

I nodded. "Oh Master I, know you would. None of us want to be the monster we are. You have a demon inside you. There is likely help for it through therapy but you won't take it. I know you. I will have to submit to your violence and cruelty or you will have to toss my collar. That is very clear. I know you will never be satisfied with loving gentle sexual congress. I am crazy but not stupid."

Master Boyd looked up in surprise. "What? You are saying you are going to submit to my perversion? Psycho, I will eventually hurt you really bad. I mean, I am sitting here in agony from just one attack. How can you take a lifetime of this."

I smiled bitterly. "I have my ways Master. You leave that to me. I always find a way to endure. If you meet me halfway, this could work. I could learn to satisfy your fetish if you can learn to control your temper and strength of attack. I am very small and you are very strong. I won't last long if you can't cool your urges a bit. Let's take this slowly and see what we can do to make us both as comfortable as possible anyway. I am getting very ill. Soon, you will suffer more than you know and have last night. I am willing to provide equal for equal, but you ever take more than your fair share again I would not want to be you Do we understand each other?" I looked at him hard.

Master Boyd held out his hand. "Yes, I do understand, and I love you even more for this. You are truly the most wonderful person on Earth. How did I get so lucky," he said as I took his hand and he pulled me into a loving embrace.

I kissed his neck. "You didn't get lucky Master, you took advantage. There is a big difference."

He quivered at the touch of my lips. "I won't deny that. I am not going to lie and say I am sorry. I am not nor will I ever be. You are everything I dreamed you would be and so much more. I will do whatever it takes to earn your love. Did you really love me once like you said?"

Master Boyd pushed me out so he could look into my face. "I sure did fool. I thought you were my hero. Turns out

I was a bigger fool than you are. You are no hero Master; you are a real asshole." I started to laugh.

He frowned. "Yeah, guess I am. Damn, I had thought better of myself."

I slapped his thighs making him gasp. "Okay enough of the sappy bullshit, Master. Time for that shower. Now take three of these and follow me. Better hurry up wretch, you smell like sweat and humiliation. It is turning me on."

We both howled in laughter at my most true statement while he did as I commanded. He was unable to walk without aid due to the severity of my thudding service. He was weaker than a kitten the entire day. My Master also could not tolerate clothing. He was forced to wear his robe and slippers.

When walking even to use his privy he required I hold him up despite the use of over the counter pain relievers. I ignored his tenderness forcing at least three more sexual romps with him throughout the day and well into the night. Eventually, he gave up trying to resist my forcing of his services. I was unable to see my children or Seine thanks to this tough love lesson with my unwilling student, but in the end, it was worth the sacrifice.

By Sunday morning, Master Boyd had engrained within his consciousness empathy for my situation when he behaved carelessly with my unit. It would be several years before he pulled anything even near what he had in the beginning of our turbulent relationship. The rapist finally concluded being too rough with your toy could result in a broken plaything.

Like my Master, I had an epiphany that weekend. Master Boyd did deeply and hopelessly love me to the core of his soul. It was also sadly clear he could never love another due to the insanity of his sickness. That knowledge upset me a great deal. It meant that if I could not work out our very serious issues, then one of us were doomed to a life of horrific loneliness and/or pain or both.

QUICK NOTE: *This fact broke my heart back then because I knew I could never love him back as deeply as he loved me. As I made clear in the beginning when I discovered his crush on me, back during the days of Julie, he and I were never meant to be together. His stupidly forcing this relationship had destroyed all the true love feelings I had ever had for him.*

I did find a deep sense of caring for the man who would hold Simon's Key for seven long years. I also will say he is my second great love affair, even though it was dysfunctional as hell (Matthew was my first, Johnathan was not love beauties).

I may have never been able to forgive Master Boyd for what he had done, for what he is, but he was not completely evil, not by far. The punishment, which did come to pass, of complete devastation should be only granted to the most demonic of souls.

If you understand that then do know Master Boyd would eventually end up overly punished for his crimes against me. Unfortunately, it came to pass because just like me, he is trapped in a sickness he never asked for, nor would he ever escape. He will become the Master we loved to hate but also hated because we loved him. That is what his story is all about. On with the show.

Sunday morning Master Boyd was feeling a bit better, but still very weak and sore. He was able to tolerate getting dressed for our visit to my children, and dinner with Dennis and Carla. My Master had been very careful to mind my every command in his position of submission to me. Gothic Barbie had enforced role reversal since my arrival that Friday afternoon, but by noon I could tell he had learned his lesson. The student was now ready to resume his place as the Master.

I returned to showing him submissive respect just after forcing him to provide me bath service.

I knelt down before him after he toweled me off. "I am now willingly submitting my will to you Master. Be careful not to forget real control starts within you. If you can master yourself, then I can grant your darkest desires. We are two sides to the same coin. If you try to overexert your power, then you will break our bond. If that happens, you will not get another chance to try again."

Master Boyd looked down at me appearing sad. "I am beginning to understand that Psycho. Being you has been horrible. I want to make your life better. Then you will love me. I will be a better Master, lover, and friend to you I promise."

I sighed. "Do not make vows you cannot keep Master. I have no doubt you will be a better Master, and perhaps a friend, but a better lover is not yet in your power. Your demon must be fed. In order to do that, you will ask a lot of me. If I am to provide for it, the cost in return will be high. I doubt you will be able to pay it. Your self-esteem is too low, and your fake outer self too proud. I am not always right. I hope you prove me wrong, but I rarely am. I know people better than they know themselves. You lie to yourself, so you will lie to me too. Honesty is the first step to trust. Trust is required to find love for another. Your reflection is both ugly and beautiful. For you to be able to find my love, you must first face the beast inside you and be honest with yourself and me about it. Only then can you be trusted to do anything more than hurt us both with lies and empty promises." I looked at the floor hoping I didn't make a horrible mistake letting this monster have a second chance.

Master Boyd reached down taking me by my waist to pull me into a loving hug. "I know you think I am not listening, but I hear you my love. I will be honest with myself and with you. I am perverted and I am truly sorry for it. I can't get help or I risk my career. If you don't meet my sick needs, I will hurt you to get what I want. I won't lie about that anymore. I won't stand your telling me no. I can't stand to be denied what is mine. I want you to love me despite all that I just told you. I am willing to kill you to keep you for myself. Now, there is the truth. What now? How can you ever get around all that when you say you need freedom of choice? Taking your freedom is exactly what I need to feel satisfied. Psycho, I am not going to let you go. You need to get that through your head. Even if you hate me, I won't let you go." He started to tear up realizing he was now being completely honest with himself for the first time ever.

I nodded in his arms. "I know all of that Master. I am glad you finally do to. We have it all out in the open. No more lies, secrets or pretending this is something it is not. This is all about your selfishness. You love me because you have no choice. You can't stand giving me what you know you don't have. You fear that I will choose to leave you alone and miserable because you are twisted. I won't choose that. You now have honesty. Next, we work on trust together. You must learn to trust that I am loyal to the Key. You hold the Key so I will find a way to work around this issue."

Master Boyd sniffed back his tears then twisted his face into a storm of anger. "Oh? You think so? I don't see how. Just know that now that you have submitted willingly I am feeling the urge to take you whether you like it or not. I am seriously pissed off over your behavior the last two days. I am not going to retaliate because I promised not to. That said, I am going to show you who the real Master is right now. Go ahead, try to tell me no and see what you get." He smiled wickedly as he grabbed me by my throat slamming me into his bathroom wall with force but without cutting off my air supply.

He began ripping at my shirt while I laughed at him. "Ah, here is the real Boyd. Go ahead, show me just how tough you think you are. No matter what you do, I will always know you are just a little bitch. You will never forget that and neither will I, Master."

Master Boyd growled. "Oh yeah? We are about to see who the bitch is." My laughter at his rage fueled his urgency and caused him to forget his pain from his bruised unit.

He spun me around forcing my face to the wall while he tore down my pants and undid his own.

My Master entered to his hilt in a single strong stroke. "Who is the Master? Say it. Who is your Master," he yelled out in ecstasy.

I gasped at the suddenness of his impact into me. "Please Master, don't, please stop. You are the Master. You are hurting me," I yelled out appearing afraid.

Master Boyd ignored my imploring him to end his sexual attack. Instead, he began thrusting roughly becoming enthralled with passion from the violence of his taking back his power by dominating me intimately.

I hid my smile while I continued begging him to stop. My seemingly earnest pleas of helplessness were driving him insane with lust. My Master wrapped his arms under my arm pits to force me down on him harder. I had anticipated this behavior and encouraged it. While very painful, it was not going to cause serious injury. I was only acting fearful. Thankfully, Master Boyd didn't realize it.

I had figured out that giving him the belief he was forcing me to fuck him was enough to feed his despicable appetite for rape without causing a real one to happen. The solution was very simple. All I had to do was push his buttons which would set off his need to regain control.

After I made him angry, I could play the helpless victim unable to stop him from fulfilling his foul needs at my expense. It would not be an easy ride for me. I would have to allow him to take out his anger demon on my unit sexually. I knew I would have no difficulty pretending I didn't really want or expect that response. It was clear if I didn't cry, beg or try to fight him off it would not appear sincere.

It was a perfect plan to solve this very serious issue. Not only would it give him the experience of rape he craved, but it also granted me the choice to decide yes or no. I could make sure not to set him off unless I was certain I was willing to take the assault that was going to follow every time.

I gritted my teeth over his harsh, agonizing, rapid thrusting and pulling. Toleration of his violence in the act was the serious drawback to my plan to attend his desires. For that, I would have to try to trust him. I could only hope he would not forget what it feels like to be needlessly harmed during the acts of lovemaking. I decided if he kept his brutality within reason, I would endure it.

However, if he ever pulled dry sodomy or strangled me again, I would murder him in his sleep. He now possessed empathy for the cruelty of such acts. I had warned that if he ever pulled those things again, he may as well hand over the key as I would consider his collar tossed.

It didn't take long for Master Boyd to reach his orgasm from his fake raping encounter. He moaned out how much he loved me while he spilled his seed deep inside my unit. I held my breath, ignoring my screaming nerve endings grateful it was over. I braced for the onslaught of cramps that were already starting to appear on the scene.

When he took me like this, it was never pleasant on my end. I would get over it. Vaginal cramping and soreness was not the end of the world. I was no stranger to discomfort during carnal congress. Master Boyd's fetish, while disturbing, was not as unmanageable as I had first assumed it would be.

My Master turned me back around engaging me in a passionate kiss. He told me how beautiful he found me. Master Boyd, in typical fashion, appeared quite loving despite the cruelty he had just shown in his taking what he wanted without asking. I sighed in relief that my false behavior had appeared to work splendidly. He believed he had raped me and was now trying to console me over it. If I was very careful, I could grant this very strange service to him and still maintain my dignity.

I looked at the floor pretending to sniff back tears, "I understand Master. I am not to say no to you ever. I will try to remember that. Can I see my children for a little while before the dinner with Dennis and Carla? Please? I beg mercy."

Feigning being humiliated was not hard as I thought it was going to be. I suppose I had enough damned practice at the real deal to know how to give an Oscar performance by now.

Master Boyd lifted my chin with his hand. "Oh of course baby. I bet you have been missing them, haven't you? I will come with you and stay on the porch. Will that be okay?" He smiled kindly.

I nodded knowing this was a trap. "As you wish Master. I will not tell you where you may or may not go. Thank you for this favor."

His smile widened. "Now that's my girl, but first the gift I promised you on Friday." He left me against the wall in the bathroom while he headed for his closet in the bedroom.

Gothic Barbie got prepared to fight sure that he would return with something foul. She was positive he decided to backdoor retaliate by claiming this was a punishment for the phone call argument of Thursday. However, to her surprise, he returned with a box.

Master Boyd handed me a very high priced long, straight blond wig that almost perfectly matched the hair I had lost in style and color. He smiled as I examined it with surprise.

"It took me forever to get this. I searched everywhere but couldn't find one that I liked. Then I finally found a woman who makes them. I let her borrow the photo I had of our submission at Darlin to match your picture exactly. I paid extra to make sure it was real hair, not the synthetic crap. Try it on. See if it works," he said appearing very proud of his ingenuity.

I stood in the mirror and switched out my wig with Master Boyd watching behind me. Before my eyes, a girl I finally recognized stared back. Psycho looked back at me while my Master hugged me tightly around the waist.

He gleefully said, "Now I have my baby back just the way she was when I found her. I love it. You are truly the most beautiful girl in the world. Especially because you are my girl." He kissed my neck rubbing his face in my newfound locks.

I nodded. "Thank You Master, I think?"

QUICK NOTE: *I was unsure what he was up to with this strange re-creation of a lost image. Something deep inside me became nervous. It seemed so silly to fear a wig or his words, but in retrospect I was right to be afraid. It would be several years before I truly understood my misgivings that day but do try to recall this incident. Its meaning was deeper than I could have ever imagined.*

Master Boyd took me to see my kids, Seine and Maiden Mary. To his credit, he always minded his promise to stay out of the picture when it came to my children. He took his usual spot on Mary's front porch swing while I went inside to visit my scattered family. I was immediately overwhelmed with happy little babies and a grateful hairy canine brother.

Maiden Mary was shocked at my sudden return to my natural look of long blond hair. "Mother, this is amazing. You look like you again. How? That can't be you, is it?"

I chuckled. "No, it is a good wig, daughter. I am glad you like it."

She smiled. "Love is fixing it all, Mother. Since you and Boyd got together you are not around enough, but when you are you look so happy and healthy. I told you he would fix everything, but you are still wearing that collar. Sheryl needs to go. If you would just stick with Boyd."

I interrupted her irritated that she had dared to stick her nose where it truly didn't belong. "Mary, I love you. That said, you ever say another word to me about my collar business you can kiss my ass goodbye. I will not have someone tell me anything about what they don't know shit about. You listening to me?" I glared at her.

Her eyes went wide in fear. "Oh, okay, yeah sure. Sorry Mother, I just, well you are right it is not my business. Forget I said a word."

Gothic Barbie continued her angry glare at Mary. "I already have. Next time I won't have a memory lapse. No more warnings. You must stop questioning my judgement. Boyd is sitting on the front porch because you seemed to think you know better than me. That lack of trust is going to eventually break my heart when I walk away from you. I know you may not want to hear that, but I know me. You betray me again, and I won't forgive you again. Do what I tell you and stop meddling in my affairs."

Maiden Mary raised an eyebrow appearing to want to ask why I had said that. It was obvious in my statement that Boyd was not supposed to be with me. She had ignored my unit language and sudden lack of parental care. Mary, like so many before her, only could see what she wanted to see. I was not happy, healthy or in a good situation. I was miserable, acutely psychotic, and being held hostage by a deranged rapist. I was now severely delusional. I was ready to blow my last gaskets or shards to be exact.

Mary nodded her head narrowing her eyes. "Yeah Mother I understand. Hey, if there is anything you ever need to talk about, I am always your friend before anything else."

Gothic Barbie laughed wickedly. "Are you now? Hmm, then remember that. I do need friends, but not a fucking mother. I already have a Master so stop trying to play something you are not."

My psychosis was starting to show through despite my best delusional effort. While I visited with my kids, my Maiden went outside to visit with my captor. She apparently asked a lot of questions based upon my sudden burst of irritation at her. Once again, she had unknowingly betrayed me to the very creature that had started the entire downslide into schizophrenic hell.

I got into my Master's car after kissing everyone goodbye. Master Boyd was quiet as usual. I didn't think too much of it. Until he took off onto a long dirt side road that would stall our arrival at Dennis and Carla's place an extra fifteen minutes. I felt my unit shudder a bit over past situations on backroads with my lusty, violent Master.

He slowed down our speed sighing. "Mary told me you jumped her ass, Psycho. She said you talked like you and I weren't getting along. Like maybe she had pushed our relationship against your will." He stole a hateful glance at me.

I shrugged. "Maiden Mary is a histrionic Master. I told her to butt out of my affairs but only because she was asking too many questions about us. She knows about Simon's Key. I told her to mind her business because I was afraid she would get wise to who you really are to me. If she took it to mean anything else that is not my fault."

He grabbed my left hand showing his ring to me. "You see this? Do you? That means we are engaged to be married. That is your collar and it belongs to me. You are going to be my wife. I am your husband and that is who I really am to you." He pulled the ring to his mouth and kissed it.

I winced. "Master, I am not allowed to argue with you about this. I will merely state the facts. I am your submissive and Simon has not approved any marriages. Plus if you recall I am still married."

Master Boyd growled. "I no longer give a shit what Simon says. I have put up with all I am going to take with your telling me no. We agreed you would not say that again. You have submitted willingly to me. I have earned the right to be your husband. The next time Mary asks about us you will tell her you love me with all your heart. I have done everything you asked me to do and still you want to deny me. That is going to stop now. Furthermore, when we get to Dennis's place you pull anything to embarrass me, I would not want to be you when we leave. Do I make myself clear? You can consider that a promise I will keep."

I glared at my Master. "As you wish Master." Gothic Barbie decided it was best not to push this very large man any further. He had everyone on his side, even my own damned Maiden.

When we arrived at Dennis's house, Master Boyd took me by the hand. He commanded I smile, keep my head down and mouth shut. I thought that would be the wisest thing to do. These were normals. Not like my Master and me. They didn't have monsters inside of them lurking in the darkness. I never had any luck understanding their type. I suddenly realized that is why my Master was always so quiet around Dennis. He must have been like me, afraid if he opened his mouth a demon would pop out and give him away.

Master Boyd slipped his arm around my waist while he knocked on the door. I was for once grateful to have him there to guide me. I already felt my unit quivering with anxiety over trying to fit in where I simply never would. He felt my shivering.

Master Boyd leaned down to my ear. "Calm down baby. Let me handle this. I have got you. You said you had to learn to trust me, then trust me." He kissed my neck then my mouth deeply.

Carla opened the door to find us necking on her front porch. "Oh my, Boyd and Psycho. Come on in you two. Ah, to be young and in love once more. What I wouldn't give." She laughed while blushing slightly.

Master Boyd pulled from our kissing, wiping his mouth. He jerked me in front of him hugging me around the waist. It was not just for show. He was attempting to hide his growing excitement from Carla. My Master never could keep his physical symptoms of sexual readiness down when we kissed too deeply.

"Hi Carla. Uhm, sorry about that. Is uhm, Dennis here," he said appearing struck dumb by his being caught wanting to fuck me on her front porch.

Carla chuckled. "Now Boyd, you know he is. Come in. He is waiting at the table. You know how grouchy he can get when he is hungry. We'd better get him fed." We followed her inside the modest home.

Dennis was indeed waiting at the long rectangular table appearing gruff. "Took you long enough Boyd. I was about to start eating my damned napkin."

Master Boyd held out my chair while I sat down appearing a bit out of sorts by that odd behavior. I was not used to being treated like a lady, especially by Master Boyd. He sat down next to me taking my hand under the table as usual. I could feel how sweaty his palms were. I assumed he was worried I would say something to get him into trouble. My Master had nothing to worry about. I had no intentions to start trouble in front of my long-time savior and father figure. I kept my mouth shut, head down and suffered through one of the most uncomfortable dinners of my young life.

Dennis and Carla yapped about church happenings, who was having a baby, and the state of the world in general. My Master was as subdued as me. He rarely spoke mostly nodding or shaking his head. I made sure to serve him by putting his food on his plate as the meal was passed around the table. I noted that Dennis watched as I fussed over my Master's needs. He appeared suspicious but I told myself it was just my guilty conscious.

I knew Dennis would hit the roof if he knew I wore Master Boyd's collar. My loyalty to the Key would not allow me to betray the identity of my Master even if Dennis had asked me outright. I was now willingly submitted, so my promises were in stone by the rules of my lifestyle.

When dinner was done, I helped Carla clear the table. While we washed the dishes together, I heard Dennis say the strangest thing to Master Boyd.

"Boyd, I know we talked about this, but I am going to remind you one more time. I see the way Psycho is fussing over you. I sure hope that is because she is smitten as you are with her, and not what I think it could be. You let me hear you have been treating Psycho with anything other than respect, I will tear you apart son. I mean it. I find out you are threatening or hurting her in anyway it won't be good for you boy. I promised your parents there would never be any more trouble out of you. God rest their soul. I will make sure that promise is kept. I am still thinking this relationship you two have is a mistake. Two people with serious problems simply don't belong together. You need a girl who can keep you in line, not one who needs help too. She is not able to

take care of herself. She has no business taking care of you."
Dennis was trying to talk softly but I heard his words clearly
despite Carla's happy chattering as I dried the dishes.

I wondered to myself what Dennis knew about Master
Boyd that I didn't. A promise to his parents of no more
trouble? Dennis said two people with serious problems and
he was aware there could be hurting or lack of respect shown
to me.

I began to realize I was not the first one Master Boyd
had come after. It was no doubt he was a virgin to sexual
congress when he raped me in the white cell, but it sounded
like my Master been caught trying to do it to another before
me. He must have been stopped from completing the act.

I stood there racking my brain. I had never heard a single
rumor about Master Boyd being anything other than quiet,
shy and odd. My Maiden had not heard of any trouble out of
him either. Maybe this was something from his very distant
past or even a kept secret?

I decided to very carefully find a way to get Dennis to
tell me what knew but was not sharing. Figuring out how to
get that information out of him was going to be tricky. I
didn't want to set off any alarm bells in my old friend, but I
believed I needed to know. There obviously was another girl.
How did she get away? I wanted to talk to her and find out.
Maybe I could escape from Master Boyd like she apparently
did.

I saw my Master flash a look my direction. I looked
down quickly mumbling a response to Carla's prattle as if I

had not been listening in on the male's conversation. I didn't need my Master to know I had heard anything of their talk. My Master went back to speaking quietly with Dennis. I strained my ears to hear, but their words were of no interest any longer. The topic had been dropped.

Finally, the uncomfortable dinner ended. My Master and I left Dennis and Carla's after several hugs from the couple, and promises we'd return soon for another visit. Both of us sighed a breath of relief when we were back on the road headed to my Master's home.

Master Boyd looked at me smiling. "You did wonderful. Carla really loves you, but not as much as I do," he said happily.

I nodded. "She is exceedingly kind. Dennis is indeed lucky to have her, the old goat."

Master Boyd laughed loudly. "Ah, you do make me smile. Dennis is lucky, but I am luckier. I have never been such a happy man. I have everything I ever wanted. One day I will be the big man in county and you will be my Carla. Loyal, sweet and compliant. Just the way a woman is supposed to be to her husband." He grabbed my hand kissing his engagement ring again.

I held back my shuddering at those words. "As you wish Master. I will need to get going soon. It will be dark before long."

His look suddenly turned dark. "You are staying with me. No more fucking Sheryl. That job is killing you. You are

112

not yourself. I should not bring it up but this whole weekend has been fucked up. I think you are sicker than you appear. I am sure you need help even though no one will listen to me. I forbid you to return to Sheryl. Not this week. You need rest. That is final."

I shook my head. "Master, I graduate in two weeks. If I don't finish my internship, I will lose my credit hours for it and it will forfeit my degree. I have worked more than four years for this honor. I am not going to tell you no as we agreed, but I beg you allow me to finish what I started long before you collared me. I will take care of Sheryl more harshly than you can imagine. She has a reckoning coming. You would deny me that?" I looked at him sternly.

His eyes went wide. "You are going to punish Sheryl? Well, baby while that sounds like something the old bag has coming. I just can't risk letting you get hurt. I checked on her. She is a raging bitch you know. Long reputation for using others for her own gain. I think maybe you should just cut your losses and come home. I will protect you from shit heads like that if you only would let me. Or if Simon would." He cleared his throat.

Gothic Barbie smiled. "Master, you have seen my work. I believe you are aware I can indeed handle myself when pushed. Allow me this mercy. I would humbly ask you allow me to finish my course work and then give Sheryl what she is owed just as I did you."

Master Boyd bite his still sore lip appearing deep in thought. "Okay, you finish college and graduate. I will stay out of it. I don't want you fooling with Sheryl though. In fact, I want you to go get Seine. Have him with you until this is all over, that is a directive. I want you protected when I can't be there. I also want you to call me every day, no excuses. After graduation, things are going to change around here. Your psychiatrist told me you should not be working any job, but this one you have is definitely not good. I don't need your doctor to tell me that. It is messing with you, making you sick. I can fucking see it. Baby, it is going to kill you and Sheryl is going to hurt you for real. I know you and I have our issues, but that bitch, that is serious shit. You have had enough of seeing blood, abuse and horror. When are you going to stop doing that to yourself?"

I began to laugh wildly. "Says the rapist Master. Seriously? Yes, I have had enough violence to last a couple of lifetimes. But then no matter where I go there it is. I thank You for your mercy, but I will not get involved in a fight with you over my choice in careers. Not yet anyway. I must get through the next two weeks, then we can talk about this. Deal?"

Master Boyd frowned. "Yeah, deal. We are going to talk but in the end, I am the Master. You do what I tell you period." He pulled the car over to the shoulder.

I looked around confused. "What are you doing? Why are we stopped?"

He smiled. "Giving you a reminder of who your Real Master is. Get to it." He pointed at his crotch demanding a blow job.

114

I did as he commanded to keep the peace between us. I knew he would likely demand special service before allowing me to return to Cumberland. One act was as bad as another, though I really hated his habit of demanding oral sex while driving down the backroads. The only good thing about it was if his hands were on the wheel, they weren't on my head forcing an already rough situation to become unbearable.

I left him with antibiotics and other soothing agents for his still healing unit. He held me as long as possible with groping, kissing and whining about my being gone a full five days from his grasp. My Master reminded me at least ten times to call nightly once I had gotten rid of the bitch Sheryl so he could hear my voice. I endured his clinginess reminding myself to check into the story of the girl who came before me.

As usual I could barely contain myself when I tore out of his driveway headed to my Maiden's house to pick up my beloved Seine. Gothic Barbie was indeed here to set Master Sheryl straight like she had Master Boyd, however, first I needed to graduate.

Kicking Master Sheryl in her woman nut sack was not smart until after I had completed the task of walking the line. It had been denied me from kindergarten to high school. I was going to be damned if I would miss my chance to see what it felt like to graduate like a normal person does.

Seine and I made it back to Master Sheryl's house just before ten that Sunday night. She was furious at the late hour but something in my face told her to 'fuck off' about using her cane. I suppose Gothic Barbie put off a vibe few could miss. The Barbie would have shoved that cane right up her ass had she dared. I was tired, had a ton of services to get on, and in no mood for Master Sheryl's punishments when she never returned even a third of the services back.

The next two weeks were a whirl of rushing from interim Master Sheryl's home to provide service, to the office to do field work plus data entry, to the funeral home, then back to Wheatly to serve Master Boyd while still finishing up finals. The day of graduation arrived just as I was ready to completely lose it with fatigue and stress.

I had started college in 1993 under great stress and with the intention of becoming a forensic pathologist. I had to drop semesters a few times thanks to inpatient treatments and terrible personal losses such as that of my beloved Matthew in 1996.

Now in May of 1998, I would walk the line with a bachelor's degree in Psychology with a minor in Biology. I was granted the honor of the gold tassel as the Summa Cum Laude (4.0) graduate. I had struggled, fought and defended my right to hold my degree in ways most people would never have imagined in their wildest nightmares. I let Simon come with me that fine day. I drove myself to the collage but was surprised to find Master Boyd there waiting for me. He told me he would not miss the event for anything in the world. He himself had not made it to college but had always wanted to go. He took my hand and walked me to join the line of students waiting to enter the area and receive our hard-earned letters of success.

Master Boyd kissed me passionately and wished me luck. I watched him go through the doors to join the other family members and loved ones of my fellow graduates. Only Simon and Master Boyd came to see me. I may have had my problems with my Master, but his coming there to witness my finest moment meant more than I can say. If he had not shown up, I would have done it alone, just like most everything else in my life.

I walked in the line with all the others and we sat down in chairs in the center of the huge auditorium. The other young people were nervous and chattering. I looked up at the bleaches all around us at the sea of proud faces. Photos snapped all around and children chased each other through the aisles. For that moment, I was one of them. Not on the outside, but a person of worth. I saw Master Boyd and Simon sitting there smiling both with looks of joy. I had made it. I had done the impossible. I had achieved the piece of paper that said I was of value and competent.

The President of the college came to the podium. He asked all the gold tassels to stand so the crowd could see the finest of the finest. I stood up alone among the students of Social Sciences. There were only five of us in the entire graduating class in any field. The crowd clapped and I watched Master Boyd stand up yelling and screaming in admiration with many others who knew the six of us. The other graduates looked at us in awe. We were the 4.0's, the perfect students, the ones who kept you from passing on a curve.

The names began to be called out. One by one the person would walk to the front to shake the President's hand while he handed them a rolled up fake piece of paper to represent your degree. Camera's flashed and mother's sobbed. Finally, my own name was called. Because I was one of the special, the President had the college's own photographer take a photo of him handing me my 'fake' award while shaking his hand.

I hated the President, Doctor Smith, more than you can ever know. He had allowed Doctor DeGrove to steal my future and forced me into a field I despised.

When I had complained of my poor treatment he had said, "Oh well, Doctor DeGrove will retire soon enough. Just wait around. You should be looking for a husband and not worrying about actually graduating anyway. A pretty girl like you could even marry a doctor if she tried hard enough."

The photo did not catch me with tears or a smile but a glare at the misogynistic asshole who let a slimy bastard screw me over. I would never forgive him for treating me like a dumb bimbo. He was certainly surprised to see my face accepting the top award. Turned out I didn't need to marry a doctor. He suddenly realized I was smart enough to be one. What a prick.

NOTE: *Only one year after Doctor DeGrove had denied me access to my chosen path of pathology, he died suddenly of a heart attack. He was touring the sights in*

London, England when the call of nature came to him. He had entered an alleyway to take a piss, what an asshole, and keeled over face first into a befouled puddle. His final gasps were in that stagnate water riddled with his own urine among heaps of garbage and wild alley cats. While that seems fitting for this creep, I wish he had done this the year before he took my future from me. Karma did get him, just too late to save me. As for Doctor Smith, I will get him back in a way he never expected but that is for another chapter. He does end up paying big time by my own hands for his part in my destruction. Something to look forward to in another chapter.

The ceremony was over. The new degree holders turned their tassels and hugged each other goodbye. Stacey walked toward me to congratulate me, but I walked away getting lost in the crowd before she made it. I went straight to Master Boyd and Simon. He hugged me tightly.

"I was so proud of you baby. Look at you. A college graduate. Oh, all those assholes in town who badmouthed you can lump it now." He kissed me with his blue eyes shining.

I nodded. "I didn't do it for the town or the bullies or anyone but to prove I am not just a stupid schizophrenic. Now I can be taken seriously," I said actually believing that was all it would take.

Master Boyd frowned. "Honey, whoever told you that you are stupid is a fucking liar. You didn't need a degree to prove your intelligent. No one I know is smarter or tougher than my girl. If anyone says differently you send them to me. I will shoot their ass." He hugged me tighter.

I sniffed realizing Master Boyd probably would shoot them too, and me as well when I told him I wasn't quitting my job. I had started to enjoy my job as investigator. At least I told myself I did. Mainly because no one there treated me like a loon. When I testified in court, arrested or interrogated, I was believed. Everyone hated and feared me for the right reasons. I was busting bad guys and bringing down child abusers left and right. I didn't want to become just a mindless submissive on her knees blowing Master Boyd after his hard day at work.

I had earned my degree so I could stop having to do that shit. It was working. I had a real job that had nothing to do with taking it up the ass or having to bow or scrap, hoping I didn't get beaten too bad. I thought I was for sure ready to be a normal now that I had the credentials. In fact, I decided I no longer need a collar a key or a Master. Psycho your next, reality will see you now.

I told Master Boyd I needed to return to Cumberland to get my things and say goodbye to Master Sheryl. He believed me and couldn't stop hugging and kissing me in pure joy. He thought I was finally giving in to his demands to live with him and give up my job with DCFS.

My Master let me go after my promising to hurry back home so we could celebrate our perfect day (yeah for him if I actually had done that.). I took off with great speed headed back to Master Sheryl.

While I had no intention of quitting DCFS, I did have plans to finally set this neglectful bitch on her ear. Well, Gothic Barbie did to be exact. I arrived in her driveway just after five, ready to kick her ass three ways from Sunday.

I pushed through her door to find her laying on her couch watching TV as usual. Her feet were propped up and she was flipping her remote mindlessly.

"Sheryl, I am here. I want you to take this fucking collar off my neck. I am done with this shit. I will no longer mind you, and you will give me back my fucking check." I growled before even dropping my purse or taking off my coat.

Master Sheryl sat up appearing shocked. "What the fuck are you talking about, Psycho? I am not taking your collar off. You are my submissive, and as for your check, that ain't happening either. Take your medication, get my supper going and shut the fuck up or I will punish you." She laid back down still flipping her channels ignoring me.

I smiled wickedly. "You apparently didn't hear me. I said now." I walked over to her TV and kicked it off the stand sending it crashing to the floor.

I turned around. "Ah, that will get your full attention won't it?"

Master Sheryl sat up stunned and angry. "You fucking bitch. I will call the police and have you arrested for that. Who the fuck, do you think you are?"

Gothic Barbie started cackling. "I am your retirement fund asshole." I kicked over her TV stand.

She stood up grabbing her cane. "You are busting up my house. I am calling the cops. You need to be in the hospital." She went for the phone, but I moved faster.

I grabbed it and tore it from the wall. "I am going to break every fucking thing you own Sheryl. You owe me thousands of dollars, so I will take it back in trade. Give me my check and take off this fucking collar or I will collect what you owe me in unpaid services." I reached out and threw her lamp to the floor shattering it.

She backed away appearing afraid. "Psycho, stop this, I mean it. You will go to jail for this."

I shook my head. "Nah, you would be too afraid of losing my work hours. Now let's see, what is a VCR worth these days?" I rushed to her toppled TV stand, ripped out the VCR and stomped it to smithereens.

While I bashed her electronics, she ran to her phone in the kitchen and made her call to the local police. I overheard her 911 call and realized I had to get out of dodge immediately. The police were coming and I knew damned well what happened the last time I got too cozy with the local cops.

I stopped bashing her stuff. I walked over to her as she hung up her phone. "You will remove my collar you useless bitch. I will be back and when I come have that key or have your affairs in order." I smiled baring all my teeth then walked out her door slamming it so hard it broke the glass from its tiny window.

I got into the Intrepid and hauled ass at breakneck speed headed for the county line. I could hear the sirens in the distance, but they mistakenly went to her house first. I made it safely past the sign marker. I was likely halfway to Wheatly before they even started looking for me. I headed right for Master Boyd's place. I had no intention of staying but for now I needed a hide-out. No better place to run then under the cops' noses with my policeman boyfriend.

I pulled into Master Boyd's driveway almost sideways from my racing without inhibition. My mind had snapped. The long time coming psychotic episode was now showing through. Not even Gothic Barbie could stop the thought disorder, communication errors, and full on loss of reality from overtaking my shattered mind.

I barely remember how I got to Master Boyd's house, and it is almost like a dream seeing him come running out to find me pacing, babbling and drooling like a loon in his front yard. He had dealt with my violent symptoms before. He called Dennis to aid him in capturing my unit fearful he would only get me hurt trying to subdue me without assistance. Until his partner arrived, he sat there on his car quietly watching his submissive ramble, twirl and dance. Master Boyd knew better than to upset me with fast movement, touching, or blocking exits.

Dennis arrived in his own personal vehicle. He kept my attention will my Master snuck up behind finally knocking me to the ground and handcuffing me so I couldn't harm myself or anyone else. The officers stuffed me into the back of Master Boyd's car and took me to the local ER off the books (without calling Cathy). I was admitted this time diagnosed Acutely Psychotic the very afternoon I had graduated the top of my class from college.

Master Boyd true to his promise kept a watchful eye on the doctor's treatment of me. He was there every day to make sure no one pulled any shit. It was determined I was suffering from a complex delusion of multiple personality shards running the unit. Under that delusion was the typical symptomology characteristic of my disease such as hallucinations, cognitive malfunction and identity confusion. Powerful antipsychotics at near dangerous levels were pumped into my system rendering me almost catatonic from the side effects.

I have almost no memory for this two month stay in a third floor psychiatric wing of a small town hospital. I do know what the results were. Gothic Barbie went back to sleep and Livevil did too. Psycho Tron, and The Chosen One did not. When July was about to end, the uneducated psychiatrist of that ward decided I was well enough to be released back into the public. Despite the obvious signs I was far from well and still acutely delusional.

Master Sheryl had been contacted and told I was in the hospital. She never bothered to visit or call me. Not a surprise. I had done several hundreds of dollars damage to her house. That she got over. Missing two months of work, now that pissed her off. She had been harassing Master Boyd almost daily demanding I be released soon. She needed me back out in the field immediately. He did not say nice things about that.

Master Boyd fought tooth and nail to keep me in treatment. He couldn't stop them from letting me back out on the streets still dangerous as hell to myself and others, but clever enough to convince them I was of sound mind. My delusion that I was a robot was completely ignored, as was my moments of continued paranoia, irritability and sudden temper outbursts. Without any fanfare, Master Boyd was contacted and told to pick me up, they no longer wanted me in one of their beds. I stood waiting with the nurse while Master Boyd loaded up my luggage grumbling that the whole psychiatric system was full of quacks and charlatans.

He gently aided me into the car continually asking me if I was okay. I was still very high from sedatives and unsure how much time was passing or even what was happening. I recall seeing a cicada bug crawling along his windshield. I was in a trace watching it move slowly when my Master got into the car to take me to his house.

Master Boyd smiled. "Well at least you are finally home with me safe at last. I am sorry they couldn't fix this. I will keep looking around for help. Someone somewhere has to have a way to make you right again." He grabbed my hand and put his engagement ring back on my finger. They made him remove it while I was in stir.

I looked at him blankly. "Affirmative Master. This scrip is running long. Our program has had to shut down and reboot. An upgrade should prevent future stalls in the program."

Master Boyd shook his head appearing worried. "Shit Psycho, you are worse than ever. Fucking idiot doctors. What have they done to you?"

I smiled from program memory files. "Nothing Master. That is the problem."

He nodded. "Finally we are agreeing on something." He drove off toward his house taking me to the next stage of my most epic psychotic episode ever recorded.

Chapter 61: Playing the Fool
Master Boyd and Interim Master Sheryl

We are charging right into these reigns of yore. Oh, what a terrible mess we have already made of everything. We have not even begun to realize the scope of stupidity of this tale of woe. Lack of understanding, impulsivity, and missed chances are the rule of these days late in 1998. Our quicksand trap was one of our design, though we could not see it at the time.

Of all the lessons we will ever learn, these chapters of extreme chaos contain the hardest of all. The scars will be so deep that we wear them like the second letter of the alphabet on our arm. We can never forget they are there.

We have achieved greatness. As a college graduate and top investigator, we are celebrated for our mental toughness and tenacity. The roar of the realm of liars is so loud we cannot hear our own warnings to not believe everything we see and hear.

What we thought we knew, we had no clue. Full of the hype we will rush headlong once more into traffic. That is to be expected. This time Dennis was not there to save us. In a repeating cycle of self-absorption we will discover one should never judge without all the facts. We had not returned a favor, but we were quick to forgive a slight. Both were terrible mistakes that took us right into the path of the vehicle of destruction.

We had forgotten sometimes one is innocent until judged guilty. Some monsters are not born, they are created. We should have recalled this fact. After all we had been human once too. Believing we were the only victims in a world known for twisting the truth was a failure most cruel. We will pay an exceedingly high price. One will suffer forever for it. The other will believe they got what they came for. Our fall from glory will be steep. This time, we will not completely recover from our injuries.

The guilt is at our own doorstep this time. Our crime was indifference. The punishment is more severe than we could have imagined in our darkest nightmares.

Ah, so it is time to get back to climbing this mountain right to the top. The air is already so thin we can hardly breath. Try not to crowd each other, there are already too many of us on this narrow slope. We do have a safety rope, but we don't trust it. Just try to remember, one foot at a time, don't rush this. What is your hurry? Let's take this really slow for a while now. See if we slip, we will be doomed.

"Did you say that there skinny law dog holding you was called Boyd? Hell's bells, Psych,. I just knew I known him from somewhere. Oh shit. Yep them there eyes of his. I should have known. No one's has them devil's eyes but Boyd. He's all grown up so I didn't suspect that was him. I were just a sprig of a girl back then, but I sure do member what happened that there summer. Oh shit, was it ever a mess with him and Maddy. You know they put him away for it."

--Angie revealing the secret of Master Boyd's past to Psycho, August 1998

Master Boyd helped me from the car leading me into his house. Psycho Tron did not give her Master any trouble but followed quietly in prefect protocol. He looked back at me several times to make sure I didn't break into a run for my own car. There was no reason to worry. I had not been granted release from his service. I never betray the collar.

Once inside he sat down asking me to join him. I did as commanded confused by the allowance of the furniture and not kneeling at his feet.

"Psycho, you are not well. I don't know what to do. If I send you to the Snake Pit, they could hurt you worse than you already are. If I do nothing, you are going to get worse I have no doubt. I want to ask you to give up DCFS. Stay here with me and I will take care of you until this cycle passes. Psychosis is not deadly on its own, but if you are left without supervision, you could end up dead by your own hand or by someone else's. Please listen to reason. I am at my wits end here," said Master Boyd while appearing sincere in his pleas for my giving into his wishes.

Psycho Tron felt the collar around her neck. She knew that while secondary, Master Sheryl had not released her from the contract to make her Area Manager. Master Boyd had not released her from serving Master Sheryl. There was no way to follow his wishes without betraying one or the other.

"Master, your coding is not following the program. This is a syntax error. It does not compute therefore it is to be deleted from our memory storage immediately," I said in a monotone voice.

Master Boyd shook his head appearing defeated. "Baby, you are completely gone. I would tie you up and make you stay, but that would not be right. I will never get you to love me doing that horseshit. Yet, letting you leave, oh what am I going to do? How can I help you? Please tell me."

I checked the data banks for information on proper response. "Allow me to return to my job and Master Sheryl. I must remove this collar to mind your commands. This program is terminal. Once Area Manager is completed, Sheryl is obsolete." I smiled without emotion.

He looked at me appearing confused. "What? I am not sure I understand. Are you saying once you make Area Manager you won't mind Sheryl and will come home to me?"

I shook my head slowly. "Negative, Sheryl must be Area Manager. It is all in the program. Once this command is completed, she is obsolete. I will be capable of re-programming at that time. The scrip is already running. Aborting of this mission is not possible. I will not delete this from our source. I am willing to fight you to keep the plan in progress Master."

Master Boyd put his head in his hands. "There is no reason to threaten me. I won't stop you this time. I suppose I must trust you like you asked me to. I promised not to hurt you anymore, and in order to make you listen I would have to beat the hell out of you apparently. The way you are now, maybe you will get arrested and sent to the Snake Pit anyway. As it is you likely will kill the old bat. I suppose I should warn her. Maybe between the two of us we can keep you from fucking yourself up. Psycho is there anything I can say to change your mind?" He looked at me appearing very sad.

I smiled mechanically "Negative Master. Thank You very much. Have a nice day."

Master Boyd snorted angrily. "Fuck me. This is beyond messed up. I can't believe this is happening. Who looks at you and says oh she is all fixed now Officer. You can take her home. This is a fucking nightmare. I am going to lose you; I just know it."

I got up headed to the door. "Negative Master. I never betray the Master program. You are the Father Board now. I will follow your commands that are not in conflict with already running script. Thank You have a nice day."

Master Boyd stood up. "Wait just one minute. You are leaving now? Psycho you are full of sedatives. It is not safe to drive damn it. If you are going to insist on going, I will take you."

He got up and quickly took me by the upper arm leading me to his car. My Master pushed me into the passenger's seat without saying a word. Then took the wheel, taking off toward Cumberland and Master Sheryl's house.

I sat there quietly listening to the coding and transmissions from 'they.' The whirling motor reminded me of the sound of fax's heartbeat. It soothed my circuits. A memory code came across my monitor. There was an error that needed repair within the unit. I would need to attend to that situation immediately before it disrupted the scrip in progress. Slow running programs were obsolete. We knew what happens to those who cannot be of service.

Master Boyd stole looks at my breasts and appeared to be longing. He reached over several times to hold my hand or pet the wig he had purchased for me. However, he didn't demand special services as we had expected. We had been inpatient for two months. It was a surprise he was able to contain his lust the entire trip.

My Master didn't even request oral sex going down the road as he was so known to do. This was confusing but I was most grateful. Perhaps, he was finally getting his impulsive urges under control. Uhm, there is a dude calling himself Reality looking for you Psycho. Should I tell him you are out to lunch?

We arrived at Master Sheryl's house just before dark. Her new TV could be seen glowing eerily through the window. Master Boyd parked the car then looked at me sternly.

"I am going to let you stay here with Sheryl watching you. I want you to call every day. Do not miss a call. On Friday I will be back to pick you up. Be here, no excuses. I mean it Psycho. You do what Sheryl tells you and mind your collars. If you don't, then I will be forced to send you away to the Snake Pit. I will be watching. The second Sheryl makes Area Manager; I want you to come home. You understand me? These are directives." He took my left hand to kiss his engagement ring.

"Affirmative Master. Thank you. Have a nice day," I said with a fake smile and very little head movement.

He shuddered. "My God even insane I want you more than you can know. Please get well soon baby. I can't live without you for long, not anymore. Now let's go. Behave yourself. Let me do the talking." He let go of my hand and got out of the car headed for Master Sheryl's porch.

I followed him three paces behind appearing unable to recall why this was not going to go well but having a sense of trouble. The heavy sedatives in my mainframe was fucking with my programming. My Master knocked as I watched Master Sheryl come hobbling toward the door.

She opened it and looked immediately angry. "What the fuck are you doing here asshole. Psycho, get in this house, now," growled Master Sheryl.

I tried to follow her command, but Master Boyd blocked me with his arm. "No you don't Psycho. Not yet. Stay there." He backed me up then looked at Master Sheryl just as angrily as she looked at him.

"Now you listen here Sheryl, Psycho is very sick. You are not taking good care of her. I won't stand for it anymore. I don't give two shits if she is wearing your stupid collar. I am her Guardian and this overworking my girl is going to stop. You will also give her those checks back. If you don't maybe I will make a few phone calls and make sure you never make Area Manager," he snarled at her.

Master Sheryl's eyes went wide. "What? How dare you threaten me you asshole. What is going on with Psycho and I is not your business. You said she is still sick? Then you suck as a human being and at being a guardian. It has been two fucking months. She should be well by now. What did you do, send her to some country quack?" She pointed her cane at him.

He chuckled aggressively. "You are a dumb bitch. Schizophrenia runs in cycles. Psycho will be well when the cycle has passed no matter how long you lock her up. As it is, she is delusional right now. She thinks she is robot and this is a problem. She won't eat or bath unless you make her do it. Now I am going to honor your collar, but you will need to keep a close eye on her. Watch for self-injury, starvation, filthiness, and catatonic behaviors. If you see any of that call me or for fuck sake call 911. Be sure to tell them she is schizophrenic or the dumbasses will shoot her. Don't threaten, yell, hit, or touch her if she is agitated. If you do then it is your funeral lady. I am leaving you some information on how to handle her and when to be afraid. I can't fucking believe I am doing this but if you collaborate with me, we can keep her out of State till this bullshit passes or until I can find real help. Do we have an understanding? If not, I will take her back home with me right fucking now, even if I have to beat both your asses." He glared at her waiting for a response.

Master Sheryl looked at me, then back to Master Boyd appearing to calm, "Yeah, you have a deal. Let me have the information and a phone number to reach you. I don't want her to put away any more than you do. I suppose I will have to play ball with you until she is well, not a robot? Seriously?"

Master Boyd nodded. "Yeah, seriously. Come on baby." He motioned me to follow him inside behind Master Sheryl.

I sat quietly watching the coding on the walls while Master Boyd discussed my care with Master Sheryl. She appeared to be interested in his warnings and instructions for safety in handling my psychotic ass. I suddenly felt faint while Master Sheryl wrote down Master Boyd's number in her address book. My head was aching as The Chosen One took over the unit.

She looked at the two Masters trying to work together to make sure to use me to both their advantages. It made the Chosen One smile wickedly at the Sinners. She would wait till the right moment and kill them both. It was what the Higher Power wanted. When the heart is black it belongs to the King of Hell. I was happy to give him back his property. All I had to do was wait for the right sign.

Master Boyd finally appeared satisfied Master Sheryl was going to comply with his requests. I chuckled at the fool. Master Sheryl only cared for Master Sheryl. She was surely only playing lip service to the deranged cop. She was not stupid. It was always easier to catch Psycho with honey rather than vinegar. He got up headed for the door demanding I follow him to get my things for my week stay with Master Sheryl. I did as he ordered despite Master Sheryl frowning in silent irritation at my minding this man.

Master Boyd handed me the luggage still packed from my inpatient stay. "Now give me a kiss baby. I think it will be okay, but we will see. Just remember, one mistake and I will not let it go this time. Behave yourself and mind Sheryl, I mean it." He leaned in for his kiss.

The Chosen One smiled with demonic glee then grabbed both sides of his head pulling him in closely. She kissed him lustfully, forcing her tongue into his mouth. Master Boyd moaned out wantonly trying to pull away from the torture of the tease. I held tighter, grabbing locks of his hair to hold him in my steamy embrace.

He grabbed my wrists forcing them off his head and pulled back with force. "Enough, I cannot keep my cool if you do that. Now go before I take your ass right here in Sheryl's driveway when I forget myself. Damn it, go." He adjusted his now protruding zipper appearing irritated at my brash behavior.

I turned to walk away but stop on the porch watching him watch me with a look of need in his eyes. "I love you, Master. See you Friday." I blew a kiss at him then went inside leaving him stunned.

Master Sheryl was standing in her kitchen waiting for me. I came in and she put her finger to her lips appearing to be listening. I stood there listening too, unsure for what though. It was at least five minutes or more when I heard Master Boyd's car start, then pull away.

Master Sheryl sighed with relief. "Ah, there. I wondered if that asshole was going to want to live on my couch too. Damn Psycho, how did you get messed up with him? What a bastard. See that is what happens when a gal gets around males. They are all trouble." She took me by my hand leading me back to her couch.

She had me sit down next to her while she looked over my unit with the same look Master Boyd often had. "Well, I was mad at you over that breaking of my shit business. Then they put you in the hospital and I realized it wasn't you at all. You are sick indeed. Sick or not, you work like a Trojan. So, I missed you a lot. Did you miss me at all?"

I narrowed my eyes at her. "Uhm, sure. What is this about Master?"

Master Sheryl picked up her notes from the talk with Master Boyd. "That is what I love about you, Psycho. Right to the point, no bullshit. Okay, so here it is. You do need my help or you are going to end up in prison or worse. I didn't really believe you had schizophrenia, but boy do you. Here is the deal, I will do all this stuff this Boyd idiot wants me to do and even give you back your check." She smiled at me appearing proud of herself for saying she would give me what she had already swore to do in the first fucking place.

I nodded. "Yeah, and so what Master?"

She frowned. "What do you mean so? I said I will take care of you and give you your check back. Isn't that what you want?"

I chuckled evilly. "What the fuck do you want in return, Master. I am not in the mood for games. Out with it. You must want something really bad to grant me what you have withheld so far. It can't be over Boyd. or losing my collar. It is something else you want? Hmmm?"

Master Sheryl sat back on the couch. "Alright you want it on the table, here it is. I was recently put up for the position of Area Supervisor in Creek County. If I get that position, Area Manager is next. It is the last step up my ladder."

I crossed my arms. "What does that have to do with me, Master? I can't fucking hire you now can I? Are you asking to suck someone's dick to get you the job?" I glared at her angrily.

Master Sheryl's eyes went wide. "Oh God, no. Well, it turns out, well, there is someone in my way. They are the one the big dogs are going to offer the job to first. I need you to get them out of my way. I am second pick."

I rolled my eyes. "I am not going to shoot someone to get you a fucking position Master nor beat them up."

She shook her head then removed her glasses. "Psycho, you are their first choice. If you turn them down, they will me raise instead." She looked at the floor hiding her irritation at what she just revealed to me.

I sat there unsure I was not hallucinating. "Excuse me? Did you say I am the one they want to hire for that job? That can't be right. I am still in probation for another fifteen days. You need seniority for that job. You must be mistaken, Master." I was not enjoying her little game.

Master Sheryl snorted. "The job starts in twenty-five days. So, yeah, they can hire you. They found out you were doing all the entry for the CHRIS program, and the big dogs went ga-ga over your numbers and cleared case load, and your cleaning out of the bullshit in the counties. It would appear I created a monster, Psycho. Your hard work got me put second to the very job you were supposed to elevate me to." She sighed while putting her glasses back on.

I shook my head. "That can't be right, Master. I never told a soul about the CHRIS program. Did Jane betray you?" I couldn't believe my fucking ears. I was being offered a job that was only one step down from big boss of the entire region and I was a new hire.

Master Sheryl chuckled. "Nah, old Jane is an old hag and a bitchy thing but not a tattle tale. It was Nora from DHS side. The nosey bitch called and told on me. She has always fucking hated me. This is her kick in my ass."

I looked at the floor. "So, if I turn down the offer, you will give me my income back? And service for service like you promised at our collaring Master? That is all I must do? Why should I believe you? Once you have the job, maybe you will rip me off again. If I take the job you are my bitch, right Master?" I smiled again full of demons.

Master Sheryl didn't take my baiting her very well. "Yeah, you can say that if you want Psycho. You have me over a barrel. However, if you play ball with me, well I can do a better job. I was wrong to ignore you, to let you suffer like that. If you will give me a second chance...I will make it right. I was stupid to get all caught up in my need to become Area Manager. I had the most wonderful thing already in my lap and ignored it. I do want to have more than just a D/s relationship with you. If I have this job, I can finally relax and enjoy you and all that we can have together, a real relationship. I can love you. Let me try?" She smiled sweetly reaching out to grab my hand.

I winced. "I seem to be getting a lot of requests for second chances lately. And a lot of bullshit about this love business too. Look, I will turn down the fucking job for control of my income. I will also want my services returned. As for the D/s relationship, I am yours to command. I won't argue with you or turn you down but please don't call it love. It is not and you know it. Stop lying to me and yourself. I will keep my promises to raise you to Area Manager, and you need to keep yours for equal service and its return of equal service. If you don't, well I would not want to be you, Master. You already have a huge debt to me." I glared at her.

Master Sheryl nodded. "Yeah, I do. No doubt. For what it worth, thank you for giving me a chance to do better and pay my debt." She pulled me in, kissing me deeply.

I pulled away from her. "Wait just a second. You want special services, but I want it in writing that my income is mine. I won't give you another second of my time till I have it."

She frowned. "I was hoping that you actually liked me a little at least. Okay, have it your way. Give me that piece of paper over there. I will write you a promise and sign it. And in my purse are your last checks. Take them, then meet me in my bedroom." She said as she grabbed the paper from me.

I went to her purse and found my last checks from DCFS and the funeral home uncashed. I put it into my own purse glad to finally have my money back. I would be able to afford to eat at long last. Most of my checks were going to pay for my children's care. After gasoline I was perpetually broke, unable to even buy a burger if I could have eaten one that is. Baby food is expensive.

I watched Master Sheryl get up and motion me to follow her back to her room. I sighed realizing I had avoided Master Boyd's unholy touch but would not be so lucky with this secondary Master. Oh well, sucks to be me.

Master Sheryl was uncharacteristically passionate and wanton that night. To my utter surprise she not only wanted to receive her own oral orgasms she spent a great deal of time treating me to my own. We tore up her room like insane lovers in deep kissing and groping.

As the Chosen One I was able to be much less mechanical. Without fail she was able to stimulate my lust drives driving me into aggressive sexual attack on her own unit. Her moaning could be heard for miles as could my own.

My cold, uncaring Master had suddenly become a druidess of epic proportions. I couldn't get enough of her touch, nor could she mine. We spent hours attending each other's needs. Master Sheryl even hazarded trying out a few of my own favored toys and playthings. It was certainly a great start to her taking her rightful place as my Interim Master at long last.

I was granted bed privileges for the remainder of my term under her reign. I happily accepted her offer. She had my attention and if she was careful, she could even obtain my Loyalty right on time. It was August. She didn't have much longer to wait if she played her cards right. My Master reminded me that on December 5th I owed her such an honor if only she could earn it.

That Monday, I was contacted by the main office and officially offered the position my Master coveted. I turned them down politely. I cited my green status as the reason. They were disappointed but told me they understood my misgivings.

Instead they elevated me to head investigator for the entire region. I now only answered to the Area Manager and Master Sheryl. Since the ruling Area Manager was ready to retire within the next twelve months, just as she predicted, Master Sheryl and I ran the region. I had already hit the high ground before I was even done with my damned probationary forty-five day start up. It was truly an honor. One I had earned through hard work, lack of sleep, oh and my sanity.

Master Sheryl true to her word demonstrated a compete turn around. She began to check on my eating, bathing, medications, and even kept in touch with my Guardian, Master Boyd. Within only two days the change was stunning. It was then my Master informed me that she would have to move to the western edge of the state to properly run her seat of power. Shit, there goes the neighborhood.

I could not easily move with her. She was placing herself one hundred and fifty miles from my children. I couldn't remove them from the county without divorcing Timmy thanks to a mother-in-law I didn't even know. She kept an eye on their whereabouts. Since Timmy and I were married, if I tried to move them where he would not have quick access, she would quickly have him file for divorce. I couldn't afford that with Master Boyd on my tail about marriage himself. I had found out the hard way when I had moved the kids to Cumberland. I received from the mother-in-law a threatening letter along with a note from Timmy that he approved the threat.

It seemed to me an easy way to get rid of Master Boyd. I called Mitchell to send a message to Timmy asking for permission to move my family out of the county. I was promptly denied and threatened again. Damn him. If I could have only moved, Master Boyd would have no power over me. If Timmy filed for divorce, I would be court ordered to return the kids to his county. Since divorces could take up to a year, Master Boyd would have my ass before I could escape. There had to be another way.

By Thursday of that week I was frustrated at the mess building. Master Sheryl was moving too far away to live with and that meant a return to Master Boyd's house. I couldn't stand the thought. I was now in charge of my income and could move myself, but I would have to leave the kids behind. I already rarely saw them. Reunifying my family was the goal, not ripping us further apart. These thoughts were plaguing the mind of the Chosen One when the police car went speeding past me headed the other direction.

To my shock he did a U-turn and turned on his blue lights as he did. I looked at my speedometer. I was not above limit. It was daytime, so no lights could be out on the Taurus. What the hell was he pulling me over for?

I rolled down the window as a white-haired police officer walked up with his ticket book already out. He was smiling as if friendly. I narrowed my eyes, what was this happy horseshit?

"Is there a problem officer," I said suspiciously.

He leaned on the car. "Uhm yeah. I am going to have to write you a ticket for expired tags little lady. Hey, are you related to the Voss's downtown?" He was scribbling on the ticket pad.

I shook my head. "Don't you want my driver's license sir. Do I know you?" I couldn't understand how he knew my name and that Master Sheryl's tags had expired by one day.

He chuckled. "Nah, never seen you before in my life. Now here is the ticket. Have a nice day and you behave yourself young lady." He handed me a piece of paper. No warning, no license or registration asked for and my name was on it perfectly. What the hell?

He got into his car and took off. I noticed the City of Wells written on the side. Wait a fucking minute. I was in Cumberland. Wells was twenty miles to the south. This was just weird.

However weird it was that this ticket signaled the end of my career with DCFS. Getting a moving violation as an investigator, even if just for expired tags, during probation meant automatic termination. I was finished, fired, gone and Master Sheryl was going to shit a brick.

I turned the car around and headed back to Master Sheryl's office to turn in my badge. No reason to attend my priority call. I couldn't testify as a terminated employee even if I did find need for DCFS involvement now.

Once in her office I showed her the ticket and explained to my shocked Master the strange pull over. Master Sheryl just shook her head groaning we were ruined. This was the sad end to all her plans and my hours of hard work. She too found it odd, but a ticket was a ticket. It was her duty to tell me to pack my shit up. I had till quitting time to get out. I handed over my badge and went to say goodbye to PC.

Jane was out with one of her many famous headaches. I turned on PC ready to give him the bad news. He whirled on smiling as usual.

"Psycho Tron, let me tell you a good one. So, what did Cinderella do when she arrived at the ball?" He bit his lip trying to stifle his laughter.

I shrugged, not really interested but unsure how to break his heart about my leaving him. "You got me PC, what did she do?"

He started laughing wildly. "She gagged Psycho Tron. Get it? She gagged."

I smiled at that. "Ah very clever old friend. Look PC, I need to tell you something. You are not going to like it." He stopped laughing realizing I was not acting correctly.

"Yeah? What is this Psycho Tron? You are supposed to be in the field? Oh no. Are your circuits hurt?" He looked me over for injury.

I shook my head. "No. I am okay. I don't know how to tell you but…" My informing him of my termination was interrupted by the phone.

I picked it up deciding to wait a moment to break his electrical core.

"Department of Human Services, Division of Children and Families. May I help you," I said still looking at my now confused computer friend.

"Uhm, I am looking for the DCFS investigator known as Psycho. Is she around," said a strange male voice.

I narrowed my eyes. "This is her. Who is speaking?"

"Ah, okay. Yeah so you have a ticket you need to have taken care of. I have the power to make it disappear. Meet me at this address tonight seven sharp and we can come up with something you can trade me to make that happen. Do you have a pen handy," said the voice.

I felt my heart speed up. "Excuse me? Who the hell is this."

The male chuckled. "Your savior sweetie pie. Just call me Charlie. You know like in the horse. Play nice or say goodbye to that job of yours. Now here is my address," he began to rattle off his home numbers.

I didn't bother to write them. My memory would capture them fine without creating a written record. I gritted my teeth angry at this fucker trying to set up bullshit like being able to fix a ticket for what seemed to be a trade in my sleeping with him. It was likely some sick joke.

He finished his reciting of the address. "You got all that doll? See you at seven. I wouldn't disappoint me if I were you. I can make you sorry for it in I ways you can't even imagine."

"I bet you can asshole. We done here? Then bye." I slammed down the phone beyond angry.

PC looked concerned. "Psycho Tron, what is going on?"

I glared at him. "Blackmail PC. See you in a bit old friend. I need to go see Master Sheryl." I flipped off my friend and headed back to Master Sheryl's office.

147

I told her of my phone call and gave her the address. Master Sheryl's face twisted into one of extreme disgust and anger.

"Fucking Charlie Welmet. That sorry ass snake in the grace," she growled so loud it made me jump.

My mind began to whirl as Looper reminded me of Master Boyd's threat the day he ran me off the road just after Maiden Mary told him about Sheryl. "If you miss calling me one time, I will call Officer Welmet in this county, oh he is a good friend of mine. Do you know him? I will have old Charlie haul you back to Wheatly on that warrant you have over hitting Christine."

I looked at Master Sheryl startled. "Charlie Welmet is a cop? He is trying to get me to fuck him to get out of this ticket. How did he even know about it Master?"

She lowered her eyes at me. "Grow up Psycho. You are a pretty woman and he wants to get an easy piece of ass. He knows if you get a ticket you are fired. His fucking wife works for DCFS so he knows the God damned rules. Shit, that fucking asshole," she growled again.

I shook my head. "Master, I have never met this man. How can he even know me? Or anything about me. He got another cop to give the ticket Master. The officer who wrote this is called Schmitz. See there is his name. This has to be an error."

Master Sheryl made fists with her hands in irritation. "Psycho, this is my fucking fault. The day I called the cops when Boyd hauled you off, Charlie was the officer who pulled you two over. God damn it. I told him you were my new worker. Shit, he got a good look at you. Everyone knows what a fucking womanizer he is, except his wife Betty. She is out of town this weekend. Charlie is making the best use of his time alone by trying to wrangle in my girl. Fuck, just fuck."

I sat down in her client chair in front of her desk feeling defeated. "Well I guess that is it, Master. I am fired because someone wanted to get laid, another fucking cop. Judas Priest. What is wrong with these assholes. What happened to protect and serve?" I wanted to cry.

Master Sheryl gritted her teeth. "Okay Psycho, take your badge and get back to your calls. Tonight, meet me here at six to pick me up after work."

I looked up at her in shock. "What? Why would I go to my calls? I am fired, Master. You have no further use for my service. I should just call Boyd now and be done with it."

She laughed. "Psycho, get your ass back to work. Tonight, pick me up for dinner, we have a date silly girl. Charlie invited us. I hope he has enough for three." She winked at me.

I smiled. "Seriously Master? You are going to get this ticket dropped by threatening this man?"

Master Sheryl looked at me with mischief in her eyes. "I am your Master, Psycho. Protect and defend remember? My collar is being threatened. Equal service for equal service. Now get your ass out there and get to work." She chuckled as I picked up my badge and headed back out to attend my priority one calls.

All day I worried about that meeting with the adulterous, blackmailing, would be rapist cop. I tried to remind myself that Master Sheryl would have to be trusted to protect me from him. However, even the Chosen One was nervous about going head on with yet another man with a badge on his chest and lust in his heart. My last battle with one had resulted on me being forced to my knees. I was in no mood to receive this treatment yet again.

That night at six I arrived at the office to find Master Sheryl fixing her hair and makeup. She had me take her to the house and dress her in her nightclub dress. I found this behavior odd, but I kept my mouth shut assuming she knew what she was doing. My Master cleaned up very nicely. She asked if I found her attractive. Of course, I told her yes, though in reality I found her silly. It was as if she was planning to fuck this man in my place. Wait, was she going to? I shuddered remembering the look Charlie gave me while I sat there helpless next to Master Boyd. I wouldn't want to be this man's wife. He was hideous.

I recalled a man of forty around five foot eight with a large gut, and piggy eyes. His brown hair was too long for his chosen style making him appear unkempt. His cheeks were scarred from teenaged ache and he had thick, unsightly lips with heavy eyebrows. Not a looker and did not seem to give a shit either. Now I understood why. He was abusing his power to get what he wanted. He didn't have to care for his appearance. He could make the girls love him whether they liked it or not.

Master Sheryl drove us to the address she already knew without my telling her. I looked at the dented mailbox as we pulled into the drive of a ranch style home. The numbers matched. Master Sheryl was right; this was the man who called me. I noted children's toys laying around the yard. I winced realizing his wife was a real fool. Charlie was beyond scum to abuse his power to fuck women behind her back and the back of his offspring too. I wondered if he had a daughter. How would he like it if some nasty cop did this to her I wondered?

Master Sheryl parked then looked at me. "Psycho, follow high protocol. You stay behind me and say nothing. Understand?"

I looked down. "Yes Master I understand. As you wish."

I got out and stayed my three paces behind while she knocked. The man I recognized as the cop from that day with Master Boyd came to the door. He was not in uniform this time. He was naked except for a pair of boxer shorts with kissing lips on them. His feet were clad in black socks with sandals. He held a spatula in his right hand. He was smiling as he noticed me standing on his porch. That grin quickly melted when he saw Master Sheryl step between his eyesight and my unit.

"Hello Charlie, we are here for our date. Oh, that smells amazing. What are we having? I didn't know you cooked?"

She pushed past the man into his house while hand signaling me to follow.

I did as she ordered pushing the man into his door while I kept perfect pace with my Master. She walked through his living room right to his kitchen were noodles and sauce were boiling on his stove. The small wooden table was set with two lit candles, two settings and flowers on the one closest to his hallway. I felt my stomach turn at his very obvious attempt to pretend an intended rape was a date. Yuck!

Charlie followed behind me appearing confused and unsure what to say or do. Master Sheryl stood there while I pulled out her chair for her. She sat down taking up the flowers smiling.

"Why Charlie, for me? You shouldn't have. Seriously, you really shouldn't have." She smiled at him while she chucked the flowers across the room at his garbage can missing wildly.

I started to fetch them for cleanup. "Psycho, you will take your place and leave that for my date to attend. I am your business not his." I nodded then returned standing behind her chair, head down, arms behind me, silent in reverence until my service was required by my Master.

Charlie's eyes went wide. "Uhm, Sheryl, I didn't, I kind of, well it is not what it looks like. I mean, uhm, can I get you something to drink?" He was not sure what to do.

I stifled a giggle at his discomfort. Master Sheryl cleared her throat and ordered I pour her water. Charlie stood there looking a fool.

"You are letting our dinner burn, Charlie. What is that, spaghetti? Oh, that is my favorite. I am starving. Let's eat." She ordered I put her napkin in her lap then she stared at Charlie appearing to demand he get to feeding her his meal.

Charlie shrugged then served up the pasta and sauce. Master Sheryl watched him serve his own plate then he looked at me. "What about, uhm, your friend? What's her name?"

Master Sheryl began wrapping noodles around her fork. "Cut the crap Charlie. You know God damned well who she is. You thought you could just come take what is not yours. Well, sit your ass down and eat. You fuck with my girl; you fuck with me. She will pass. She eats for me asshole not for you."

Charlie looked frightened. "You aren't planning to tell my wife are you? She would be, you know, upset."

Master Sheryl chuckled while shoving in his food. "I should. She'd cut your balls off. Sit down and eat asshole. I want my date. Be nice and maybe we can figure out something in trade to make this whole thing disappear," she said repeating the words he had used to me on the phone.

He nodded finally appearing to understand the situation. Charlie didn't say a word as Master Sheryl ate like a pig and then demanded seconds. I did my best not to giggle at how damned rude she could truly be. He would try to sneak a look at me standing behind her. When he did, she would poke his arm with her fork and demand he keep his eyes on her. It was amazingly funny to see this Master give this shady cop a poke he didn't expect or want.

Master Sheryl finished two plates of his Italian meal, then demanded desert. He initially insisted there was no such a thing. She continued to argue and he begrudgingly finally got the strawberries and cream from the refrigerator. Master Sheryl looked at them and rolled her eyes asking Charlie how damned stereotyped he could get.

She demanded I serve her this sensual meal. I spooned them into her bowl while she moaned in ecstasy. "Oh baby, remember the last time we had these?" She looked at me appearing dreamy.

I knew we had never had such a thing since I couldn't eat this but nodded. "Yes I do. It was wonderful."

She smiled and winked, then had me feed her the strawberries by hand while she stared at me lustfully in front of Charlie. He just sat there flabbergasted. Finally, when I reached the final berry, she pulled me in for a deep French kiss. Charlie gasped at what he realized was a huge mistake. He had put the moves on Sheryl, the ballbreaker woman.

He looked at the table appearing embarrassed. "Uhm, hey uhm Sheryl, no hard feeling. huh? I uhm, didn't realize, I won't be bothering your uhm, lady friend anymore."

Master Sheryl broke from her kiss. "God damned right you won't Charlie or get ready for divorce court. Leave all the girls alone in fact. I will keep my ears open. I hear a breath of you fucking with another girl I will make a phone call to the little woman. Got it? Now, I want that ticket. I know you didn't turn it in to the courthouse. Give it to me or so help me you will lose more than your wife."

He got up and ran to his room. Charlie came back with the sister ticket that should have been turned in by the cop that wrote mine. I was safe. No record of the stop would ever be recorded. Master Sheryl took the paper and ripped it to pieces then put them in her purse. She stood up motioning me to follow.

We left Charlie standing in his kitchen alone in his shorts. The last time I turned to see him looking scared and dumb holding his spatula and limp dick in his hands. Charlie Welmet would never bother Master Sheryl's girl again. This time it was the cop brought to submission, not the Psycho.

Master Sheryl and I laughed our asses off at Charlies idiotic attempt to blackmail me into his bed. She made fun of his shorts, meal and looks the whole way to her house. Once parked she barley could contain herself pawing at my unit chasing me, as fast as she could run given her poor hip, to her bedroom. Once again we enjoyed the act of carnal congress together. Master Sheryl was as lusty as the first night of my return.

Apparently intimidating police officers was a real turn on for my manhating Master. Charlie's loss was my gain. I enjoyed several hours being both adored and adoring my collar holder. She had proven her worth by stomping down the foul creature Charlie and protecting and defending my collar. I made sure my special services were equal to her service to me that night.

The next day was very slow with no calls to go into the field. This was a rare occurrence. I decided to catch up paperwork at Jane's office with PC. Jane was back, but as usual sleeping at her desk or in the breakroom most of the time. I did a statewide search of childhood and teenaged offenders. I looked at almost every single case of rape, stalking or alleged rape from the years of 1977 to 1987.

I was looking for any evidence of this so-called trouble I had overheard Dennis discussing with Master Boyd. My Master was six years older than me. I assumed if he had done something horrible it had to happen before his career as a cop. Since he became Dennis's sidekick in 1987 at twenty-one years old he had to have done whatever he did around those years. I spent the entire day combing through hundreds of reports all around the state for that decade.

Nothing even close to his name appeared. I included all inconclusive cases, still nothing. Whatever Master Boyd had done, it was off the record. I sighed as Master Sheryl told me it was time to go to the house. I looked at the clock realizing Master Boyd was likely already on his way. I would have no choice but to go as promised.

If I didn't find a way out come September I would be stuck living with the creep full time. I got up wishing PC a peaceful weekend. I shuttered bracing myself for a rough one myself at the hands of the rapist cop Master Sheryl had not been able to save me from.

On the way to her house I asked Master Sheryl if she could see that I was put on call for all foreseeable weekends. My Master almost fainted with shock.

"Are you sure? I mean you will never get a day off, Psycho. That is, well, let me think about it okay. I mean how are you feeling? Boyd says you need rest. I have been going easy on you since you are supposed to be delusional thinking you are a robot or some shit." She glared at me.

I chuckled. "Uhm, did I seem like a robot last night? Come on Master, do you really believe that nut?"

She narrowed her eyes., "Wait, aren't you engaged to Boyd? I saw you kissing the idiot. That seemed pretty real to me."

I smiled. "Master, he is a cop. My husband is a prick and I must watch out for the outlaw fucker. His whole family is a pack of scumbags. I married far too young. I can't get out of it easily. My children are held hostage in that God forsaken county. Boyd can protect my family while I mind your collar. If I must pretend to like the devil I will. If that makes me crazy, then many a mother is."

Master Sheryl smiled back. "Why you clever bitch. Ah, I knew you didn't love that bag of gas. Wow, damn remind me not to cross you. You're a manipulating little psychotic, aren't you?"

I chuckled. "Got you wrapped around my little finger don't I, Master?"

She snorted, "Damn right you do. You fuck like a champion, work like a mule and still find the time to go home and deal with that asshole. Girl you have my respect."

I sighed. "Yeah, but he has my Guardianship papers. Until that shit can be ended, I am stuck. Master, where would someone go to find out if a secret crime was ever committed which was then covered up by the local boys in blue?"

She gasped. "Huh? Now that is a strange question. Do you know something about a cold case, Psycho? My suggestion is you keep that shit to yourself. Charlie is a fool, but some of these local assholes make people disappear forever you know. It is good old boy land. You best watch yourself if you are digging around for shallow unmarked graves."

I shook my head. "No, I don't know anything that could get me shot, Master. I am looking for an old story that is a rumor. It is only for my own knowledge, nothing else I swear it. Where would I go to find stuff not maybe in the record? Someone to maybe ask without stirring up shit?"

Master Sheryl paused appearing to think for a moment. "Okay, you would go to the lower rungs of these small towns. The hill people. Hell, those folks know when an opossum farts honey. If there is some dirty secret, they tell it over shine and bone fire catfish get togethers. If you ask an old hillbilly from around these parts, they will know. They can't read or write so they are often ignored. They always know where the bodies are buried and who put them there too." She frowned.

I followed her sightline noticing Master Boyd's black car in her driveway. "Oh, he is early Master." I frowned too.

She grimaced. "I am not surprised. Look, you bring your car next week. I will get you put on call. I understand why you asked. I wasn't thinking."

I looked at Master Boyd's car, "Thank you Master. I do appreciate the favor."

She groaned. "He's that bad, huh? He must be for me to ever hear a DCFS employee thank me for working them 24/7 without overtime. I am sorry Psycho. Is there anything I can do to help?"

I nodded. "You just did, Master."

She pulled up and Master Boyd got out of the car smiling at me. "Ah there is my girl. You are looking better than ever. Where is my kiss? Come here, I have missed you so much."

I looked at Master Sheryl who rolled her eyes and slammed her door hard. "Psycho, go get your stuff. Boyd, give the girl a damned minute. She just got off work. It has been a tough week."

I stood there unsure who to mind. Both Masters stood there. One said give him a kiss, one said go get my luggage. Who was in control?

Master Boyd's eyes filled with storm clouds. "I said come here Psycho, now."

I went to him without pushing him any further as I recognized the danger in his look. Master Sheryl saw it too. "You are a fucking bully, you know that? One day you will get what you have coming to you." She huffed into the house leaving me in the claws of my rapist Master.

He smiled as the dark skies of anger melted in his gaze. "You feel so good. I almost couldn't stand it. You know, I started to come to your office. Now give me a kiss, then get your stuff. We are going by to see the kids, then home, our home."

I nodded as I kissed him briefly. "As you wish Master." I started for the door when Master Boyd reached out and swatted my backside.

I winced but assumed that meant hurry up. When I entered the house, I found Master Sheryl making the call to get me put on the list for duty every weekend. She smiled bitterly at me and gave me a thumbs up.

I smiled back mouthing. 'Thank you Master.' She nodded she understood.

My constant calls out every weekend would put an end to Master Boyd's hold for up to six weeks I hoped. He would surely hit the roof when I informed him of this change. I couldn't find another way to avoid being stuck with him full time when Master Sheryl moved. Until I could find the girl who had escaped him, it would have to do. She had gotten away. I just knew I could too.

Master Boyd yapped non-stop about his busy week with collaring offenders the whole ride to Maiden Mary's house. I pretended to listen. I was trying to wrack my brain about who I could find old school and native to the county that may know a dirty little secret and the address of the victim I sought. I stole a look at him sitting there happily chatting as if everything was cheerful and great. He made me sick at the very sight of him. I hated him so bad for stealing Simon's Key and all so he could force sex. He was just a rapist with my Key and collar, nothing more. Why didn't he just rape me and leave my delusions alone. I thought he was my friend. He was no better than all the others.

I looked at his lap wondering when he would attack me again. I saw his gun around his waist and had a flashback of him forcing my submission. Then I thought of Mickey's headless unit and Angie. Angie was a hill person. Master Sheryl said the hillbillies knew the secrets that the counties try to hide. I needed to talk to her. I hope she can tell me what happened and where to find the girl or girls who got away.

Master Boyd had gotten quiet. I looked at him smiling sweetly. He saw me gazing at him appearing enthralled by his person.

"What are you thinking baby?" He smiled back appearing very happy to see me appearing to notice him.

I laid my head on his shoulder feeling him tense up suddenly with interest. "Oh, just that after we go see the kids I would like to go by and wish Angie a happy birthday really quick. I mean it is her I must thank for getting us together. Do you mind taking me there for just a moment?" I rubbed his thigh noticing an immediate tightening in his lap.

It was of course not Angie's birthday, but I prayed he didn't know that. He grinned feeling very wanted and secure by my appearing to adore him without his force and the lack of talking like a robot.

"Sure baby. Whatever you want. But you make it quick okay? I want to get home and show you what I got for you. You will just love it." He put his arm around my shoulders pulling me close.

I closed my eyes trying to ignore my disgust at his touch. "Oh you are too good to me, Master. I do love you so," I lied.

Master Boyd kissed the top of my head. "I am truly happy. You are well and you finally love me. There is nothing I can't do now that I have my wife by my side. My job is doing great and soon we will be together all the time. I heard Sheryl got a job way the hell off and is moving. You can finally move home full time now."

I grimaced. "Oh, wow, news travels fast doesn't it, Master."

He laughed. "Small towns baby. Can't do anything without someone knowing about it."

I smiled. "That is a fact. Well you would know. I am not from here, Master."

Master Boyd snorted. "You are lucky. I was born and raised in that damned county. I am going to die there too. At least now it is easier knowing I won't be alone until that happens. Thank you, Psycho, for being mine."

I closed my eyes. "I believe I didn't have a choice in the matter, Master."

He sighed. "Yeah started off a bit rough but it will get better, already has. Just give me time. I will treat you right and one day you will be glad it all happened, you'll see. We can forget the bad and just focus on our future together." He smiled then kissed my head again as we pulled into Mary's yard.

Master Boyd took his place on the front porch swing, as I went inside to visit with my youngsters. I had missed them terribly. Maiden Mary never brought them to the hospital to see me due to some issues with her vehicle. Master Boyd had offered to bring them, but I had refused him access to them or Mary. I wanted my monster as far from my innocent children as possible. Especially my daughter. I may have had to tolerate his foul obsession with forced carnal congress, but I would be damned if he would get a crack at pulling that shit with my little princess.

Seine was so thrilled to see me he nearly knocked himself out twirling, dancing and jumping. My furry friend was a true joy to see. I decided to take him back to Cumberland with me when I returned on Sunday afternoon.

While I was visiting the kids and looking over their latest get-well cards they had made for me, my bug-eyed buddy snuck out the back door. He had decided he and Master Boyd had an argument to settle. There is no telling how long it had been since I noted he was missing.

Frantically I ran outside assuming my Master was putting a round of bullets in Seine's bulldog head. I came around the front porch to find Master Boyd sitting very still looking afraid. I followed my Master's eyes to see Seine sitting quietly staring at my Master while breathing hard but not moving any closer. The two of them were in a silent stand-off. I was grateful to see my dog had not done anything stupid yet.

"Seine get over here now," I yelled at my canine friend.

He looked at me then back to Master Boyd appearing to want to attack. Master Boyd looked at me with begging eyes but didn't dare breath a word.

I yelled for my fur buddy to come once more. This time Seine trotted back to me appearing to want me to reward him for holding that bad man at bay. I spoke soothingly to Seine then picked him up putting him safely in the house. I could see the relief on Master Boyd's face when both were broken out of that uncomfortable meeting without anyone getting bitten.

After his near canine attack, Master Boyd was ready to take me to see Angie, then to his home. I said goodbye to everyone but promised to return the next day. I rushed to Master Boyd's car in a hurry to get going for a change. I needed to see Angie right away. My heart was racing with anticipation of what she may know and fear that she wouldn't know at the same time.

My Master had no idea what my real plan was to see Angie Bruiser. He chatted appearing in good spirits about how great Seine was looking and how big my children were getting. I only nodded and smiled unable to focus on anything other than figuring out a way to talk Angie into helping me with my problem.

I knew she herself would likely not be of much help regarding Master Boyd's past. It had been clear she did not know him when he was stalking me back when I wore her collar. He had approached her about me several times asking about me and she had not even known his name. She always called him 'that skinny law dog.' I hoped maybe she did know who knew him and maybe even knew his secret.

Master Boyd pulled into the driveway but let me out to walk to Angie's shack house. He didn't want to get his black car stuck in the ruts of her washed out driveway. He told me he would drive down to Darlin, turn around and then pick me up from the road. That should give me time to visit with my old Master. Then we would head to his home.

I jumped out walking fast as I could hoping to glean as much time as possible with my old friend. She had seen Master Boyd drop me off and came running out to hug me squealing with glee.

"Ah, my Psycho. You are back for a visit. Come in. Damn, you never did change none, now did you," she drawled out nearly beside herself with joy.

I hugged her back. "Angie, I can't stay long, my ride will be back. Can we talk for a minute? I have a favor to ask you if you wouldn't mind helping me out?" I looked at her appearing very serious.

She waved me into her house and promptly told Joe and the twins to 'skedaddle' right away.

I sat down and looked out the window hoping Master Boyd was not around anywhere to hear. I took a deep breath steading my nerves. "Angie, I need to know a secret about someone in this town. Something bad they may have done when they were just a kid maybe? A rape but possibly a rape and murder or even a stalking and rape? It was done by a cop, so it was hidden from the law. Who would know a rumor about something like that?"

Angie's eyes got wide and she looked around also appearing afraid that I had even uttered such words. "Oh no, Psycho. Some law dog done killed some poor hill girl? Is that what you're asking?"

I shook my head. "Well, that is the problem Angie. I don't know if she is dead or if there is more of them. I don't know what has been done. I need to know if there would be someone who could tell me about a rumor maybe about something Boyd Simmons may have done."

Angie almost fainted as her eyes rolled up in her head. "Oh my word, Boyd Simmons. I hadn't heard that there name in an age. I hear he become a law dog, oh no, wait. The skinny law dog that just dropped you off. Oh shit Psycho, that there was Boyd. Oh Lord, sonofabitch."

I jumped back as Angie fanned herself appearing terribly upset. "Oh my God. You know Boyd?" My heart began to pound hard in my chest. "Angie please, you have to tell me what you know about him."

She took a deep breath. "I done swore to Maddy never to talk about that there business, but because you're is with this troubled person, well Psycho, I will talk. You see, Maddy was my bestest secret friend so she done told me everything. This includes stuff that no one around here knows. I can never forget this messed up story. It all started when Maddy was thirteen and Boyd was fifteen."

Chapter 62: The Cruelty of Public Opinion
Master Boyd and Interim Master Sheryl

I sure hope you brought your coffee and eager ears today. This chapter is all about gossip, rumors and secrets whispered behind closed doors. Ah, the guilty pleasure of hearing dirty details of another's failures is such a sinful delight. We all know better, but we all engage in this nasty little bad habit.

Usually, it is just a bit of comforting fluff in our own dark worlds. No one gets hurt, and we rarely believe even half the crap we hear. Most of the time there is a grain of authenticity to the tune we spin. When that small seed is given enough attention, it can be cultivated to grow into a monster reality. In our space behind the shattered looking glass sometimes fact is stranger than fiction. It is quite easy to cause lies to become the truth when unprovable tales spun have legitimizing effects.

Ready to take a ride back to a past that never should have been? Awesome. This time we will ask you to step out of our way and watch us fall to our knees begging forgiveness. You need not carry this burden, for it is our cross to bear. We are taking off our hat while look at the floor in shame. We are being forced to remember never to judge anyone's behavior before we know why. When we are quick to assume, we will get hurt.

There was always another path, but we were too busy to remember the kindness that had given us such a luxury to still travel at all. Small kindnesses, gentle patience, loving protection when kicked enough can become hatred. Madness is not a realm we own. There are others in this place. They got here just like us, against their will. This time we asked to be there, and we will have to endure the punishment alone.

"Actually, I was expecting you. I found the camera this time. Hey, I love the blond on you. I went and even blew some cash on the good coffee and creamer. Damn, it sure is good to see you Purgy. Johnny is in the back...want me to go get the little bastard for you?"
--Nikki to The Chosen One, second meeting, September 1998.

I sat there watching the window fearing Master Boyd would somehow jump out of the curtains to kill Angie and I for daring to discuss his crimes. I did my best to focus on her tale of the creation of my rapist. Her look of terror made my heart pound like a bass drum. I was not sure I could handle hearing about the horrors the girl(s) before me had been put through by this monster. I braced myself for the worst.

ANGIE'S STORY ABOUT BOYD AND MADDY:

Angie took a deep breath and continued her story. *"Maddy was my cousin, you know, but the kinfolks, they were feuding at the time. So, Maddy and her biggest sister Suzy would come on out to meet with me for fishing without anybody knowing. They were just hill folk like Joe and me. We were nobodies too.*

Maddy, she was a real pretty girl for thirteen. She was well built like she was already grown up. The boys they was like bees to her honey. But she was playing hard to get and never accepted no beau. She was a Bruiser like me. She was expected to get hitched to another hill boy someday.

Maddy thought much of herself. She was not willing to set her eye at no hill trash. Then comes this boy called Boyd. Well, you see, Boyd was this town boy. He was handsome and, you know, smart. He could read and do ciphering. Well, he got the sweets for Maddy. She was all smitten with him, and him with her. Now Boyd, he was from real God fearing folks. Not like regular but from them crazy church folks around here.

His momma, she was a mean old snake. She done found out Boyd was cutting his eyes at Maddy. She threw a tantrum. She told old Boyd that Maddy was not good enough for him. So, Boyd and Maddy they snuck around the old heifer. There wasn't anything that could break them two up.

Maddy done told me she'd tried to kiss him but he'd always get all scared and ran off ever time. She'd hold his hand and he'd get all sweaty she done said. That made her giggle a lot. He was very shy and just cow eyes is all. Nothing serious, nothing but silly kid stuff. They was just young ones, both of them.

Boyd he'd done bring her lover stuffs like flowers and fishing lures from the store. He spent his earnings on her. Maddy was loving that. Suzy and I got all flustered that we didn't have us a Boyd. We both want one of them there town boyfriends like Maddy had, you know.

The two of them would meet at the end of her old driveway for handholding and sweet words. This went on for the whole spring. Maddy said Boyd was going to run away with her and the two of them would live in some big city someday, with him going to school to support her and their kids. He planned to run away from that mean old momma of his to be with her. Maddy told Suzy and me she hitch to Boyd as soon as he got enough scratch to afford a place.

Then when the summer done come, Maddy got all quiet. She told Suzy and me she had done broke it off with Boyd. Suzy and I were like why? Them two were so in love during spring and now she said no to him. We thought it was Boyd but is wasn't him. Maddy told us there was something wrong, but it wasn't Boyd. She just cried and said she was not good enough for him no more.

Then Maddy done come to see me by herself. She had done left Suzy home. She took me out our fishing hole and done told me a secret. Her big brother Paul, who was about seventeen years old, was forcing himself on her. She done told me now she'd been all ruined for Boyd, not being fresh you know even though Boyd was waiting for her. So, she'd broke it off with Boyd because she was so ashamed.

She told me Boyd was taking her pushing him away very poorly. She told me he was calling her crying, begging, and asking what he had done, but she wouldn't say anything. She told him it plumb broke his heart and hers as well. Maddy couldn't tell him what was wrong with her. So, she says she is going to kill herself to escape Paul and because she'd thought she would never get to be with Boyd now. Maddy loved Boyd and if she couldn't be with him she'd rather be dead.

I did my best Psycho to tell her not to go and do something so dumb. Boyd was going to love her because she done fought Paul like a bear, but he was too big for her. I done told her Boyd wouldn't care she wasn't a maid. He loved her enough he'd never care about it for sure. She didn't hear or believe me.

That next day them law dogs found her kilt by her own knife. She done run it deep cross her wrists in her and Boyd's meeting place. She was holding a piece of paper Boyd done written to her telling her he was tired of her not telling him what he'd done to her to make her break off their plans. Maddy was pretty badly soiled (raped). The laws found that letter from Boyd in her cold hands.

Then they all thought that Boyd done that soiling of Maddy. The law dog told Boyd that Maddy kilt herself over his words and his soiling of her. I heard Boyd was near crazy from finding out Maddy was dead and used like that. They had to take him to the nervous hospital at State. They called it the Snake Pit in them days. Well, while him was there with the crazies, Maddy's kin press charges on Boyd for soiling their Maddy.

Boyd got found guilty because of her words in her hands. He didn't say nothing about being with her like that. Only that he was angry she done stood him up too many times. The courts and the law didn't care none that there was *no proof. They sent Boyd off to the Boys Home for six years until he was the age at twenty-one.*

His own damned mean momma helped them there law dogs put Boyd away. She said he was full of the devil for loving Maddy. She wouldn't tell them law dogs that Boyd was at home with her when that trouble with Maddy happened. Can you imagine her sending her own boy off to the big house just because you found out he done went against your saying no to his pick of a girlfriend?

Them law dogs said that Maddy was scared by Boyd saying in his words ta her he was going to stop calling on her because she wasn't coming to meet him anymore. They said Maddy was broken hearted because she was ruined and Boyd had taken his fill of her or that he was saying she didn't come give him what he wanted so he left her. That was why the law said she done kilt herself.

Psycho, Maddy never told Boyd but she couldn't read a lick. She was like all us Bruisers, she couldn't even write her name. No matter what them words said she didn't get mournful over them as she couldn't cipher them. She weren't no more threatened by his words than that there man in the moon.

The whole mess was all covered up here in town. Folks here knew about old Boyd, but it's all hushed because his momma was some crazy bitch in her church. Old Boyd was never forgiven by her for fooling round with hill trash like Maddy.

When Paul got turned in years later fur soiling another girl, he done told it was him who done Maddy dirty that day she killed herself. He laughed because a dumb town boy got the blame. Trouble was that Boyd did the time that should have been Paul's punishment. Them law dogs didn't want to say they done punished the wrong boy.

So, the folk still wag their tongues that Boyd was still the one that hurt Maddy though he didn't do it. I know that for sure. Maddy told me herself. She said Boyd was too scared of his momma and God to do more than hold hands till they were hitched. She said he never even tried to get her to do kissing.

It was Paul. Her own damned brother. So, I heard old Boyd, well now he has a powerful temper over them years doing time for nothing and what these damned folks round here say about him. I heard he is kept away from the women folk and not allowed to do much because no one trusts him none. I can see why he'd be powerfully mad too. The town folks all think he is a raper and call him one behind his back.

Then that church of his momma's, well they done cast him out. His own kin was ashamed of him. That made him go become a law dog, them telling him that was the only way he'd get any forgiveness from God. They all still think him a raper man. He never got that schooling or run off to that big city that he and Maddy were going to run off to together. Can you see that? He spent all those years in jail, then he has spent years being a law dog. That sure would make me powerfully pissed too.

Well, now I see he's done gone and taken a shining to you. Psycho, he's likely pretty mad still about all this past stuff. You would be in deep trouble if you set off that powerful temper I heard he has. I done seen that craziness in his devil's eyes when he done come to ask about you.

Girl, I heard he done gone to the devil over it all. He ain't that sweet little boy who was shying away from Maddy all them years ago. Now I'd be willing to bet you. I am a guessing if you are asking about this mess he may have done that he turned bad like I'd figured he would. When folks kick a dog long enough it will get awful mean.

It is so sad I lost my bestest friend Maddy and that Boyd, well he got hurt really bad for loving a hill girl. There is no doubt Boyd did love her and that Maddy loved her Boyd. But that nasty old Paul, he messed them all up. Well that is what I done know about Boyd Simmons. Is that what you'd wanted to be know?" Angie sniffed tearing up while she recalled the loss of her beloved cousin Maddy.

I sat there with my mouth open in disbelief. The Boyd I had been so cruel to when he had shyly asked me out was the real Boyd. The monster who raped me in the cell, forced my submission and delivered amazingly vicious attacks was a Boyd that false imprisonment, incorrect rumors, and harsh judgement had created. My Master was more than just harboring a demon. He was like me, severely mentally ill. His mind had been shattered by the grief of losing his first love to a rapist, and her own hand.

My Master's anger was understandable. He had not only spent time in teenager jail for a crime he didn't commit, but he was also forced into a career that he never wanted. Stuck for life with reminders all around him of the prison he came into his manhood within. Worse, after having to suffer for six years, the brutal judgement of social shunning was waiting for him. Now, trapped in the small towns who had whispered the rumors, he would not be forgiven nor treated with kindness. No woman would ever consider dating a man who had raped, then caused the suicide of a thirteen-year-old girl.

My mind whirled back to his many clumsy attempts to date me. I had turned a cold shoulder towards him. I thought of his stuttering, sweating, anxious invites. Master Boyd was afraid of me then. He likely was being very sincere, but I judged him a pest. I viewed his stalking me as sinister. I could clearly see now that was his way of trying to work up courage to try again, and his way of finding out more about me. If he could find some passion I loved, he could maybe coax me into being his lover.

In my self-absorption I had forgotten all the kindnesses he had shown me through the years of my own hellish existence. I had been too caught up in my own pain to recognize his. A twinge of guilt hit me when I understood I had let him down when he needed me the most. It would not have killed me to go out on one dinner date. It also would not have been horrible to be his lover either. If only I had known why he was acting so nuts. The trouble was I was not interested, nor did I have any concern for anyone but myself.

I believed horrible things of this man who had shown me nothing but respect when he was just lonely.

After all, he had been there for me all those years. When I needed a ride home from inpatient treatment, I called my good friend Boyd. He had hunted for years looking to make Tammy pay for her crime against me. When I woke up from being tortured by Master Julie, I found him sleeping in a chair. He swore to hunt down and kill the person who was hurting me with fire in his eyes. It all made sense now. Master Boyd had lost his first love to a predator. He wasn't going to stand to lose me too. I started to tear up realizing he had always been a great friend to me, but I had not been a fair to him in return.

I remembered his tears when I verbally bashed him in Mistress Heather's parking lot. I now understood I had kicked him right in the heart. I thought I was doing him a favor. I didn't see his desperation. Master Boyd was thirty-one years old, never had kissed a girl, never likely to find a mate.

He had followed me silently for years, wishing, hoping, yearning. I never bothered to notice him. I thought of how I would have felt if I had finally gotten the courage to ask out the girl of my dreams after so many fails in life. Boyd was thinking he and I were friends. He knew I needed help. He was without a lover and I was without a protector. I didn't care about public opinion; he was not subject to any hope of regaining their trust. In his mind the perfect solution to both our problems was to unite.

Likely, when I made it clear I would not ever consider him as a potential partner, his deep affections for me spiraled into hatred. His vision that I was different was shattered to pieces when I acted just like everyone else toward him.

I realized then the white cell was not planned. He never intended to rape me but when given the chance his pent-up urges and anger at my continued denials caused this impulsive act. He had wanted me so badly, but I continued to tell him no despite all his finest efforts.

When the chance came to force me to be his lover, he figured why not? Everyone called him a rapist anyway. He had already done the time for it with interest. He was beyond angry at me for not giving him the time of day. It was justified in his mind. All he had to do was prove he could do it and then I would be his forever. He was sure he would marry me, thus undoing his moment of weakness.

However, once he had done the deed, he developed the addiction for more. Simply put, he had worked so hard for years to find a lover but was chronically denied. Once he took it by force, he found success. This violence curbed his inner rage at being unjustly punished, it gave him pleasure and he was finally able to be in control of something in a long life of no choice.

His whole life he had been held as a prisoner unable to go where he wanted or even asked what he thought. No one trusted him, especially his own parents and Dennis. No one believed his pleas of innocence. Now he had found a way to have all he had lost. Master Boyd could be assured the complete domination of one uncared for, unimportant schizophrenic who called him Master.

I shuddered when I finally realized; Master Boyd would kill me to keep all he believed he had recouped by holding Simon's Key. Master Boyd was hooked on the violence of raping me by sheer accident. He crime had resurrected his lost love and given him his power back. Escape would not only be beyond difficult; to try and fail would mean death.

Most of all, it occurred to me, I had perhaps played a minor role in setting this very disturbed, righteously so by the way, person right over the edge into the abyss of madness. While Paul had caused Maddy's death, the courts had wrongfully imprisoned him, and the town gossip, and Dennis, had cockblocked him. I too had let him down by demonstrating indifference to his plight. I understood fully well why he hated the word no. That is the only word he heard from everyone since the day Maddy had taken her life.

I still could not forgive Master Boyd for raping me because he felt justified by my refusals to date him. I could not overlook his cruel treatment of me or violence toward my unit once he had found me that day in Darlin Cemetery. No matter what he had been through, that didn't give him the right to take it out on me.

However, now I could certainly understand why he did it and what was driving his inner demons. Angie had indeed given me the answers to my many questions. It was not the response I had expected nor wanted to hear.

Angie sat there wiping her eyes. "Uhm, I sure am sorry for having not told you this before. I swear I didn't member him cause he is all grown up. Is he hurting you, Psycho? I could get old Joe to ask about. Maybe get Boyd sent to hell. He's a mad dog no doubt. Probably be best for him too. I can see this here life ain't none too easy for old Boyd with that kind of talk about him."

I shook my head. "Thank you Angie but it is not like that. No reason to hire guns over this. I will be alright. I appreciate your telling me the story. It helps a lot. It will make things easier now I think." I smiled at her.

She nodded. "Okay then. Promise you'll never tell anybody what I done said here. I mean if them there law dogs found out I know Boyd was not the raper, well they likely would send someone to make sure I was killed for talking." Her big brown eyes were wide in fear.

I chuckled. "You are safe with me Angie. No one is going to find out what you said, promise. I wanted to give you a birthday gift before I go." I reached into my pocket and pulled out four twenty-dollar bills and handed them to her.

She looked at the wadded-up cash. "Girl, you know it ain't my damned birthday. What is this for?"

I laughed hard. "Well I do know you are going to have a birthday and I seem to remember you never have any fucking toilet paper around this house. So, I gave you four sheets to keep you till next time I see you."

She looked up realizing the joke. "Ah hells bells, Psycho. You're too good to me. When do you want to go fishing with me again?"

I saw Master Boyd pulling up into the drive. "Soon darlin, soon. I must go for now. Kiss the twins for me and say hi to Joe. Get some fucking groceries of worth will you? Damn, I am sick of always smelling bean and potatoes when I visit you." I hugged her while she chuckled at my bitching over the smell of her supper cooking.

I walked to Master Boyd's car feeling the air around me seeping into my pours. Nothing seemed real. I could see his face looking concerned through his windshield. It was impossible to hate him now that I knew the truth no matter what he had done to me personally. I was like him. Punished for life, shunned and treated unfairly. These were things he could truly empathize with me about.

Yet, I couldn't stand the thought of being trapped with him as his Stepford wife forever. This was something I would have to discuss with Simon. Master Boyd would never give up that Key, and I could never give up my right to choose. A reckoning would surely come one day between me and my unfortunate Master. Until then, it was best to do try to meet his demonic needs without getting hurt in the process.

"Did your visit go well?" He smiled happily as I got into the car.

I nodded. "Better than expected. I suppose I am ready to go home now." I smiled at my Master bitterly feeling more lost than ever.

My Master perked up smiling even wider. "You called it our home. Yes Psycho, wait till you see what I got for you. You are just going to love it."

I closed my eyes. "It is not fishing lures is it, Master?"

Master Boyd took off down the dirt road a high speed appearing excited to get to his house. He didn't answer for a moment appearing confused.

"I didn't know you liked to fish. I can of course get some if you need them." I opened my eyes to see him unsure what to say to my odd statement.

I shook my head. "No Master. I am fine. I am sorry for upsetting You."

His look told me Angie's story was true. Maddy had just crossed his soul. I knew the look because my own shadow named Matthew. When I thought of him it often made my eyes look like rain would break out as his did just then. I reached out and took his hand startling him both from his disturbing memories and because I had never done such a thing before.

He looked at my hand holding his appearing unsure what to think. "Psycho are you okay baby? I mean, Sheryl said you were better this week. Maybe the medication is working?"

I didn't answer him. I understood Psycho Tron and The Chosen One were still plaguing my unit often. I could only take control at times. Luckily, I had been able to speak to Angie without their interference. It had been a calculated risk that either could show up in the middle of my fact-finding discussion. For a change, the shards were still. I needed this time of peace and quiet to decide if a confrontation with Master Boyd regarding whether my new information would help or hurt our bonding. I was within still debating as he pulled into his drive and parked the car.

I got out only to be grabbed by my overly happy Master and carried into the house like a bride over the threshold. This strange behavior of his was annoying. It often set off fear within due to it demonstrating how much stronger he was than me. I was not a helpless child and could walk just fine.

Once through his door he carried me straight to the bedroom. My heart started speeding up with fear he was going to sexually assault me. Instead he put me down gently on my feet and went to his closet.

I watched him rifle through the police uniforms until he reached a long white dress covered in plastic wrap. He turned around to show me a very expensive wedding dress made of white lace. I nearly fainted from dread.

"See, I got your dress already and my suit is in here too. As soon as we are rid of Timmy, we can walk the aisle and make it all official and legal." He smiled then asked if I liked the dress he had chosen for me.

I nodded. "Sure Master. Make us official to who? God? The town? Dennis? Or someone else maybe?" I heard the words come out of my mouth before I could stop them.

Master Boyd hung the dress back up appearing stunned by my statement. "Someone else who? Psycho, what is wrong with wanting to marry you? I want to be your husband forever. I am not ashamed for everyone to know it. You say Simon says you can't marry a Master. Maybe you really mean you won't marry me?" He looked at the floor.

I walked into his living room feeling the urge to scream at the unfairness of the world. It was all just so wrong. Nothing was wrong with Master Boyd, but nothing was right either. I was so tired of all the cruelty and unfairness humans did to each other. How could we call ourselves higher species when people like my Master and me exit because of direct injustices?

Master Boyd walked out of his room behind me looking me over trying to understand if I was demonstrating psychosis or something else.

I took a deep breath then turned to look at him. "Master. I want to apologize for not being a good friend to you. I cannot undo that but we both know I already have been punished for it. I realize that now. In the world of D/s once punished, an infraction can't be brought back up. So, I won't ever call you a rapist again. You have heard that word enough for a lifetime I think."

Master Boyd looked at the floor and I could almost hear his heart sink with those terrible words. "Oh, I guess you heard. That is what this is all about? How long have you known?" He walked to his armchair sitting down seeming very defeated.

I sat down on his couch. "Long enough to know it wasn't right what happened to you."

He looked up surprised. "What? You mean you don't believe I did it?"

I chuckled bitterly. "I happen to know you didn't do it. You didn't even know where to put your damned cock when you took me that night in jail, Master. Only a virgin would be unsure. A seasoned rapist would have known where everything goes."

Master Boyd smiled sadly. "Yeah, I suppose they would. I wasn't sure you remembered that was my first time. I shouldn't have. I was stupid to, well, I am a rapist. This time I am guilty."

I nodded. "Unfortunately, that is true. But you weren't. I want to tell you, I forgive you, but I would be lying. You hurt me, but now I realize I hurt you first. You tried to date me in the proper way. I ignored you and hurt your feelings. I see that. Truth is we hurt each other. Equal service for equal service works both ways." I looked to see his response to this revelation.

Master Boyd snorted. "I suppose you could see it that way, but now I can't stop. It is all I think about, all I want. I hate it Psycho. I can't make it stop. Every time I see you it crosses my mind, makes me want to hurt you, hear you say

185

my name, see you afraid. I want to rape you again and again. So, it turns out I really am the devil after all. Just like everyone always said. I killed her by being an asshole. She died because I couldn't control my temper. Now, I likely will lose you or kill you too because I am just so fucked up." He put his head in his hands beginning to sob.

I got up and forced my way into his lap holding his head on my breast while he wept. "You didn't kill Maddy, Master. She never read your letter. Maddy couldn't read at all. She died because she couldn't face not being perfect for you, not because of your anger."

My Master looked up startled. "That is not true Psycho. I told her I wouldn't see her anymore and she killed herself. The rape had nothing to do with it. She got raped, then read my letter and thought everything was lost. That is what they told me." He trailed off with the sudden understanding that Maddy was hill folk. They are often illiterate.

I ran my hand down his cheek softly. "Master, they lied. Maddy couldn't read. You didn't rape her. It is okay to be upset but be mad at yourself for the right reasons. You did nothing wrong. Maddy's death was someone else's crime. You got wrongly accused and there is nothing I can do or you can do to change that. But you didn't have anything to do with Maddy killing herself. She loved you, like I do."

He looked at me with tears rolling down his face. "Do you really mean that, Psycho? Are you just having a psychotic episode?"

I laughed. "I am probably having a psychotic episode. Master. Do you care? No matter what I say you are hell bent to keep me here. You won't give me Simon's Key back, nor will you release me from your grip. I am trapped just like you are in this hellish little backwater town full of cruel hateful people. You have made yourself my Master. Your sickness must be dealt with or I won't survive your demons. I suspect neither will you. I am your last and only chance to not be left to die a very lonely person. If you are smart, you will keep trying to battle your urges to strike out at me. I know it will be hard and I will help by meeting your addiction if you keep it to a tolerable roar just as we agreed. I will return the service by trying to understand you and adoring you the way you need to feel whole again. That is all either of us can hope for given our, what did Dennis call it? Oh yes, our serious problems. There is no cure for schizophrenia and there is no going back in time. Likely, you are as damned as I am to be eaten alive by your illness."

Master Boyd closed his eyes and hugged me tightly. "If I could go back in time I would protect you and Maddy from those bastards that destroyed the most beautiful souls ever born into this shitty world.."

I ran my fingers through his hair "Master, I think maybe you have to face the fact you also needed protection. That is okay. I am here to do that now if you will let me."

We began to kiss deeply as my Master continued to rain down his feelings of regret onto my face. I didn't feel his excitement rising as we held each other in this act of tenderness. He was not turned on by my showing him kindness and affection. His internal torment had completely blocked his lustful drives.

Instead he held me while he emptied his liquid despair through his soul portals. Over the hours I listened to him speak privately of the years of pain and loneliness suffered in silence. We were both exiles from the realm of the real. Neither of us were valued, honorable or wanted. For those moments, we clung to each other feeling a little less afraid of the monsters we'd become.

Master Boyd and I had once been like all of the normals, but now we realized there was no hope of rejoining the world of the living. Once your humanity is taken, there is no going back.

I could repeat the things he told me of his childhood, his love affair with Maddy, his unjust incarceration, his feeling about his mentor Dennis and his lost dreams and hopes, but I will grant him mercy. Master Boyd had suffered needlessly is all I will ever say about it. His secrets and words were his most heartfelt gifts to me. I will be selfish and never share them with anyone.

He and I fell asleep in each other's arms that night. No sexual assault or carnal congress of any kind occurred. Only tears, confessions, and the gentle touch of lovers. Master Boyd had managed to withhold his urges through my two months inpatient treatment and the entire week I had been free.

Thanks to his staying platonic, that night I met the real Boyd. I began to feel true adoration for the man I had once called a friend, then a rapist, now my Master/lover. My second great love affair had begun, just as it had with Matthew, by being tethered by a short leash around our necks. The difference was it was psychological this time instead of real.

QUICK NOTE: *As it had happened in those bright happy days of my D/ss family I had essentially been forced to learn to find love for my enemy or find myself facing death. Master Boyd and I had become a strong D/s relationship that would last for the next six years. Despite our horrible beginning of rape and forced submission (along with his perversion), Master Boyd would prove himself a worthy Dominant and loving partner. He had become my second most powerful Master to ever hold Simon's key. Only Master Jon can boast more power, understanding of the D/s relationship, or being more loving than the reign of Master Boyd. So, what went wrong? Ah, that is a good question. You will have to read on to find out.*

The next morning we awoke to find both of us were cramped from the unusual position we had found slumber. I laughed as my Master bitched about advancing age while I went to the kitchen to cook his breakfast.

The phone rang and Master Boyd picked it up while making lustful demands of a brunch he would like to have served to him in the shower.

"Hello, it's Boyd what do you want," he said still smiling at me while I blew kisses at him from his stove in a tease.

"Huh? What? Wait, slow down. Can you repeat that? Uhm, okay hold on." Master Boyd held the phone out to me "Psycho, it is Sheryl. She is pretty upset. I can't understand her she is blubbering so badly."

I raised my eyebrow with concern while taking the phone. "Sheryl? What's wrong darling?"

Sheryl sobbed. "Psycho, please come home. It is horrible. I just can't, this can't be happening. Oh God, help me," she wailed.

I took a breath. "Sheryl please, you have to tell me what is wrong. You are scaring me."

She sniffed loudly. "I had a biopsy of my breast last week. I didn't tell you, Psycho. I didn't get the message yesterday on the machine. I called. It's cancer. Its advanced they say. Oh God, Psycho, I need you. Please help me," she screamed in terror.

I gasped. "Okay, okay, calm down. I am coming. Just take deep breaths. It is going to be okay. I am on my way." I hung up the phone to a thankful Master Sheryl.

Master Boyd was eating his eggs looking at me now also concerned. "What do you mean you are on the way? Psycho, what is going on. You are home. Can't that old bat handle a case by herself. You need your time off. It is not healthy to call you in on weekends," he said appearing irritated.

I looked at the floor. "I apologize Master for not getting Your permission before saying I would attend her. Sheryl has just found out she has progressed breast cancer, Master. She is alone and upset. She is requesting I come be with her to help her adjust to this tragic news. May I request your release? I will return once she is calmed."

Master Boyd put down his fork looking at the table. "Breast cancer, shit that is tough. Yeah, sure baby I understand. Sheryl needs some comfort if you are feeling strong enough? I want you to call me when you get there safely. Wait, do you want me to come with you?" He leaned forward appearing ready to roll if I requested him.

I chuckled. "Thank You Master but I think this is a girl thing and Sheryl doesn't like you very much to boot. I will be okay. I promise to call you and come home when she is stable. Can you call Mary and tell her my status Master? I need to go now. She is terribly upset."

He got up and embraced me, kissing briefly. "Yes, I got this end of things. You get going and come home soon. I believe you owe me brunch." He smiled playfully.

I nodded returning his smile. "As you wish Master, and maybe dinner too." I winked then left quickly headed to Cumberland to deal with my most distraught secondary collar's devastating news.

I rushed to Master Sheryl's side. When I arrived at her home, she didn't come to the door. When I had waited over five minutes, I kicked it in, finding her collapsed in the floor. An empty bottle of pills lay by her side. I groaned as I called

911 to send an ambulance and did my best to awaken her from the sleep of eternity she had been seeking. I found she did have a heartbeat though it was weak.

The emergency team showed up in record time. I was told she was alive but would need her stomach pumped. I rode in the ambulance with my unconscious Master answering the responder's questions about her as best as I could. We arrived at the hospital ER and she was taken back for physicians to work to save her life.

I called Master Boyd to inform him of Master Sheryl's suicide attempt. He asked to join me and once again I told him to stay home. It was not even clear if she would survive at that time. My Master stated he understood and would inform Mary I was unlikely to return for the entire day. I told him I would call as soon as I had more information.

Four hours after arriving at the hospital a physician informed me they had successfully resuscitated my Master. She was well and resting. He asked me if I knew why she had tried to kill herself. I gave him her news of the cancer diagnosis. The doctor nodded his head informing me that was a common reason for suicide attempts in females her age.

I waited another two hours in the admission waiting room before I was finally allowed to go back to see my Master. She was heavily sedated, but her color was better. I sat with her holding her hand as she smiled telling me how grateful she was I had found her in time. Master Sheryl hoovered between sleep and dreams.

The doctors informed me no one else was coming to sit with my ailing Master. I volunteered to be at her side if they would allow her company. The doctors thought it would be helpful to have someone there to keep an eye on her in case she decided to try again.

I called Master Boyd to inform him it appeared I would not be returning the entire weekend. He was at first incredibly angry. I reminded him that she had been looking after me during my darkest hours. I believed I owed the service when the shoe was on the other foot. He finally begrudgingly agreed but made me promise a rain check on his requested services. I had no problem making that promise now that he and I had come to an understanding of his place in my dark world.

The entire night I slept in the chair next to Master Sheryl's bed. She didn't wake up appearing very tired. The next morning her doctor came to visit. I offered to leave the room, but she asked me to stay.

"Well Miss Fressman, the cancer has spread to your liver. A mastectomy, radiation and five years of chemotherapy may put you into remission. I won't sugar coat this, your cancer is extremely aggressive. Even with treatment, the average survival rate after diagnosis is only three to five years. I am truly sorry. This type of cancer is usually seen in mature ladies who never had children. I wish I had better news, but that is the facts Ma'am." I tuned the doctor out as I felt my Master's hand tighten around mine.

I looked at her laying there, frail, thin, afraid and weeping silently. Her life would be ending soon. There was no way out. Even with treatment, the demonic cancer would come back like a thief in the night to steal her breath away and make her a corpse. I wished there was something I could do to make it better, but there is no cure for death any more than there is for monsters forced upon the unfortunate ones.

The doctor left and I held my wailing Master as she tried to accept her horrible fate. All her life she had been hard, tough and capable. Now, she was like a frightened child in my arms unsure how to cope with the coming darkness of eternity. I said nothing as I rocked her listening to her cries of helplessness. There are no words of comfort for the unwilling dying. You can only hold them and let them understand they are not alone, not yet anyway.

Master Sheryl laid in the bed unspeaking most of the day Saturday. She would have fits of tears and refused her meals. I sat with her taking breaks only to pee and call Master Boyd to post him on her status. My poor Master did seem to be a broken woman. I feared she would promptly give up and try to cut to the front of the line to her destiny once more the second she was released.

Sunday started the same, with no change. I stood there looking down into her staring eyes. She was not speaking or eating. I sighed with frustration then pulled my chair next to her and sat down.

"Master, I beg your forgiveness, but aren't you wasting precious time acting surprised that you are mortal? You surely knew we all die. Everything dies. Now you are told your time is short and instead of kicking ass and taking names you behave like a pussy. I thought you wanted to be Area Manager? Well, you still have plenty of time to make that dream come true. I don't understand any of this. I thought you were tough, smart, independent and ready to battle to the death. Well, time to put on your fucking armor and sharpen your sword bitch. Death is coming. You had better hurry before he catches you," I yelled full of rage as The Chosen One whirled into my unit control room.

Master Sheryl blinked then turned her head to look at me. "You are right Psycho. I am tougher than this. I can beat this. I can. I have always survived all the shit ever thrown at me. Oh my God. What am I doing? Get my shit, we are going home. The food here sucks, and this bed is killing my hip. Tell the doctor to get his ass down here and sign me out." She sat up her eyes bright with the fires I had come to know well.

I smiled wickedly. "Take no prisoners, Master. They will move aside or take them to hell with you."

She smiled back with a hint of mischief. "You bet your sexy little ass, pumpkin. Now get your butt up and get that doctor. That is an order Psycho. Don't come back without the prick."

Without further argument I did as she told me. The doctor of course wanted to hold my terminal Master for further observation. She gave him a tongue lashing that few would have been able to tolerate. She was released with his blessing in another two hours. I drove her to the house and was surprised by her sudden call for special services of the collar.

That afternoon Sheryl fucked like the doctor told her she would be dead by morning. I was scratched, pawed, groped, bitten and everything in between. There was no doubt after her third demand for an orgasm my Master was back to her old grumpy, mean self. I would have breathed a sigh of relief that this crisis was over had she gotten the hell off my face to let me. Okay, too much information and totally unnecessary to share but both true and funny. Nurse, meds over here. Hey, has anyone seen that fucking nurse?

I called Master Boyd to let him know of Master Sheryl's recovery from the edge of depression. While he was happy to hear she was better he was irritated at his lost weekend with me. Especially since he and I had also just dealt with some heavy shit before Master Sheryl decided to demand all the attention. It was late Sunday afternoon and driving back to his house then returning would be reckless and a waste of gas. I had to return to work by six in the morning and he was heading to his own shift in only two hours.

I made many heartfelt apologies and pledged to make the loss up to him the very next weekend. I could tell by the sound of disappointment in his voice, he was going to have a rough week waiting it out. I hung up the phone thinking he had certainly earned his special services by behaving himself like a gentleman for an unheard-of amount of time (for him that is lol). I made a mental note to make sure to be super solicitous of him when providing his needs that Friday.

Monday arrived with a powerful storm. The electricity was knocked out through the entire town. Without a way to get faxed priority investigation calls I was forced to sit waiting by the office phone. All day the foul weather kept me from getting the full information to attend the emergency child abuse allegations. When the weather finally calmed, and power returned to the building, quitting time had arrived for everyone else.

For the Chosen One, work had just started. Fax informed me I would be burning the midnight oil. It would be an all nighter. I dropped Master Sheryl off at her house making sure her mental health was stable. After she assured me she was over wanting to die, I took off across the five counties I handled. It was a wild night of chasing down offenders in order to beat the twenty-hour response deadlines for the cases held back by lack of juice to my machine co-worker.

At eleven o'clock I managed to corner the worst of the alleged monsters. He was a well-known child rapist in the town of Wheatly. My priority one had been called in by a neighbor who had been told the secret by the victim herself.

It didn't take long to get the young lady to spill her trauma to me. I had the mother of the girl take her to the ER for a rape kit to be performed while I called Cathy for assistance from the sheriff's office. The local boys in blue known as Mark and Will showed up and my pray was hauled to the local jail in cuff. I had the shit head weeping thanks to my informing him that even criminals hated baby rapists. I had crudely stated I hoped he had friends on the outside who would pity him enough to send him lube. He was going to need it.

Mark and Will were laughing as they told Cathy of my foul statements to this hated town icon. They were impressed by my moxie and lack of fear of the very large suspect. Cathy told Mark and Will the suspect should have been the one terrified. After all, he had just met the Psycho herself.

I rolled my eyes as Keith and several other old hands from the jail joined the loafing officers. Stories were being recalled of my youthful antics and infamous crude verbalization. I was trying to fill out my paperwork on my collared offender quickly as possible to escape the waves of laugher over my very tarnished history with that piece of real estate known as the county jail house.

I was walking out to head to my next call when Dennis and Master Boyd sped into the parking lot dragging out their own cursing prisoner. I let out a breath of irritation realizing I had been held up just long enough to have to encounter my Master while we both worked to keep the streets and homes of our world safe from beasts just like us.

Master Boyd saw me immediately, but not before Linda who pulled in behind them had come running to hug my unit.

"Psycho, wow, look at you. I heard about your arrest; I mean the arrest you made." She chuckled at her clever catching of that strange statement.

I nodded. "Yeah, Fisher is in stir. Hey, if the jailhouse catches fire lose his key will you? Cindy is down at the ER.

I must go collect those samples and head off to Jessieville. Great to see you. Stay safe sister." I rushed past Linda trying to make it to the Intrepid before Master Boyd could catch me as well.

However, I never was a lucky one. Master Boyd had already come back outside. Dennis told him to go see his fiancé while he did the intake on their detainee. He smiled then hurried past Linda holding me in a loving embrace. Linda watched his inappropriate public display of affection momentarily then cleared her throat to remind him of her presence.

"Damn you Boyd, you are making me jealous. Can you do that somewhere else please," grumbled a mildly irritated Linda.

Master Boyd pulled back from his deep kiss blushing while pushing me in front of him. "Oh shit, sorry Linda. I wasn't thinking." He looked down appearing ashamed while I stood there tolerating his hard on in my back.

"Psycho was just leaving Boyd. Come on you owe me lunch, buddy. No more sneaking out of it. I want to grill you about what is like to sleep with this beautiful woman." She chuckled while admitting to her interests in my sex life unabashedly.

Master Boyd snickered. "I never kiss and tell you know that. Besides, I will be taking this beautiful woman of mine out for lunch instead. I will catch you tomorrow night."

I growled. "Okay you two, now I must be the one to break this up. I really need to be going. I have a lot of miles to cover before the sun comes up and runs me back to the coffin. If you will excuse me." I jerked out of Master Boyd's grip feeling sudden irritation at his presence overcoming me.

Linda looked down feigning fear. "Uh oh, looks like your offer to 'eat out' was turned down there big boy," she said poking fun at Master Boyd being shot down in his offer to take me to lunch.

I just shook my head and began heading for my car. "See you later lover. Got to bolt. Have a great night. Enjoy your lunch."

Master Boyd apparently didn't like my attitude which I suddenly realized was being driven by him. His sexual frustration left over adrenaline from chasing down an offender, and likely mild hunger had somehow bled into my own mood. My mirror for him had become enormously powerful. Even a buzzing mosquito irritating him likely would have been felt by my psyche I had become so sensitive to him.

He reached out grabbing my upper arm harshly. "Hey. Where are you going? I said come to lunch with me. I have a thirty-minute break. I am not asking for you to take off for five fucking hours." The dark clouds of anger were filling his eyes.

A storm of intense outburst was deep within. The Chosen One was aware that if she didn't release this tension quickly by the weekend it would burst into terror. I made a split-second decision to attend his perverted need for control in this thirty-minute break rather than the chance of being alone with an explosive fury over a two-day weekend. I did have a lot of cases to attend but keeping myself from being severely harmed or even killed by a Master with an out of control temper was truly an emergency.

I looked at Master Boyd glowering. "Let me go damn it. I have shit to do. Go eat lunch with Linda and let me get to work. I don't have time for this Boyd." I jerked my arm from his grip heading to my car slow enough to be caught but fast enough to look angry.

My Master took my bait. He stormed at me grabbing my upper arm again growling like a beast under his breath. By now, Keith, Will, Mark, and Cathy had come out for a smoke break joining Linda as the audience to the argument I had purposely contrived. There was awed silence among the watchers. No one could believe their eyes. The quiet, calm, easy going Boyd was pushing the buttons of the infamously hot-blooded Psycho and he didn't appear afraid.

"I have not fucking seen you in months, Psycho. Don't tell me you can't take thirty God damned minutes of your time to have lunch with me. I don't see any fucking fire trucks headed out. So where is the fucking fire," yelled Master Boyd.

I jerked my arm away again. "I am busy, God damn it. I am not going to lunch with you, not now," I growled back.

He put his hands on his hips with his eyes now flashing rage. "Are you fucking telling me no, Psycho? Is that what I am hearing?"

I smiled evilly. "Uhm, yeah. That is what I said Boyd. No, I am not going."

Master Boyd could take no more. He grabbed my arm dragging me to my car jerking the keys from my hand. He shoved me kicking and cussing into the passenger's side slamming the door behind me. My window was down so the audience of police officers heard me call him a pushy asshole as he got behind the wheel and started the vehicle backing out wildly in obvious displeasure.

Mark yelled out, "Hey Boyd. Where are you going man?"

Master Boyd voice dripping with irritation yelled back through his window. "Fucking lunch. Clock me out. I will be back in thirty God damned minutes." He spun rubber hauling ass right for the edge of town.

He pulled the Taurus off a back road parked it and jumped out coming around to my side. Without saying a word, he ripped open my door jerking me out by my upper arm. He dragged me into a heavily wooded area until we reached a small clearing surrounded by nothing but darkness of the forest all around.

He pushed me hard. "Tell me no again. Go ahead and see what happens."

I was nearly out of breath from his rapid stride. "No! Happy now, Master? Do you think you are a big man picking on a little girl? Come on you bully asshole. Bring it. I am not afraid of you. You are just a little bitch." I forced laughter.

Master Boyd blew his gasket at my jabs. He flew at me grabbing me by both upper arms pushing me up against a neighboring tree. His weight had me pinned tightly.

"Oh yeah? Well you will be afraid. You seem to have forgotten who the Master is here." He smiled crazily at me his eyes flashing in pure violent pleasure.

I glowered panting from his weight. "Get off me you fool. You are the Master. Stop this bullshit."

My mild pleas to stop finally snapped him. I was almost relieved, almost because it was taking forever to set him off. When he finally spun me around. I gritted my teeth as I prepared for his vicious entry while he tore down my pants, undoing his own while telling me he was going to make me plead for mercy.

He didn't make me wait long to start pleading. Within moments his eager harsh thrusting had begun as he pushed my unit hard into the trunk of the tree. I did my best to hold it together, but it had been a few months since our last sexual romp. I couldn't take the pain of his rough carnal lust.

I panicked as my pleas became real. Master Boyd was in his zone out feeding his beast and could no longer hear me. Before I could stop myself, I caught him off guard by elbowing him in his stomach. The sudden move knocked his weight off me. I was sent to my knees in agony with a sudden surge of vaginal cramping.

I couldn't get up or catch my breath from the discomfort. Master Boyd recovered quickly. He grabbed me by my waist attempting to re-enter from behind me. I rolled sending him sprawling to his back with me. This fighting him was only making his interest worse.

Before I could utter a word of protest, he was back on my unit pulling me back onto my knees. This time he successfully re-engaged and held me still by latching onto my shoulders from behind me. I couldn't escape his debauchery this time. I screamed out in agony while he forced himself into me wantonly without restraint. His climax was thankfully not long in coming, partly because it had been awhile and partly because of the extreme aggressiveness of our battle for control. He had won at last. Master Boyd now felt content as he took his power back by dominating his prize intimately just as his perversion demanded.

As usual, as he spent his seed, he called out how much he loved me. I gasped and panted cursing myself for forgetting the true strength of my Master. I would need to be much more careful about allowing this urge inside him to build to such a toxic level in the future or be sorry for it.

I moaned out with displeasure. "Fuck, Master, that was rough."

He had finally come back from planet 'monster asshole.' "Oh God. Baby. I am so sorry. What the, oh hell, I lost it again. Please Psycho, are you going to leave me? I messed up again…I don't know why I keep doing this." He was still coupled with me already trying to undo his explosive outburst of outrage.

I chuckled bitterly then moaned again from the cramping. "Of course not Master. However, I do have to get to work if you are satisfied now? I can take you back to the station, but you have missed getting to eat."

Master Boyd realized he was still in his mount he jumped up reaching down to aid me to stand. I held my lower abdomen grimacing as the cramping began to lessen slightly.

"Psycho here let me help baby. Don't worry about my eating. I have a snack in the car. How about you? Have you eaten? Are you taking your meds," he said while aiding me to redress while adjusting his own uniform.

I nodded. "Yes Master I took my medication earlier today. I don't recall whether I have eaten or not. I will try to remember later."

He kissed me once after we were clothed properly once more. "I love you baby. Thank you for not being angry with me. I will keep trying to stop acting stupid like that." He took my hand leading me back to the Taurus.

I looked at him. "Master do you even recall what you are doing when that happens? I mean do you know you are doing it?" I had noticed he didn't appear himself during the attacks.

He shook his head while aiding me into my seat. "Actually, come to think of it, not really. I mean I get angry and it is like I can't stop myself. I know but I don't know? I want it to stop but it is like someone else is running the show. Does that make sense? Like I am dreaming?"

I looked at the ground. "Yeah it does Master. Thank you for sharing. I will see what I can find out about what happens to you when the fits come on."

Master Boyd got behind the wheel looking at me appearing grateful. "You will? Do you think you can find a way to stop them?"

I shook my head. "I doubt it, but maybe we can find out what is causing it. It is a start, Master." He took my hand and kissed my engagement ring then took off headed back to the jailhouse.

We pulled up to change drivers so I could get back to work. The entire jail house staff was standing around outside. All of them were trying to appear like they all just happen to be getting a smoke at the same exact moment. I saw our audience realizing exactly thirty minutes had elapsed since Master Boyd and I had left in a huff. He rolled his eyes as we both got out noticing our fans too.

I walked behind but was stopped briefly to engage Master Boyd in a passionate kiss at his request. "Be safe baby. See you on Friday. I am counting the seconds. I love you, please never forget that. Call me later if you have time."

I nodded while still in his arms. "I love you too Master. Will do around nine in the morning. Does that work? I won't be done till then."

He smiled. "Sounds perfect. I can hear your voice before I go to sleep. Wait, are you getting any rest?"

Our audience was starting to murmur while watching our show of affection. "Uhm yeah, sure Master. I will sleep tomorrow, promise. I must go. See you soon." I hoped in the car leaving Master Boyd walking across the parking lot to deal with the sea of nosey onlookers.

I finished my night without missing any deadlines. It was a close one, but I got my cache emptied before the latest of the new calls came pouring in through my fax buddy. At nine, just as promised before I took off back into my five-county chase of abusers, I called Master Boyd.

"Uhm Master, it is me, just as promised," I said while trying to pack my black case with files for the day's workload.

Master Boyd moaned out happily while sounding very sleepy. "Hey baby. Did you eat? When are you going to sleep?"

I shook my head. "I forgot to eat Master and I will sleep tonight, I promise."

He growled. "You will eat right now and sleep today, Psycho. Don't make me come out there to kick Sheryl's ass. It wouldn't look good to beat up a sick woman but honey you must look out for yourself too. I worry. Now, when you get off this phone eat something, that is a directive. You are looking thin again. I will need to weigh you this weekend. I am not so sure you are not still suffering Acute cycle. Baby, you can relapse so no stress. That is an order." He coughed.

I nodded. "Did Linda give you any shit after I left Master? I worry she may be suspicious You are the Master. You know she is aware of it."

He chuckled. "Nah, she didn't but everyone got a good laugh at me and you anyway. I uhm, next time we see each other like we did last night in the woods remind me to brush off afterwards, uhm you know. I mean if we are, well just remind me."

I raised my eyebrow. "Oh? Why Master?"

Master Boyd laughed nervously. "Well, when I got back, I was asked by several of the boys where we went for lunch. I told them Darla's Drive Inn so they bought it. I went to file the paperwork on the perp, and well Mark and Keith were snickering and watching me. I just ignored them. You know how juvenile they can be. Anyway, Will came up and shook the back of my uniform collar. Leaves and crap spilled all over the office floor. Everyone has been teasing me all night that Darla's has now increased their delivery service. They teased all night that included over the Psycho Mountains and into the woods for important customers like Officer Simmons." He apologized again for his momentary lapse of consciousness and violent sexual assault.

I rolled my eyes. "Master we discussed this. Keep the demon within reason and I will serve your proclivities as best

I can. As for the other officers, don't allow them to get you down. They are just jealous is all. Let them tease. You will be sleeping with me while they sleep with their hands down their pants all alone." I chuckled.

He laughed out loud. "You are right. They are jealous but you are mine. I love you so much, Psycho. You have made everything so wonderful. How can I ever thank you?"

"Keep us both out of the Snake Pit Master. That would be a great start." I sighed looking at PC smiling at me on the monitor.

Master Boyd groaned. "Yeah, neither of us will see that place again, you have my promise. No matter what I must do. I won't let them get you again."

I smile. "I won't let them get you again either Master. I love you. Now I must go. I just recognized a name on my list. It is one I have been waiting to see come up again."

Chapter 63: The Beast Within
The Rise of the D/s Power Couple
Master Boyd and Interim Master Sheryl

It is starting to get very strange in the world behind the shattered looking glass. Even in our most odd existence the end of 1998 stands out as one of the most bizarre. None of it was ever supposed to happen, it completely deviated from our plan. We had come apart at the seams trying to serve a Master of misunderstanding and a secondary collar of no worth. In the end our delusion was mixing with the real, further confusing our most turbulent journey to the wrong destination.

Master Sheryl is dying. Her womanhood has betrayed her by calling out for the reaper. To show compassion is a human condition, just like mortality. We had forgotten we were not human anymore. In our wish to feel normal we mistakenly allow robbery most cruel. We tended another's failing garden and let our own become overgrown. We will starve this winter while our Master enjoys the fruit of our tender care. She will not appreciate what we sacrificed assuming it is her right. It goes to prove not much can grow in the darkness of Eternity. We had forgotten we were always farming a barren field even in the growing season.

Master Boyd is growing in power. His Domination of our insolence is teaching him a lesson that will serve him well. The clever Master will recall his vows and force us to surrender to his return of affection. Inside the D/s pair the monster's growing in strength. Well fed by the other they will rise from the bottom of the muddy waters of obscurity together. They will become a double threat of reckoning. When the couple are at the height of social awe, the schizophrenic within us will falter. The Master will push us to our knees and stand guard while he takes the blow. The 24/7 lifestyle perfection shall be achieved.

Ah, do you feel that? It is the winds of change in the air. This is something we vaguely recall from our dark past. Last time we had one Master and two collars that worked together (D/ss). However, in the end it crushed our heart to smithereens. This time, there are two Keyholders and only one circle of silver (Dd/s). Our heart is being patched together by the Dominant, but our mind will be kinked by the vanilla with a twist.

Ready to see what happens when we forget why we follow Simon's orders and think we are normal? Great! This time grab the electrical tape, a knife, and that extra wire. Set your alarms for 'never.' Say goodbye to the sandman, he is no longer your friend. Now you start running, …but do know we are already at the bottom. We have been there for quite some time waiting on all of you.

"Well I don't know what has gotten into Boyd. He used to be quiet and minded his manners. Now he is cussing out the other officers when they fun him. The boys have always teased him, it doesn't hurt nothing. Then the other day he told Cathy to mind her business when she asked him if he was tending his momma's grave. He used to listen to me and do what he was told. Since you and he started dating he is, well, different.

211

What are you doing to my officer Psycho?"
--Dennis asking Psycho about changes noted in Master Boyd, early October 1998.

The Chosen One pulled by the mailbox at the bottom of the hill. Nikki Pools old trailer house loomed at the top like a wart on a witch's chin, ugly and hard to miss. I looked up to see that Nikki was already standing in the doorway smiling at me. She couldn't have heard the Taurus pull up. I narrowed my eyes at her wondering how she could have known I was due to arrive. Unless someone had informed her that a call of child abuse had been made. I began the long climb to the top ready to haul her son Johnny off to a foster home if any of the story from the wire to me was correct.

"Purgy. Ah, you are blond now. Love it. Come in. Come in. I have coffee and creamer already waiting for you. I expected you about an hour ago. Guess the severe weather yesterday held you up," Nikki yelled down appearing happy to see me despite my grim reason for the visit.

I looked up at the overly ecstatic Nikki irritated by her careless attitude of dragging me out to check on her parenting. It had only been two months since my last visit on a charge. This gal was quickly starting to become a pest.

"You seem in good spirits. You appear to know why I am here, Miss Pool. Let's sit down and chat shall we?" I said almost out of breath as I reached her tiny porch.

She nodded eagerly "Oh hell yes. I really love the blond. Suits you better than the black. Hey, could we get the photo first?"

I raised my eyebrow at her. "Miss Pool if I find out Johnny's teeth are really in the shape the call says they are in, we have a problem. I may have to arrest you. Still want that picture knowing that?"

Nikki rolled her eyes still grinning like a possum. "Uhm duh, yeah. Besides, Johnny's teeth do suck but I didn't do it. The dentist wants too much cash to fix them. It is natural ugly, nothing I did wrong."

I glowered as I followed her inside. "Miss Pool you have an open case. If Johnny needs his teeth adjusted the State must pay for it to get him on track if you are unable to afford that. This is a caseworker issue, and not what was reported."

She laughed. "Oh, I know what the report said. Someone said I punched him in the mouth, but I didn't do that. Hell, the kid would murder me in my sleep if I dared. He's too much like his daddy to take any kind of hitting. Look for yourself. His mouth is ugly but not punched." She called for the child who was late for school already.

Johnny came out with his books in a rush. "God damn it, you old heifer. I heard you the first time. I know I am late. If you would get off your lazy ass and wake me up once in a while I wouldn't oversleep. Shit. What good are you," he growled at Nikki.

My eyes went wide at this most inappropriate lack of both respect for his mother and foul language for a seven-year-old. I looked at Nikki stunned to see if she would indeed punch him in the mouth over his insolent retort to her calling

213

him. I know I likely would have been tempted my fucking self if it had been my son.

Nikki chuckled. "Oh get over yourself, Johnny. I wanted you to show Purgy here your mouth. There was another report. They said I punched you." She pointed at me while directing him to show me his mouth.

Johnny sighed with irritation then opened his mouth dramatically almost in a taunting fashion. The child's teeth were crooked, and a few were rotting with observable cavities, but there was not a sign of a fist causing the issue. Just neglect of oral hygiene.

Nikki smiled. "See just ugly as homemade soap but not from abuse. Now, get your ass to the neighbor's house and catch your ride to school since you missed the fucking bus again."

Johnny ran past me flipping off his mother with his right middle finger while heading out the door to catch his ride.

I stood there feeling I had slipped into a time warp. "Uhm, your relationship with your son is, well, not my business. Look how did you know what the report claimed? It was called in anonymously. Do you know who made it? If I can get a name and prove it, we can counter-claim for harassment." I took out my pen ready to write down the name she surely knew to have all the information the caller claimed.

Nikki's eyes went wide. "You mean that is illegal? To call in a false report I mean?"

I put my pen back into my case letting out an angry sigh.

I stood there glaring at Nikki realizing my false reporter was standing in front of me. "Miss Pool, yes it is. Calling in false claims costs the State money in man hours, and paperwork, not to mention it pisses me off when I have real abuses to investigate all over this God forsaken land. I am not saying it was you, but if it was then stop that right now. I have better shit to do," I yelled angrily.

Nikki looked at the floor appearing embarrassed. "Wow! I didn't know. Are you going to tell on me? I mean if I did it, not saying I did. But if you thought it was me will you tell my caseworker?"

I grabbed my temples trying to shake off my fatigue. It had been hours since I had slept and days since I had a bite to eat. My head was starting to throb from my neglect of both necessities.

"All I want to know is why? Tell me that and I will let it slide this time if you never pull this crap again that is." I sighed while looking at her face hoping she would answer honestly so I could move on to my next call.

Nikki shrugged. "I didn't know when the next time my mother-in-law would call in a fake one. Johnny finally found the camera and I wanted a photo. I thought why not just do it myself. I wanted to have coffee and hang out with you. I was hoping we could become friends. So, I made the first move to get to know you better. I called it in myself."

My eyes went wide. "What? You called in a report of abuse on yourself just so I would have coffee with you? Are you insane? How fucking lonely do you have to be to risk my arresting you just to make a friend? Miss Pool, I am a DCFS investigator. I cannot hang out with clients." I couldn't believe my ears.

Nikki looked hurt. "You think I am not good enough to hang out with because I am poor and all that, right? Well, I am just as good as the Richie riches around here. More honest too. If you want friends that back stab you go ahead. If you want a real friend come, see me sometime without me having to call in a lie," she whined out acting if she was the one that was badly used by her impulsive behavior.

I almost passed out from shock at her lack of empathy and insight, to her disregard for my job duties. "Seriously? This is not happening. This conversation is over. Don't call yourself in again. Get out more. You are going stir crazy or something. I will let your case worker know you need a mental health assessment. Good day Miss Pool."

I left her house and stormed down the hill feeling more lightheaded than ever. The world was losing its mind faster than I was, it seemed to me. I felt the pager in my belt begin to vibrate wildly. It was Master Sheryl's office number. I was not far from her. I decided to head back, see what she wanted and file the unfounded paperwork on the Pool case before heading one hundred miles to the north after my next priority one case. I didn't bother to look back at Nikki's trailer nor pose for that fucking photo she kept asking for. What a weirdo.

When I arrived at the office, I rushed to Master Sheryl's to find her still paging me every few minutes frantically. It had gone off over five times while I was driving to meet her. I had become panicked thinking something was wrong. She surely knew I may not be able to get to a phone quickly. I would have gotten to her as soon as I could. Her constant paging scared me that tragedy had struck again somewhere in my world. I pushed into her office door out of breath in a full-blown anxiety attack.

"What is it? Did someone die? Was there an accident? Oh shit, are my kids okay? Master what is going on," I panted out my eyes wide.

Master Sheryl glared at me appearing irritated. "Uhm, no. None of that. I paged you and you didn't answer me. Where the fuck were you that you couldn't get back to me when I called?"

I looked at the floor suppressing my anger. It seemed Nikki was not the only one with a total lack of giving two shits I was working and had no time for foolish visiting.

"I was investigating Nikki Pool and working my caseload Master. You know, doing my job," I growled back.

She narrowed her eyes. "I don't like that tone Psycho. You had better watch your little attitude missy or I will make you sorry for it. Next time I page, fucking call immediately. Got it?"

I nodded. "Yeah, loud and clear Master. Now, what is the problem that caused the page in the first place? I have a lot of shit to do, and no time to do it."

Master Sheryl leaned back appearing to soften as she removed her glasses. "I want you to go to Julia Stubbs after you leave this office. She needs a friend right now and thinks the world of you. Then this afternoon I have pre-op for the mastectomy. You spend the morning with Julia then come back here pick me up and be with me while I deal with these medical dickheads." She smiled at that.

I again felt I may faint at the incredibly stupid sentences coming out of my Master's mouth. "Uhm, Master, I am not sure what you are thinking but I have twenty-five calls across a two hundred mile stretch of Earth to cover today. I will have more by morning. I can't just go hold the hand of an upset ex-foster parent or run to hang with you to get your blood drawn. I will be there for the surgery and take care of you during recovery, but this pre-op you don't need me for. I can't remember the last time I ate anything, and I have not slept in days. I need to finish this shit so I can have tonight to rest. I can't pull another all-nighter."

Master Sheryl stared at me hatefully. "You will do what I told you to do. You are on flex time. You have all day and all night to meet those deadlines. How can you stand there and let a good soul like Julia suffer after all she did for those little girls? What kind of a heartless monster are you? As for me, you will come with me because I fucking said so. I need some support and you are it, pumpkin. You are young. You don't need rest and you know it. So cut the shit, get to Julia's and get out of my sight until one or so help me God," she yelled out.

I shook my head. "If Julia needs someone why are you not going Master? She is your friend. I don't even know her. She can't think the world of a stranger. I met her once. You have known her twenty years. I will come back for your Pre-op but can't you handle Julia?"

Master Sheryl snorted. "I have been. I can't snap her out of it. I am hoping you can do for her what you did for me. Do remind her why life is worth fighting for. Go share your spirit to battle with her and help her out of her hell. She knows it was you that is fighting for her murdered babies. She has asked to see you and thank you in person many times. Now today she will get her wish. No more arguing, go now." She answered the phone while wagging her cane at me in a threat for a beating later if I continued to deny her command.

I faked a military salute while frowning angrily at her in a sarcastic gesture of severe irritation, then left her office. I rapidly filed the unfounded form for Miss Pool then got back into the Taurus starting the still hot motor to fly off like a bat out of hell to meet up with the grieving Julia.

"What is in the fucking water, I mean coffee, these days," I yelled out loud to no one in frustration while waiting at a stop light.

Simon opened the door and jumped in shot gun smiling at me. "How you doing Psycho, or Psycho Tron, or The

Chosen One, or well whoever the hell we are today." He chuckled.

I glared at him. "Et tu, Brutus? What the fuck do you want now? Coffee and friendship too? Sorry cupcake, my dance card is filled. So, spit it out, and then get the fuck out."

His eyes showed fear., "Psycho, errr, hey look we need sleep. If you don't eat and you lose any more weight Master Boyd said he is going to punish us too. I believe he gave us a directive to eat? Did we forget already?"

I frowned. "I didn't fucking forget Simon. I haven't got time. Shit, just shit. I need more time. Coffee counts as food anyway. So I was not breaking directives. Look I don't need another mother hen here. I don't want any fucking friends either. I just want to do my job and be left the fuck alone. How God damned hard is that to understand? Do you think Jane has to go have coffee and offer support to her asshole bosses, co-workers or clients? No, this is bullshit," I yelled so loud the lady in the car next to me at the red light looked at me then locked her door assuming I was nuts. A correct assumption, by the way.

Simon looked at his shoes, "Psycho, please listen to me. Leave Sheryl. Leave this job. It is going to kill us. Master Boyd is right. Sheryl is stealing services and you are not normal. Stop trying to be normal. Did she ever visit you in the hospital, call or care? No. Is she looking out for our needs? No. She is still overworking us. She has not changed. Plus, she stole from Master Boyd. We were not there this weekend thanks to her and we got hurt in those woods over a service that was overdue to a Master that was owed a debt. Please listen to me. Leave before she kills us with her selfishness."

My eyes went wide, and mouth dropped. "Why you fucking cold hearted motherfucker. How dare you? Master Sheryl is dying Simon. She is scared. How can you say leave her to die alone? God damn you. Get the fuck out of my car and don't come back until you grow a soul," I screamed at the top of my lungs at him.

Simon snapped his head up to my words. "Psycho, do you hear yourself. You are telling your inner self to get out. We are not fucking normal. Stop trying to play by their rules or we are dead. We need help. We cannot help us much less others. Get it through your fucking head."

I started through the light turning off toward Julia's. "Simon, I mean it, get out. I am going to pull over and you leave. I can't believe you are here to preach to me about stolen services to Master Boyd or condemning my attending a human fucking being in need. She almost died Simon. If I had not come she would have. I am not going to stand by and let her suffer just because you are mad she never came to see us at the hospitals. Get out, get out now." I pulled over to the shoulder and pointed at the door angrily.

He looked at me starting to tear up. "We are going to die Psycho. This Sheryl is a monster, but you can't see it. She is dying and plans to take us with her. This job is no good for us and she knows it. She doesn't love us. Sheryl is using us, manipulating us by promising to give us what we can never have. We are never going to be able to save others from our fate Psycho. She is lying to us. If you want to help, we must find another way to do it that can allow for our weakness. Our sickness is too deep. Can't you understand? We can't save the abused from drowning because we are drowning too."

The fire raged in my eyes from my inner anger demon. "Get out, God damn it. Out now." I reached out and pushed his shoulder.

Simon nodded then got out of the car walking down the road, not bothering to look back. I watched my old friend in the rearview mirror. I couldn't stop fuming in intense fury wanting to run him over while he retreated. I hit the steering wheel losing my temper to the point of busting a piece off the dashboard. I was just so sick of everyone trying to tell me what to do. I couldn't stand it. Every time I wanted to do anything, I heard the word no. Wait a moment, uh oh.

I looked in the rearview mirror to see the melting storm clouds in my blue eyes while my outrage calmed. Master Boyd's own crazed gaze looked back. I suddenly realized I was developing an explosive anger disorder not unlike his own. My own inner beast was growing stronger with each violent coupling with my aggressive Master.

I felt a feeling of extreme relief and fatigue wash over me. I really needed a nap or a cigarette even though I didn't smoke at the time. The feeling was better than an orgasm. It was beyond pleasurable to have let off the steam that had been building in my psyche. I smiled wickedly finally understanding my Master like few ever could or should. I decided I had to agree with Master Boyd regarding this hostile and destructive way to release pent up aggression. It worked well to make me feel so much better.

I started the car quickly speeding off to meet with Julia Stubbs as I had been commanded to do. I was no longer full of resentment. In fact, I felt very gentle and friendly for a change. Just the right mentality to deal with the mourning woman and perhaps even become good friends.

It never once occurred to me that I had just dismissed the only connection I have to sanity. It didn't matter that I had not slept or eaten in days. I only thought of minding the orders of someone who was treating me like an endless river of strength, comfort and energy. That was okay too. After all, I am not human anyway. I am a robot. The ability to keep going without food, water or sleep was all in my programming.

I pulled into Julia Stubbs driveway still feeling high from my intense anger outburst only minutes earlier. I wondered how long the euphoria lasted before I would have to blow up again. It seemed to me keeping an eye on that would be helpful to learn Master Boyd's rhythms. This could be information that would work to my advantage in keeping his violence under control.

QUICK NOTE: *Too bad I forgot my own anger Devil would soon need similar aid if I too was developing the monstrosity within. In typical schizophrenic fashion, and because I had dismissed Simon, I forgot my own needs* *while worrying only for those of everyone else. My countdown to psychotic episode had just begun yet again. This time the explosion would demonstrate just how dangerously ill I had become. I was in serious trouble, and so was everyone around me.*

I knocked. After several moments Julia came to the door. The pretty middle-aged blond I had met that spring had aged a decade in only months. Her eyes were swollen from countless tears shed over her murdered foster babies. She looked at me with her dull soul portals appearing either sleepy or drugged out of her gourd.

"Mrs. Stubbs? Sheryl told me you had been asking to see me," I said unsure what to say to the sad woman.

She looked at me appearing startled. "Oh? Sheryl, oh yeah, you are the one who is fighting for my girls. They said you are testifying in court that DCFS killed my babies and so did that horrible woman. Oh my God, my babies. My beautiful little babies. Ruined. Oh, they died in pain. God should have taken me instead," she wailed out suddenly while falling to her knees in a total emotional breakdown.

I stepped back almost running for my car in terror of her sudden movement and pleas of mercy from the Christian Deity.

She looked at me putting her hands into a praying position. "Bring them back, please. Tell me it was a lie. I will forgive you for lying. Tell me you hid them and that they are okay. Please!" Her face reddened with tears flowing like water down a turbulent river.

224

I looked down at her with pity in my eyes. "Mrs. Stubbs, I am not here to tell you a lie. I am here to help you find your way back. The girls are gone. They can't be hurt anymore. You on the other hand are suffering. Take my hand. Let's find peace for you together. The babies have peace now. Don't you think they have earned it?" I held out my hand to aid her to her feet.

Julia looked at me shaking her head. "No. I want them with me. Don't you hear me? I can't live without them. I need my girls back in my arms. Go get them. Get them now. Do you hear me?"

I kept my hand out frowning. "Do you believe in a life after this one, Mrs. Stubbs?"

She looked down nodding still wailing.

I stepped closer. "Then you would take their freedom from brutality for your own selfish hurts? Why? Do you think that DCFS will give them back to you if I could get them? No. They would hand them to another shitty foster home or back to that beast momma. They would suffer again, and again. They are beyond all that now. The moment of pain for them has passed and they have moved on to a better place, far from the nightmares of this world. I know wherever they watch from they will not want to see you like this. They love you. You must be strong and love them enough back by letting them go. Take my hand Mrs. Stubbs. I need some coffee and you need a tissue." Julia looked up at my hand with frightened eyes but took it while I helped her to her feet.

"I don't know how to go on. I am so lost," she mumbled still weeping.

I smiled with gentleness toward this bereaved mother. "It is okay. Take it a minute at a time. Let's start by walking to your kitchen, then from there we can decide what to do next."

She nodded trying to wipe her eyes. "Yeah, you are right. Coffee would be great right now. Come on in. You are Psycho right?"

I chuckled,. "Uhm, yeah most of the time."

She looked at me appearing confused then smiled finally getting my clever response, "Ah, that is funny. I love that. Your nickname is like a joke."

As I followed behind her I snorted. "The nickname is the truth. The joke is me."

I sat down at her kitchen table while she poured us both a cup of coffee. For the next several hours I listened to her talk of her feelings about the murders of her foster daughters. She showed me tons of photos she had taken of them and her during their lives together. I held her while she wept the tears of deep loss. I could do nothing but sit, be calm and talk softly. To lose a child, or two as she did, to the reaper is one thing. Having your beloved kids brutally raped then slaughtered is another.

The fact that one was only five and the other just seven, was beyond heart wrenching. I doubt the toughest soul could have handled knowing, or seeing as I had, what their final moments had to be like. The terror and their screams called out to Julia in the darkness. I have spoken to many mothers who lost children to killers. They all told me the same thing. In the night they can hear their babies crying, begging, and saying 'where are you momma?' Why are you not here to save us?' I cannot even, nor do I desire to ever, begin to know the pain a mother must endure when their little ones are taken to the grave this way.

I let Julia draw her strength from my own ebbing waters that morning. I believed she needed an empathetic ear. Just a hand to hold, someone to care. I felt very helpless. I cannot bring back the dead or undo injustice. I had suffered when I lost my Matthew, so I knew there was nothing that could be done for Julia. If she decided to join her foster daughters, she would no doubt do it. With that in mind, I did my absolute best to remind her that her husband and his two sons needed her to stick around. The girls were safe now, and they would still be waiting when her right time had come.

Slowly, just as my time was ending, I could hear the acceptance of her fate in her voice tone. Julia was coming to terms with things that can never be changed. There was no guarantee she would stay on the mend.

Often grief yo-yos many times before the person gives up or learns to live without the one they miss. The only thing that was clear was she was smiling, joking and mildly laughing at silly stories about life in that town I shared with her. Those emotional displays were a good sign that Julia would eventually recover even if she would never feel whole ever again.

I reminded her that time heals all wounds when I got into my car to leave her. It was time to attend Master Sheryl's pre-op appointment.

She smiled bitterly. "My mom used to say that. I would watch the clock wondering how it could fix a cut. I know silly, but I was just a kid. Thank you, Psycho, for being here. Thank you for fighting for my babies. I will never forget what you are doing for me and did for them. You are an angel on Earth. Come by again for coffee anytime. I had fun, well fun as possible given the circumstances."

I chuckled. "Yeah, sure Mrs. Stubbs. Please remember to take care of yourself and don't be afraid to ask for help. That is what those lazy counselors are for. Hell, make the bitches earn their money just like the rest of us."

She chuckled too. "Never thought of that. Okay, you bet. Tell Sheryl I said hi and send my sympathy over her troubles. If she ever needs anything she can call me."

"She will be okay. She is tough as an old goat. Plus, she has a Psycho helping her out." I winked as I shut the door.

Julia smiled. "No doubt. Lucky bitch indeed. See you soon. Oh, and for the last damned time, call me Julia, will you?"

I nodded then took off rushing back to the office like my trunk was on fire. It was only one in the afternoon and I already felt like a week had passed. Master Sheryl was waiting for me outside. She opened my door telling me to get out while she demanded I allow her to drive.

She and I raced to her appointments. It took all afternoon to get her blood drawn, medications, pre- and post-surgical instructions, and general physical. I kept falling asleep in the waiting rooms, awakened roughly by my Master when she kicked my legs or pushed me off the chair. She thought it great fun to watch me freak out as I woke with a start. My scrambling was likely comical to watch but down right mean to do. I did complain to her asking that she cut it out. My Master informed me my antics kept her from being bored, and I was supposed to be entertaining her without sleeping.

When we finished her arrangements for her surgery the next week, we returned home. I went directly to the couch and was asleep before I hit the damned thing. Less than two hours later Master Sheryl rolled me off into the floor telling me the pager was going nuts. I looked at the number irritated that I had yet another emergency added to my already impressive number. I got up grumbling at my lack of intimate time with my lover the sandman. I made a thermos of coffee. Without a word to my Master I grabbed my coat and files, then rushed off into my father darkness. I spent the entire night hunting down the demonic shadows that haunt children's nightmares.

That week was horribly punishing for me. I didn't get two hours of sleep each day and only could recall eating a couple of times. I was always on the run to one call in a county with the pager going off with three more spread out across the five-county catchment area. I was ordered to visit with Julia Stubbs two more times that week.

I did pity the poor woman, but her taking up two to three hours of my workday sobbing over children long lost was a problem. I had kids out there who needed aid at that moment. I began to view her demands to my Master as irritating. I was already spending countless hours testifying, answering lawyers, questioning the offenders, and filing paperwork over the murders. Having to then coddle the foster parent was beyond torturous. I was never getting much time to be free of those accursed images of those two little girls and their lifeless, mangled little units.

By Friday, I was ready to go home to Master Boyd. I didn't think I would ever be happy to see that man. However, the crushing scheduling, lack of sleep and non-stop demands of my frightened Master Sheryl were taking a toll. I needed a break. Even sleeping with the Devil would have looked like a holiday.

I was getting into my Intrepid when Master Sheryl chased me down handing me the pager. "Psycho, you forgot this. You are on call for the next six weeks. I went ahead and signed you up for the remainder of the year too. You can thank me later, but you had better get now. I don't need that asshole Boyd calling again wondering when you are headed out. He is getting on my nerves."

I was stunned. "Huh? Master did you say the rest of the year? I can't. Why did you do that?"

I couldn't believe she had been so cruel. I would be 24/7 for the next five months without holiday, vacation or weekend off work. I was a salaried worker which meant I would receive no overtime or holiday pay for the long, grueling hours put in extra. The State law prevented anyone from doing on call service more than six weeks a year. Master Sheryl was second in line and had gotten a special waiver from the Area Manager to force me into this overwhelming workload.

Master Sheryl looked at me smiling. "Now old Boyd won't be getting any of my girl's affection. Not unless he can chase you from county to county every night and day. You have all five counties. The caseworkers are going to love you. Now they won't have to fight deciding who will give up a weekend or take turns." She slapped the top of the car chuckling turned and walked back inside.

I looked at the pager that began to vibrate with a number over sixty miles to my west. I almost threw the fucking thing on the ground and ran away right then. Truth is I should have. No one, not even Psycho Tron, could work non-stop without a break. Endless cases, endless faces of the abused, the offenders, the lawyers, the judges, the mountains of paperwork. I was feeling sick to my stomach.

I went back inside and called the number taking down the information. I had no time to go to Master Boyd to explain my situation before I would have to head off to track down the monster. With great fear I called him before taking off to hunt baby rapists.

"Psycho? What is wrong baby? Is the car not starting?" I heard Master Boyd's voice breath out appearing upset.

"Uhm, the car is fine Master. You see, I am on call. I just got a priority one down in Jessieville. I must go attend it. I will be a few hours late. Forgive me Master?" I held my breath waiting for his anger to erupt.

He sighed. "Yeah, okay. Go take care of it. I will be waiting. Try to hurry. I barely was able to make it this long. I really need you home. Now hang up and get going. Sooner you get it done sooner you are home."

I nodded. "Thank you Master. See you soon." I ran to the car feeling grateful I had not been promised death for having to attend a late case.

I lucked out for a change and the call was false. Within only two hours I had cleaned up the mess. My trip to Master Boyd's house was one of the fastest I had ever made. I called ahead to the local cops in each county between me and Master Boyd to warn them I was rushing through. All the police officers in the catchment area knew my status as a State Police Investigator. They also knew my Intrepid and the Taurus.

Since I was always on an emergency timeline like most cops, I could break speed limits when on my way to crime scene without punishment. I always showed respect by calling ahead to make sure the local boys knew it was me rocketing by them as if the devil were chasing me. This was one of the only times I called ahead and said I was flying through but there was no child abuse case at the end of my destination. I was trying to prevent my own beating by speeding home.

When I pulled into Master Boyd's driveway, I was sideways from nearly driving past it. My fatigue was fucking with my mind. I was almost in a trance fighting off the coming unconsciousness of incredible weariness. To my horror I hit and knocked over Master Boyd's mailbox as I had in a previous vehicular incident. I pulled into his yard, then rushed back hoping I was dreaming I had just taken out the new mail holder by its roots. He had cemented it in this time. It was not a figment of my imagination. I had done it again, shit.

I picked up the now demolished postal box dragging it out of the middle of the road feeling sick to my stomach. I looked up to see Master Boyd coming shaking his head. He had seen my little oopsie moment.

"Psycho, damn it. I just replaced that. Why do you hate my mailbox so much?" He put his hands on his hips chuckling at his statement.

I breathed a sigh of relief. "You are not angry Master? It was an accident, I swear it. I think maybe I am very tired?" I looked down hoping he wasn't just luring me into a sense of security that he was not pissed over my damaging his property.

Master Boyd grabbed my arm pulling me into his arms hugging tightly. "No Psycho, it is just a stupid box. I can get another one. It is you I can't replace. You look very tired. Come inside. You are also very thin. I think that we need to discuss this job of yours. But not tonight. Tonight, I just want to enjoy my girl being home at last. Now come inside, get

233

your stuff. This time I won't let you leave to go anywhere." He started pulling me with his arm around my waist towards the car to grab my luggage.

I looked down at my pager. It sat there with its one big eye appearing to glare back. Fear made biscuits down my spine. I worried I would see its evil green eye as it quaked in fury any moment with yet another emergency. There was no way it wouldn't at some point. Five counties would never be calm an entire weekend. Telling Master Boyd of my stupid move to agree to six weeks, much less the rest of the year, was not something I was in a hurry to do. I decided to wait till I had no choice. I was just too tired to fight or do much of anything else for that matter.

Once inside the house, Master Boyd made me sit down at the kitchen table. He reached into his refrigerator and got out his dinner plate and one for me. He warmed them both in the microwave and sat down demanding I eat where he could verify that I had finished at least one meal.

While I did as he commanded he yapped about his busy week, troubles with everyone teasing him about our parking lot argument that Monday, and that Dennis being particularly nosey wanting to know when we were getting hitched. I winced realizing this was going to end in another discussion of walking down the fucking aisle with Master Boyd as Mrs. Boyd Simmons.

I did my best to keep all signs of emotion out of my face regarding Dennis pushing the idea. I was beginning to wonder if maybe Dennis was behind my Master's frantic attempts to make me a so-called honest woman and not him trying to undo his guilt at having taken me by force in the white cell. Dennis did have a very powerful hold on Master Boyd. This was all thanks to the promise Dennis had made to my Master's parents to keep him out of further troubles. The possibility that Master Boyd didn't want to hurry marriage but was being pushed was curious to me. However, my fatigue caused me to dismiss my asking about it.

After dinner I really wanted to get some sleep. I assumed granting special services of the collar was in the cards but asking him about them forbidden. I decided to try to accelerate his interest by offering bath service. To my surprise he said he was not interested.

"Maybe later but right now I want you to go into my room and put on the wedding dress I bought for you. Then come out here and let me see you in it." He smiled as he gently pushed me toward the bedroom door.

I gasped. "Ah, Master, I am super tired. May I beg mercy. Maybe another time?"

I couldn't stand the thought of even putting that thing near my skin suit. Marriage was not my thing. I was already collared. I am not the marrying type.

My Master looked at me stunned. "What? No. Go put on the dress. I want to see you in it now." He sat down on the couch to wait for my wedding dress fashion show.

I looked at the door then back at Master Boyd. "Uhm, please Master. I just can't do it. Maybe give me more time.

It is all just so new to me." I looked at the floor unable to push myself to follow his order even if it resulted in trouble.

He shook his head. "I am not going to tell you again, Psycho. Put on the fucking dress. You are starting to piss me off. Fuck, I am not demanding you go to church and stand in front of the preacher. I just want to see it on you." He was now glaring angrily.

I tried to go and mind him, but it made my stomach lurch. "I am sorry. This is not something I think I can do Master. It would seem I have to request punishment at your pleasure."

I winced as I heard those words come out of my mouth. Master Boyd was not someone to fool with. However, it was the rule. If I couldn't mind an order no matter the reason, it was my right to request punishment instead. It was up to him how to handle my insolence.

It does seem strange I couldn't do something as silly as try on the wedding dress. It was not the dress that bothered me. I believed I should not do anything to feed the idea we would marry soon. With Dennis pushing, and now this weird request, I was feeling very nervous that Master Boyd was developing yet another obsession that could get out of control. It was bad enough he made me wear the blasted engagement ring. That dress was a symbol of completion versus the symbol of promise around my finger.

Right or wrong I was ready to stick to my guns refusing to cater to any further reminders of a union I was going to make damned sure never happened. I was already collared and he had my guardianship, that would have to be good enough or too bad for him. I was willing to submit on my knees to a Master but not submit on my belly to a Husdom.

Fire began to blaze in his eyes. "Fine. Come here and kneel now."

I shuddered but did as I was told. I knelt in front of Master Boyd with my gaze cast to the floor. I could tell he was beyond angry about my refusal of his order. He stared at me as if thinking. Then he leaned forward telling me to look into his eyes. I looked up locking his attention into mine.

"You won't put on the dress because you don't want to marry me. I am not stupid, Psycho. You say you love me, but you don't. If you did, you would be happy to be my wife. I tried to treat you like a real girlfriend without the collar. You didn't want me that way. You told me no. You said you followed the collar and only the collar. Well, I got the God damned thing and now you are here. I tell you to fuck me, you will do it. I ask you to put on my ring and wear my dress and you refuse. I am trying to make you my honored lady, but you won't let me. You would rather I treat you like my whore. I don't want you to be my whore. You are better than that. What I want doesn't matter though does it? I had to beat that collar out of you. You don't want me. I get it. Well, then I guess I will have to be happy with a fucking whore. So, I will treat you the way you seem to think I should." He reached into his front pocket retrieving wadded up money and change then slammed it on the coffee table behind me making me jump from the noise.

He glared at me hatefully. "So is this enough? What does a good whore charge? I guess I should have given up wanting a true lover for all my own. God won't let me have one. He took my beloved with a pure heart and now he teases me with the girl I have always loved that has no heart. What a fool I have been. I should have realized no matter what I do, I will always be the rapist and you will always be the whore. You are right. We are never going to be acceptable. Not to the town and not to each other. You are so full of hate and I can't stop wanting to earn your hate. We are monsters, both of us. We have the Devil inside and this is how our sick love will always be. So, what are you waiting for? Play you part. Get to it, whore. Suck my cock and you can keep the money and I can rape you when I can't afford you. Then we can both be happy in our own little love nest in hell." He undid his pants grabbing my head forcing my head onto him.

I heard his words that were echoing in my Looper around my head buzzing and stinging like angry bees. I began to try to do as he commanded me by providing oral sex, but he pushed me back before I could even start. I sat there confused as he sat glaring back. He seemed even more angry that I was not fighting his choice of punishment, or that is what I assumed it was. None of it was making any sense to me.

"Master I will do as you ask for punishment. I will not fight you. However, you must allow me to follow the command." I said keeping my eyes down unsure what else to do to calm him down.

He growled. "Yeah so you take the punishment and I can never bring it up again. I am learning the rules, Psycho. You have a way of teaching that I am not soon to forget. Forget it. I am not going to punish you for being honest with me. Don't put on the fucking dress. Burn it if you want. I won't say a fucking word. Throw away the engagement right too if you want. Tell you what, I will give you back the Key if you want it too. I am ready to do whatever you want. I can't keep wishing for something that is never going to happen. Watching you suffer is killing me. Not just from your disease but from my touching you. You hate me for a damned good reason. I have tried to stop acting stupid. I can't. I am already taking medications. I can't see a therapist or I will be fired. Then it is factory city. I don't have a fucking education like you do. I am almost thirty-two, Psycho. I can't just start all over with nothing but dreams. I am not as strong as you. I am stuck in this shit town till I die. I can only hope to succeed Dennis one day. All that aside, the only thing that I can't deal with is that you don't really love me, never will and that is final. I should have listened when you told me to fuck off years ago. All I ever wanted to do is take care of you and have you as my very own. I wanted to love you and I will never stop that ever. Well too fucking bad for you old Boyd. Psycho loves the collar as long as it is not you holding it," he yelled then got up and stormed from the house slamming the door behind him.

I stayed there kneeling feeling tears starting to flow. I was so confused. Master Boyd was doing his job as my Master very well. Yet, he was right. I couldn't love him, but

I didn't hate him either. I was starting to feel something for him, but it was just too early to know what it was.

He and I were too much alike. Our demons were feeding each other, growing them into mature monsters of the worst kind. I never could stand cops, and he was one of them. I looked around his room. There was no television, no magazines, no leisure items of any kind. He never drank, did drugs nor did he engage in gambling or dancing. He had a small radio but often didn't listen to music, only the news. His life was like his home was clean, plain and dark. The only passion he ever had was the root of passion, lust.

Master Boyd had lived in a prison cell all his life, never tasting his food or feeling the warmth of the sun. I understood that like no other could. It was my life too. Neither of us knew how to relax, enjoy life nor even feel comfortable in our own skin units.

All we did is what we were told to do day in and day out. Service, sleep, then more service. One day bled into the next, marching endlessly without holiday. What was wrong with his wanting to be loved? Why couldn't I learn to love him even if it was not normal? What was wrong with having someone to be at your side while you suffer and they suffer too. It could never be a vanilla love, not like Matthew. He could make me feel normal because he was able to be my equal. I was aware it was possible to love a Master the way he wanted me to, but I was not ready for that kind of step so early in his reign. His metal had not been proven long enough to even be sure he would not eventually toss his collar.

What I could promise to him was to be his full partner. One would be more powerful that the other, but both would be hunters. Both fighting side by side to survive one more day. This I was willing to offer. We could hold each other through the brutal storms of our shitty lives and at least never be alone if nothing else. The only problem is I was not sure he could be satisfied with a true D/s marriage of the Key and collar and leave God and the State out of it. My mind began to whirl with the possibility of uniting with Master Boyd in this way. Would it be enough to calm his need to feel loved?

I decided I would stay married to Timmy at all costs. I would have to in order to hold off his obsession with making our D/s relationship legal through marriage. At least till I was sure this is something that I was able to do for good. Once married to a Master it would be impossible to remove the collar without serious implications. The mixing of legal with psychological is never a good idea unless you are damned sure. Master Boyd and I had serious mental illnesses. I didn't want to chance the damage done if I got caught in a turbulent marriage that could not just end with the tossing or stealing of a key. Maybe one day, but for now I was not willing to go there.

I wiped my eyes and went to his room. I took the wedding dress and removed the plastic. It was very beautiful with an intricate rose pattern weaved into a white lace. It was very low cut to accent my ample bosom. That made me giggle. Master Boyd would intend to show off his prize even while walking it down the aisle of no return. I suppose after many years of suppression, hurtful rumors and denials of affection he had the right to brag if he wanted. Though it was all in his head like most belief systems people have.

I quickly put the dress on finding the fit perfect. Master Boyd had apparently had it made to my measurements. If so, it was expensive indeed. I was grateful to find no veil in the wrapping. I don't bother with undergarments such as hosiery or underwear. For all I knew he wouldn't want to see his dress any longer now that I had hurt his feeling for likely the hundredth time. I didn't bother to look in the mirror. Such pomp and primp was not for the likes of a silly Psycho who only wanted to please her Master.

If he wanted me to wear the fucking dress, I would stop being an asshole and mind him. If he told me to wear it to work I should have said yes Master instead of acting like I had a choice.

Master Boyd was right. He had tried to make the relationship vanilla. I had refused him. I had told him I only follow the Key and collar. I am not normal, so his attempts to date me failed. He took by force what it took to have me for himself. That is legal in the lifestyle, just as all the others before him had done. His tenacity to take what he wanted, and strength wielded to hold me, proved him a worthy Master/Dominant.

I needed to stop treating him like he was less than any of the previous Keyholders. He had the right to anything he wanted as all those who came before him. I had no right to deny him his services that night in the back of the squad car. I had no right to lie to him and sneak to Darlin the night he

242

branded me. I also had no right to deny him his wedding dress fashion show. I was fighting him. He was taking the blows despite all my protests, even taking a beating from a psychotic Gothic Barbie. That proved him the right holder of Simon's Key and a Master unlike any I had known before.

Boyd/cop/friend/rapist, none of those things defined him to me the second I submitted to his collar. From that moment forward he was the boss, my leader, my lover and I needed to stop being an asshole. I don't get to always choose the Master. I don't always like the pick. Boyd or not, he held Simon's key by right. I needed to get over myself and get back to my fucking station in life, attend my duty, or take off the collar and go die.

I walked out of the house onto the porch not seeing him anywhere. I saw both cars parked but still no Master Boyd. I finally walked over to my Intrepid parked next to his black vehicle. I saw him heads in his arms weeping at the steering wheel. He apparently had been considering leaving but thankfully had not made the trip to wherever he was headed. I knocked on his window. He looked up appearing irritated though his face was drenched in grief.

My appearance in his fancy wedding dress reflected at me through the glass. It was very lovely. Master Boyd's tears stopped as he looked at me appearing in awe. I smiled then turned around so he could see the back. "It fits, but do you think it makes my butt look big?" I giggled at my silly joke since you couldn't see my backside because of all the layering of stiff silk in the back.

My Master shook his head while opening his door. "No, it looks so beautiful, you look so beautiful. Just like I always imagined," his voice trailed off as I took his hand while doing a silly little dance that shook the layers and spread the bottom wide from my motion.

"You can kiss the bride, Master," I snickered while still spinning and shuffling.

Master Boyd's eyes were full of adoration. "Do you like the dress I picked for you, Psycho?"

I smiled while he pulled me in for a hug. "I do, Master. I do. Please forgive me. I understand now. I have figured out, I do love you like you love me. We are the same, you and me. I cannot marry you before your God, not yet. But if you are patient with me, it will happen one day. Until then, can you be happy with just a collared submissive fiancé all your very own?"

He closed his eyes appearing very grateful as he hugged me tightly. He knew this time; I had finally understood his attempts to woo me were sincere. Even if dysfunctional, violent and misguided in the beginning, I could love him as my Dominant and my lover. I was just not ready for romantic feelings, but maybe one day it could grow. Stranger things had happened.

"I am happy to have your love anyway I can have it. It is all I ever wanted. I will do my best to not hurt you anymore. I will take more medication, fight my anger, and take care of you my love." He sniffed while kissing my ear.

I chuckled. "Oh now Master, let's be honest here. You are super angry inside. You are going to blow up from time to time. You like violent sex and can't stop yourself. I am schizophrenic. I hit people, talk to people you can't see, throw tantrums and run over mailboxes. It is okay. I love you no matter what monster is inside you because you love me despite my own. I will help you; you will help me. We are a special kind of couple."

Master Boyd sighed then frowned. "Yeah, a fucked up one. Psycho, how can you love me if I keep hurting you like I do? I just know you are going to leave me. You are right, I can't seem to stop. If I lose you, I just can't lose you."

I smiled. "I am the only kind of girl that can love you despite your demons. I wear your collar Master. I will deal and you will pay me back. You are a great Dominant. The best one I have ever known and the fairest. You still have a lot to learn, but you are getting there fast. I would have dropped Sheryl's collar but the poor woman is dying. I would beg your mercy to allow her to finish her reign, but it is your choice Master. I will never disobey you openly again. You are right. You have earned my respect and deserve all the spoils that come with the title. Can you ever forgive me for being such a shit to you?"

Master Boyd's eyes went wide. "What? Are you serious? Baby, I am the one who should be on my knees begging forgiveness. I hurt you and liked it. Worst of all, I will most likely do it again. You should be running for your life not asking me to forgive you for doing what? Being unfortunate enough to be caught in my fucked-up fantasy?" He shook his head not believing what I had said.

I nodded. "Yeah, you will hurt me again and like it but I will hurt you just as much Master. How many times have I hit you with chairs, kicked you, spit on you, smacked you and worse over the years? I mean you have been around my psychotic shit for over a decade and you foolishly decided you love me? My love, you are truly something else. Crazy, but my kind of crazy. About Sheryl? Can I have your permission to finish her reign?" I looked at him noting his pure love reflected in them.

"Yeah baby, finish it if you want. Then you come home to me for good. That is the deal. Simon or no Simon, I want to look after you the way only someone who loves you can. If you will agree to that, I will not interfere with her collar." Master Boyd smiled kindly.

I nodded. "Deal Master. Now if you don't mind, the dress is itchy and I am very tired. Can we go to bed now?" I scratched at my shoulder feeling the lace poking into my skin unit.

Master Boyd laughed. "To bed my wife." He picked me up like the bride I appeared to be carrying me once again across his threshold to his bed.

He gently laid me down engaging me in a passion filled kiss as I began to wantonly remove his clothing. Master Boyd began to moan with ecstasy while I backed up allowing him to crawl between my legs and lift his wedding dress. I gasped as my Dominant entered my willing unit. My Master took to orgasming with a lover's coupling of intense voracity.

Our emotional responses to that lovemaking session were no doubt reserved for those who were bonding on a higher level. That night he proved the novice, shy, clumsy cop named Boyd had matured into a powerful seasoned Master with all the skills of an expert in the art of carnal congress.

We took it slow and fast, violent and calm, in almost every position possible for mating plus a few that I would never try again. I called out to the anyone within miles the name of the one who brought me to several climaxes. Master Boyd was brought to his own monstrous orgasm only after making sure I was begging for release of his incredible prowess. No longer my rapist he had become my heart.

Master Boyd's blue eyes were cloudy with satisfaction as he smiled laying in my arms. "Thank you for living out the fantasy I have dreamed of since I was fifteen years old. I always wanted to have my wedding night with a beautiful woman I could call my very own."

I gasped with horror at my misunderstanding of why he wanted to see me in the dress. "Oh Master, that is what this was all about. You wanted to see me in the dress to, oh my love, I am so sorry I was such a bitch. You just wanted to see what it was like," I trailed off realizing once again I can't know everything (or anything it seemed).

My Master stroked my face. "Forget the argument. I said and done things I shouldn't have said or done too. I will likely keep fucking up, and so will you. We will get better at this. It is new for both of us no doubt. The important thing is to talk to each other. You said it, remember? No secrets, no lies. We are going to fuck up. I will forgive you if you will forgive me, service for service, right?"

I nodded. "Yes, you are right Master. I think though this dress needs to go to the cleaners." I looked down at the now disheveled dress half torn from my unit during our lustful triste.

Master Boyd looked at me feigning surprise and indignation. "What? Hell no. It looks perfect just like that. Let me call Preacher Wilkinson. I bet he would love to have our wedding this very night down at the Freewill Baptist Church. If not well shit, you can just kick the fucking door in and make him. When you are done, run out the back way to the woods and I can rape you to consummate our unholy vows." He smiled at his teasing both of our nasty little histories.

I laughed wildly. "Damn kick in one fucking church door and no one ever forgives you."

Master Boyd jumped up pretending to be ready to attack me. "You are telling me about the town that is never forgiving. Why little red riding hood, what big boobs you have. I am Boyd, the big bad wolf, come to steal your daughters and eat them." He growled playfully biting my bosom.

I let out a fake scream giggling from the attacks of my Alpha wolf mate, just as my pager began to freak out loudly.

I gulped in fear ready to start explaining my on call situation when Master Boyd's phone started ringing off the hook. He went to take the call. It took only moments to discover we had been hailed to the same police station. Trouble had come to Wheatly. It was so big it required the immediate attention of both the rapist cop and the schizophrenic investigator.

Master Boyd asked me to ride with him to the scene of the crime and I agreed. We quickly hurried to dress for our public appearance as social warriors on a night that few would ever forget. When the sun rose, a man who had it coming would be on his way to die and there would no longer be any doubt that Master Boyd and I were a mating pair. The new D/s couple were about to partner up right in front of the whole fucking town.

We are about to encounter a real beast unlike any you would ever want to meet on a dark street or crowded sidewalk.

Chapter 64: I Hear the Train a Coming
The D/s Power Couple
Master Boyd and Interim Master Sheryl

The ride to hell is really revving up now. In those dusky autumn days of 1998, we had no idea our path was leading right to the mouth of a place of no return. We apparently didn't think we had collected enough personal nightmares in our already tragic life span. So, we decided stupidly to gather some from those unfortunate souls around us. You know what they say, 'double the trouble, double the psychotic fun.'

The newly minted D/s couple are about to have their animal instincts tested. They are both hunters of evil most foul. One protects the pack and one protects the young. The lupin order will be maintained through constant battling for supremacy which is all for show. The Alpha will serve his submissive mate. She will return his loving favor with a gift of pure understanding. The two will bond tighter than ever in a twisted dance calling to them from the wild.

Dennis and Linda are full of the green-eyed monster of jealousy. One fears the growing pup and one dreams of making a trophy of the exotic. Both will challenge the mating pair trying to split them apart. Singularly, the two are manageable but together they are an unstoppable force. This hunt is canned. Master Boyd and Psycho will find an escape through the second silver ring.

So off we go for another dip in the sewer called our memory. Are you all ready to go? Awesome! Our time is short since we are already late to our next emergency call. Set your pagers to vibrate, grab your pens and don't forget to oil those handcuffs. You will need them.

"Now that Sheryl has moved away, where are you going to live? Darlin is no longer acceptable. No fiancé of mine is living in a filthy outhouse God damn it. You need to be with your children anyway. This separation from their momma has gone on long enough. So here are your choices: You and the kids move in with me for good, or you and the kids move in somewhere close to me. No arguments. No more homeless schizophrenic bullshit. I will help you get into a suitable home anywhere you need it, but the cemetery is off limits. That is a directive."
--**Master Boyd's directive to Psycho regarding her chronic homelessness, late September 1998.**

I recognized the address Master Boyd was speeding us to from my past. The home was located right next door to the yellow house I had once called my own. I felt queasy having to be so close to that horrible place were my dreams of a real family had been shattered. I vowed I would never return when I had left that place after finding Matthew's suicide letter to me. So much had changed in such a short time since that dark November day in 1996.

I looked over at my new lover feeling again the sensation of disbelief. How had everything gone so off the tracks so fast? I was supposed to be working in a laboratory in Dallas, Texas, as a forensic pathologist. My keyholder should have been Mistress Ginger. The lover I wanted was my brother collar Matthew.

Yet, it had all gone terribly wrong. I was on my way to a crime scene with my old cop buddy Boyd, while I myself was an investigator. Boyd was not my friend anymore. He was my Master and full D/s partner. He was also my fiancé and lover. For more than a year he had been the one person on earth I hated the most. He had been my rapist, my stalker, and had been crueler to me than I cared to recall. He forced me to submit and he stole Simon's key. Now, I trusted him with my life and heart. How the holy fuck could this even be happening?

The air around me seemed to be thin. My lungs could barely find the oxygen in it. My hopes and dreams were not even close to what I had worked so hard to obtain. I had missed the mark more completely than a blindman throwing darts. I watched the darkness rushing past the windows of Master Boyd's black car. I briefly considered jumping out to my death. If this was to be my life, I was not sure I was not ready to forfeit before shit got any worse. I had always hated the cops. Somehow, I had not only become one, but I was also engaged to one.

My mind wander to the vision of a police officer legal union. I wondered if we would say our nuptials before the prison priest in the white cell. Perhaps I would toss my bouquet of mace and handcuffs to the prisoners to be. I could see me walking around the jail to make sure there was enough wedding donuts to go around. Master Boyd and I could even get mugshot photos of the grand day to hang on the wall in pride. Bet that strip search before walking the aisle would be a real hoot. At least if I gave that job to Linda,

I could be sure I was wet and ready for my rapist hubby on our honeymoon night for a change. What a fucking joke.

Master Boyd's voice in the darkness called me from my imaginative imagery of our horrid wedding night. "Did they tell you anything about the situation? Cathy just said Dennis wanted me there. As usual she didn't seem to think I needed to know why," he grumbled.

I nodded. "Yeah. It is Cindy Slater. I was told there has been a gang rape and I am to take her into custody immediately on a FINS emergency case. Her mother has been unable to get her to comply with the caseworkers." I sighed.

Cindy Slater was the town slut. She was only sixteen years old and already had an impressive arrest record for prostitution and drug related charges. Her mother was doing all she could to get the child off the streets and off her path of self-destructive behaviors. It was not that Cindy was really a bad egg, nor was her mother uncaring. This poor child had been stranger raped at the age of ten when abducted from a softball game. She had taken a break to use the little girl's room when a nasty predator had snatched her away. Cindy was one of the lucky ones in that someone heard her cries while the monster took his fill of her in the woods. He had been so wanton he could not even wait to get the pretty redhead off to a more secluded spot to steal her childhood.

The man was capture and doing life. Cindy was defiled but survived to find herself unable to deal with the indignity. Over the years she had used the nasty drugs, alcohol, crank, then methamphetamine to numb the pain she felt inside from her trauma.

Her mother had done all she could from counselors to the finest in drug rehab centers at the time. Cindy would always return to her life of drugs and petty crime. She would sell her unit to both feed her habit and to further punish herself for something she did not deserve to happen to her.

In fact, I had just arrested a town child molester called Fisher that previous Monday. Cindy had been his victim this time. Cindy had gone to Fisher willingly to sell herself, but the nasty baby rapist had refused to pay up once the deed was done. I had arrested Fisher since Cindy was underage and warned the FINS caseworker that she would need to be put into rehab once again.

As usual, I was ignored. Thanks to that, Cindy was now the victim of a cruel gang rape. Her twenty-one-year-old boyfriend Javier, an illegal alien, had tied down the drugged-up child and sold her to his friends for sport. The neighbors had heard the girl screaming and called the police. I was told by the reporting officer that Cindy was inconsolable, terrified, and beaten half to death beyond the horrors of two days of gang raping. I was ordered to take her statement, assume custody for the State and make sure a rape kit was done. Another fun Friday night for old Psycho, and sadly for Cindy it appeared.

Master Boyd winced. "Gang rape? Oh shit. Javier? That sonofabitch. How many do you know? I am sure there must have been quite a few if they are calling me in off shift."

I sighed. "I am told they have four or five in custody. They are talking to them and to Cindy trying to see if there are more. Javier is not among them. They have an APB out on the bastard."

Master Boyd nodded. "We'll get that shithead. However, they will just send him back to Mexico and he will be back next week just like last time. Dennis and I have arrested that little asshole about three times already. They haul him to State, he gets deported then is back on the next bus to do it again. It never ends with this creep."

I looked at him shocked. "He has raped other girls? Seriously?"

He shook his head. "Nah this is his first rape. He has been robbing the hell out of the local stores. He is wanted for murdering his pregnant girlfriend down in Mexico and is married in that country too, can you believe it? Dennis thought for sure they would throw the piece of shit in the Mexican jail to rot where he belongs. Never happened. He just keeps coming back. They will let him go this time too. Watch and see." He snorted angrily.

I rolled my eyes. "Leave it to Cindy to pick a winner. Guess she hoped he would kill her too. Poor thing. This is going to leave a bit of a mark on her already darkened soul."

My Master looked surprised. "You think she was dating Javier hoping he would kill her? Really?"

I nodded. "Yeah, Cindy is looking to be killed but doesn't have the guts to do it to herself. She doesn't know it but that is why she keeps on hurting herself like this. No one is really listening to her. They just see a whore or a druggie. She is a little girl in pain. She wants out but doesn't know how other than to put herself in danger. It is really very sad."

Master Boyd reached out and rubbed my cheek. "You are too big hearted for this job, Psycho. Cindy would cut out your heart and sell it for drugs if you let her. That kid is lost and has been lost for years. You should stop trying to save dead cats."

I glared at him through the darkness. "Are you lost Master? Am I? You know we are Cindy. Should we be left without care too?"

My statement startled my Master. "Uhm, I guess no, but we are different. No one helped us. We didn't take to drugs or prostitution."

I chuckled bitterly as I flipped my collar,. "Oh is that so? What is this around my neck? I believe it is the world's biggest cock ring, at least now it is. And you Master, no you don't drink or do drugs. You don't whore like me or Cindy, but you are an addict too. Make no mistake, sex is your drug Master."

Master Boyd paused appearing upset. "Yeah, I never thought of it that way. I suppose you are right. We are more fucked up than anyone else I know, maybe more than Cindy."

I nodded. "Damned right we are, Master. Cindy still has time. You and I are fucked for good. Too old and incurable. So, if I can save just a few of them, isn't it worth it?"

My Master smiled. "Yeah, you are right Psycho. That is what I love about you the most. You are always ready for a fight and braver than anyone I have ever met."

I chuckled again. "No, I am not Master. I am more terrified than you can imagine. I just don't have a choice. I fight because if I give up I die. I suppose unlike Cindy I am not ready to go yet."

Master Boyd looked at me adoringly. "That is exactly what I want to hear. You want to live. That means you have decided to stay with me for good. I am one happy man."

I stifled my look of irritation at his statement. I was only starting to not hate him so much. We were a long way from my wanting to spend my life with him. The way I saw it, he had been the number one reason for several months that I had considered taking the dirt nap. However, if his believing that kept down that nasty anger demon inside, I would not be the one to correct his errored thinking.

His big smile of contentment began to twist into horror. I could clearly see his change of mood in the flurry of red and blue lights that lit up the dark like a giant Christmas tree. Squad cars, an ambulance and even a fire truck were surrounding the white house that neighbored my former residence. Master Boyd parked the car in the driveway of the yellow house unable to get any closer thanks to the swarming emergency services vehicles.

We both got out in a rush heading to the front door to assess the scene and be of aid. Master Boyd was called to attend Dennis who had four Hispanic males on their knees with hands in cuffs. Several other sheriff deputies were standing about discussing what they had witnessed. Dennis was taking notes with the aid of an interpreter as he questioned the detained offenders. My Master split off mumbling 'good luck' as I walked inside to find my ward Cindy.

I walked through the living room that was in a shamble. I could hear the ER staff struggling with a cussing and crying Cindy behind a door off from the small, cluttered kitchen. Trenton one of the local cops was guarding the door I assumed was the bedroom where Cindy had been held hostage. I walked toward it only to be stopped by the big cop.

"Hey, Psycho, what the fuck are you doing here? This is a crime scene. Who let you in," he growled.

I glared. "I am with DCFS investigations State Police attachment asshole. Move aside. That is my victim in there. I have been ordered to assume custody. Get out of the way." I showed him my badge.

Trenton looked at the badge narrowing his eyes. "Ah, very funny Psycho. Did you make that yourself while at the State Mental Hospital? Hell, they are sure getting awful sophisticated. I thought they only allowed you nuts to make ashtrays and shit." He chuckled at what he thought was a clever joke.

I snorted. "Very cute, Trenton. Move your ass. I am not kidding here. I must get in there and calm Cindy down. Don't you hear her? She is scared to death."

I was now very angry and about to blow as I heard Cindy crying out in terror. This fucker was about to get plowed. That was my kid in there and he was getting in my way.

Trenton looked at the door. "Well, I guess she shouldn't have been opening those legs for that Mexican trash. That is what you get when you fool with the big dogs."

I had enough of Trenton I felt my arm start to rear up for the backhand of a lifetime when arms went around my waist pulling me back. I turned startled ready to beat the hell out of someone when I saw the devil blue eyes of Master Boyd. Immediately, my inner sense of protocol kicked in submitting my anger demon to its knees.

"Trenton get out of the way. Psycho is with DCFS State Police. You move aside or I will kick your ass. She has a job to do just like you and just like me. Move," said Master Boyd sternly.

Trenton snorted. "Boyd, we should have known your slimy badge would be around this kind of case. Hey, tell me, does it bring back fond memories of youth when you work a case like this?" I felt Master Boyd tense up at that nasty accusation.

"Go on inside Psycho and take care of Cindy," Master Boyd said ignoring Trenton's rude remarks.

I nodded realizing my Master was right. Trenton didn't matter. Cindy was my client and she definitely needed me based on her screams of terror at the all-male ER crew. I pushed past the asshole Trenton rushing into the room.

Cindy was on a filthy mattress with no sheets. The frame was metal and apparently, she had been tethered by her wrists to it. The nylons were still around her wrists. She was backed into a corner bleeding, bruised, naked and screaming out of her mind in terror. The ambulance staff was backed against the other side of the room trying to convince her they were there to help, not hurt, her. She was insane with terror having three men coming at her with bags and needles. I could understand that very well.

The biggest of the crew looked at me. I showed him my badge saying nothing. I motioned for them to stay put as I walked toward the terrified teen.

"Cindy, look at me. It is Psycho. Remember me? We met last week. I was with your mom. We spoke." I looked at the floor not directly at the child.

Cindy wailed. "My momma. Someone get my momma, please. Help me." She grabbed her knees pulling them toward her battered unit.

I walked a bit closer. "Cindy, I have called your mother. She is coming. Let me help you. You are hurt. Will you let me help you get dressed?"

Cindy looked at me in desperation. "Those men, they are here to hurt me. Help me please, Psycho. Don't let them near me. Help, please, I want my momma."

I nodded. "She is coming little one. I won't let those men hurt you. Come here and let me help. Come here to me. I will keep them away till your momma gets here. Cindy, listen to me, you have to come here for me to protect you." I held out my hand taking small steps toward her panicked little unit.

She suddenly ran across the mattress on all fours grabbing my arm and pulling me tight into a hug holding on for dear life. Cindy was shaking and weeping hard. I wrapped my arms around her waist and sat on the mattress to manage her weight while rocking her and rubbing her back.

"Hush, it is okay now darling. You are safe now. The men are all gone. No one is gonna hurt you anymore. I got you. Calm, breath, it is over. Come on Cindy, breath with me slowly. There you go. I got you." She quivered and calmed down sucking her thumb like a small child.

She was traumatized beyond imagination. I began humming to her while the emergency staff stood there looking at each other confused. I glared at them daring them to come any closer. Cindy needed a moment to breath. They would have to wait. There was no sign of deadly injury to her unit, but her psyche was near melted down. I felt her slowly begin to relax as her tears began to dry. She sniffed listening from wherever our minds go when bad things happen to us. I let her have as much time as she needed. My legs were numb from her weight and my own fatigue threatened to send me straight to hell, but somehow I found the endurance to keep this child from slipping off into a catatonic horror.

Finally, I felt her heartbeat slow. She was mentally strong enough for the medical help at last.

"Cindy, I want you to stay here with me while this man gives you something to relax. It will help you sleep. Will you let him come do that for you," I said still holding her tight.

She stiffened up in fear. "No, Psycho, no. Don't let those men come. You promised me."

I nodded. "I did, and I will keep my promise. If you choose to let the one man give you a shot, you can sleep and when you wake up your momma will be here. I won't leave you. I will watch for trouble while you sleep. You are ready for sleep. yes?" I realized Cindy had regressed to a very small child in her head. This was not a good sign.

She pulled back to look at my face trying to read my eyes. "You will watch out for the bad men if I sleep a little while? You promise me?"

I nodded smiling at her. "Yes Cindy, I will guard you with my life. You need sleep little one. Let this one give you medicine to sleep okay? Just the one man. I will stay here and watch him too. He won't get us both."

She nodded. "Okay, just this one man, only if you stay."

I looked at the ambulance worker nodded that he could bring the heavy sedative now to calm the child. He came forward slowly and gave Cindy the shot. She panicked a bit when he touched her arm. I told her to look at me, not to look at the man. She minded. Within only a few moments her unit went limp as deep sleep overtook the injured child. I laid her down gently and sat next to her while the ER crew prepped her for transfer to the hospital. True to my word, I did not leave her the entire time only moving out of the way so the crew could do their job.

Cindy's mother Eva arrived just as she was ready to be taken from the room. I was notified by Dennis that Eva wanted to ride to the ER with her little girl. I nodded that it was for the best despite my having legal custody of her at that moment. I assumed I could catch another ride from one of the officers, maybe even my Master to attend the girl once she was in a room stabilized.

A rape kit had been ordered. Luckily, Cindy would be out cold and never have to endure the added torture of that nasty procedure. Never a fun thing to do to a lady after she has already been violated enough. Sadly, it was necessary to make sure that those monsters didn't walk away free.

I walked out to find Master Boyd still hanging around the door waiting on me. I looked at him thinking a simple rape kit in his case would have saved him years of false imprisonment and shame for a crime he never committed. He saw me and came over quickly to make sure I was alright.

"Yes, Cindy will be okay. I will send her out to the Girls Colony when she has recovered. They have a great program there for rape survivors. I have several young ladies who have gone in wrecked and come out shiny once more. I hope it will help this child too, but one never knows. I have a feeling this may be her wake up call. Did they catch Javier?" I looked at Master Boyd who was staring at Trenton.

He shook his head. "No. They are checking the neighborhood. His friends say he heard the police and ran from the room. None of them are talking much. The nasty bags of shit."

Trenton walked up smiling wickedly. "Now what are you doing, Boyd? Hell, even Psycho isn't crazy enough to date the likes of you. Bug off. Psycho come with me and I will buy you a coffee and we can discuss you and me, and whatever else pops up." He started to laugh at his crude statement.

He apparently had not heard the news. Oh well, too bad for him. He was about to find out.

Master Boyd's eyes lit up with fire. "Trenton, you will apologize to my fiancé right fucking now for your foul mouth. Then, we can take this discussion outside where no one can watch me wail the piss out of you."

Trenton's eyes went wide. "Fiancé? Bullshit. Boyd you couldn't handle a spitfire like Psycho. You stick to little girls you can sneak up on. Leave the wild woman to us real men." He chuckled as I saw my Master's veins pop out on his forehead and his jaw grind. Uh oh.

264

I grabbed Master Boyd's arm quickly. "Baby leave this bag of wind alone. Save your strength for me. I am ready to go home and finish what we started. It is all I can think about. Please? I am so ready to go." I pulled myself between the two men grabbing my Master's head with feigned desire forcing him to look in my face instead of locking eyes with Trenton.

You could have heard a cricket drop a grain of sand it got so quiet in that room. Every damned officer was privy to my begging Master Boyd to take me home to his bed. My Master also was stunned at my brashness in public as I continued to rub my arms across his chest keeping his attention away from the abrasive Trenton.

Trenton spit in the floor in full shock. "What the Sam Hill. Nah, no fucking way. Psycho, do you know who that is? Do you know what he did? I think you have finally blown your last gasket. Girl, you need stronger medication if you are asking Boyd Simmons to take you home for loving. He can't do shit for a woman like you. Besides, he doesn't even like a willing girl."

Master Boyd was pushed beyond his limits of handling the insult to his submissive and to his own false reputation. "That is enough, asshole. You will apologize to my girl and then meet me outside. Or are you too pussy," Master Boyd yelled angrily.

Trenton came forward as Master Boyd pulled me behind him. He pushed my Master in the shoulder growling.

"Why go outside child rapist. Let's dance right here. Ain't nobody looking." Trenton smiled.

That was all it took. Master Boyd took off plowing into Trenton knocking him into the wall hard. The force shook the floor under my feet as the two big men collided. Suddenly the closet door flew open and Javier came running out right at me. He knocked me to my ass as he ran into the now empty bedroom. I watched him jump from the window while yelling for someone to stop the sonofabitch.

Master Boyd and Trenton both ran towards the window jumping out after the offender. Luckily, Dennis saw the creep fall to the ground and was already giving chase. I ran to the window with two other officers watching as Dennis and Javier jumped the chain link fence of my old yellow house.

Javier was no match for the near Olympic running ability of the officer. Dennis knocked him to the ground before the man could get across that back yard to the other side. I smiled with glee truly able to appreciate the stunning prowess of old Dennis from a witness view for a damned change. I made a mental note to never try to outrun that old bull ever again. The man was simply fucking incredible. For a little guy, Dennis sure could scoot.

Javier was cuffed and stuffed with the other scum to be hauled away to the jail. Each would be transported to the capitol for deportation within the week. Master Boyd and Trenton eyed each other hatefully but their brawl was done for the moment thanks to that little distraction. I breathed a sigh of relief. I realized that had Javier not jumped out, not only would Cindy's offender be allowed to run free, but my Master would be in the unemployment line.

It also was not beyond me that my Master had stood up for me. I was already thinking over how I could repay this very special gift he had granted. Master Boyd was not known for standing up to anyone. For him to do this just to defend my reputation had opened my eyes to his true dedication to our D/s promises to protect and defend each other. He had just risked his job over a few nasty comments. That was something I could not just ignore.

Trenton and the other officers shot my Master evil looks as Boyd and Dennis secured the prisoners. Though they all tried to puff up looking tough I could sense a bit of fear in the air. The quiet, shy, butt of all jokes Boyd was not as mousey as they had assumed. His sudden defense of me and himself scared the shit out of them. They knew he had plenty to be angry at them for. If he were indeed about to start paying them back, wow, they were going to be in for a lot of ass kicking.

I watched as Trenton glance at the wall next to the closet. I had noticed my Master had slammed him hard enough to make a hole in the sheetrock. Trenton had shaken his head then stole a look in my Master's direction with what appeared to be confusion. I understood what Trenton was thinking. He was trying to figure out how the skinny law dog had just thrown his huge bulky unit like a rag doll.

They all assumed Master Boyd was just a rail thin weak fellow. A clumsy, stuttering, nerdy fraidy cat they could pick on as the runt of the litter. They were dead wrong. I had also been fooled myself. However, I was now intimately familiar with what Master Boyd had always hidden from all observers.

Trenton was the biggest bully of all the police officers because he was so damned big. That was just because he was a pot-bellied jelly donut. He had been a football star in the local high school in his teens. When he became a cop, easy living in a small town, with a low arrest rate led to his going to seed quickly. Most of the fear and respect he got from his fellow officers was residual from his days as a big man on the sports team.

Now it had just become stunningly obvious Trenton would have had his ass kicked to hell had my Master continued to release his beast on the idiot. Trenton like all the other good old boy cops had no idea what kind of a rough customer Master Boyd could be when he set his mind to it. No one had ever been able to stir up Master Boyd's anger before. No one knew he was strong as a bull. On the surface my Master just seemed like a tall, skinny fellow without any real tone. That couldn't be further from the truth. He was nothing but muscles.

My Master's no fat, tough physic came from years of taking out his anger on an old shed and punching bag behind his house. In order to keep from blowing up and burning down the whole town, like he probably should have, he would spend hours a day beating the hell out of those items.

He had shown me the shed to prove he was trying to gain control of his problem long before it had gotten out of hand with me. Well, what was left of it after years of his beating the holy terror out of the walls and floor. Yikes!

His daily rigorous workouts with a plain diet, not a lot of sugar, had created the illusion of a thin fellow. That was in part thanks to Master Boyd's height. The other factor in this oversight were his uniforms were always a bit too large. It was easy for him to get away with no one knowing he was built like a Spartan under his clothes. Trenton had just found out of what I sadly was already aware. Master Boyd was not someone you wanted to piss off.

Master Boyd and I loaded up into his car so he could drop me off at the hospital. He had to hurry and meet Dennis at the jail house to book and interrogate the prisoners plus file the reports. We sat in silence for the first few moments. Finally, he cleared his throat appearing unsure of what to say.

"Uhm, I am sorry about that bullshit with Trenton back there. I shouldn't let him get to me like that. He's always been an asshole and always will be one," my Master said flatly.

I nodded my head. "Yeah he is, Master. For what it is worth, thank you for standing up for me and yourself. You deserve to be respected just as much as those pricks."

He chuckled. "Well at least we found Javier huh? I will try harder to stop getting so angry. That was a close call there. Had I hit him, well how would I ever support you and the kids? Fine husband I would make without a job."

I winced at his bringing up marriage yet again. "Ah, no worries Master. I have heard the State fair prize money for pig tossing is pretty decent. You are no doubt a champion just waiting to happen. I have never seen anyone toss a tub of swine farther or with such panache as you did tonight. We could live off your first-place earnings if we pinched our pennies." I laughed at my teasing him.

Master Boyd smiled. "It did feel good to throw that sonofabitch around a bit. I have wanted to do it for years. Okay baby, I will be back for you in a couple of hours. Stay out of trouble please? I don't want to throw out my back tossing anymore of the town folk tonight." He leaned over to kiss me as he pulled over in front of the ER doors.

I kissed him deeply. "Are you sure you wouldn't want to come in. Perhaps we can get a private room for a few moments?"

He moaned out in frustration. "Stop that. You know better. I can't keep my cool when you come on to me. You are right. I think I am addicted to sex. At least sex with you."

I nodded. "Oh that is true. I will stop Master. You do what you must and I will go hold up the walls till you get back."

My Master looked at me suddenly appearing concerned. "Hey, Psycho, when was the last time you slept? You look very tired baby. Why did they call you in tonight instead of Frankie? She is the caseworker for Wheatly not you."

I shook my head getting out quickly. "Uhm, I am on call this weekend Master. We can discuss this later perhaps?"

His eyes glared at me. "You're God damned right we are going to. This is pure bullshit. Sheryl is already working you to death. This is unacceptable. You need rest. Fuck!"

I looked down quickly. "As you wish Master, but now I have to go."

I moved my legs like the Russian Army was two paces behind me firing cannons. There was no way I was getting into an argument with my Master. Especially in the parking lot of the hospital that tended to lock my ass up on the third floor every few months.

I arrived to find Eva sitting with Cindy holding her hand. Cindy was out cold filled with sedatives that would for a bit bring her a peaceful and much needed rest. Eva was crying silently looking at the daughter she had such high hopes and dreams for. I motioned for Eva to come join me in the hallway in case Cindy was conscious at all. I never assumed that one cannot hear what is said or recall it just because they appear asleep. I often appeared unresponsive but was not.

Eva came out looking worn. "You are taking her into custody I hear. I reported her missing two days ago Missus Voss I swear it." she sniffed.

I nodded. "Missus Slater, this is not a case against you to take personally. We are trying to help you help Cindy. Her problems are simply too big for even the most loving mother to handle. I do hope you understand this is not intended to be an insult to your parenting skills. No child comes with a manual. Some need special help."

Eva looked at me seeming grateful. "I am just so tired of being afraid for her. Every call I expect to hear, I can't even say it, I would just die. If only I had not left her alone those years ago then she would be okay. I let that monster get to my baby. She ain't been right since." She began to weep again.

I wrapped my arms around the grieving mother. "Don't you dare take the credit for this Missus Slater. You did nothing wrong and neither did Cindy. You both need to stop letting that monster and the one from tonight continue to keep you prisoners to their crimes. I am taking her to a place I hope I can wake her up, but you know what? You need help to handle this too. I will have the FINS people set you up with your own counselor Missus Slater. You need someone to talk to. Cindy is not the only one hurting here. Say you will go? She needs your strength, all of it. Believe me you need someone to lean on when the going gets tough." I looked at Missus Slater to see if she could hear my words.

She looked up appearing grateful. "Yes, I will go if you can recommend someone. I just want my Cindy happy and healthy again. I don't care what it takes. I would walk on hot coals for my baby girl."

I smiled at her. "You know Missus Slater you may be the most beautiful creature I have ever seen in my life. Cindy is very lucky to have you. I hope and pray she will see what a treasure she truly has before it is too late. Here let me get you that number. I will take her to the crisis center in a few days when she is feeling better. You can visit her as often as you like but do make sure you remember to take time for yourself too. A tired mom is of no use to a sick child."

Missus Slater thanked me while I wrote down the number of a therapist in town that worked with victims of crimes. The woman was a true empath and had worked wonders by reputation. I watched Missus Slater go back into Cindy's room. She took the girls hand sitting there praying, weeping, hoping, loving her child. I admit, I was in awe and maybe just a tad jealous too. I could have watched that angel on Earth for hours, but I had an appointment. I needed to repay another kindness I had encountered that horrid night before I passed dead away from crushing fatigue.

I had seen Linda standing at the admissions desk when I had approached Missus Slater. She was likely there to try to talk with Cindy for a statement about the rapes. I knew that Cindy was in no condition to answer any questions for the night. I walked out to greet a very perturbed officer who understood the child was sedated but wanted to get her report in as soon as possible.

"Well, hello Goddess," I said happily startling Linda who had just started for the doors out.

She turned smiling. "Ah Psycho. You are here. Wait, why are you here? Are you here inpatient? Do they just let the psych patients walk around free now or what?" She narrowed her eyes at me.

I rolled my eyes. "Damn it, why does everyone have to keep bringing up that shit tonight? No Goddess I am here for Cindy Slater. I took her into custody."

Linda's eyes went wide. "This late? Where is Frankie? You've seen Cindy? How is she? Did she say anything?" Linda questioned me like machine gun fire.

I snorted. "She has been gang raped for two days, Linda. They have her flying with the swans in neverland where the poor thing should be. As it is, this is gonna be one nightmare she will have a tough time working through. You can give up talking to her tonight and likely tomorrow. Her mind has snapped. I had to sit with a sixteen-year-old baby. She is regressed pretty badly. Hopefully, she will get better in a day or two, but I would watch how they interrogate her. She could melt down pretty easy, okay?" I looked at her glancing at her notebook sternly.

Linda nodded. "Ah okay, gotcha. I just assumed with it being Cindy that you know the way she lives and all, she would be tougher you know."

I growled, "How dare you Linda Hendericks. That was uncalled for. Cindy was raped. Rape is always rape even if it be a prostitute. Working girls have pride and feelings too. She is just a fucking little girt to boot. Shame on you!"

274

Linda looked down realizing her error. "You are right Psycho. Shit, I guess this job makes a person forget basic human feelings sometimes. I don't want to become a hard ass, that is for sure. Thanks for reminding me that Cindy deserves respect no matter what she does or doesn't do in her life choices." She appeared truly apologetic.

I grimaced. "Yeah. You are okay. Just watch out that you don't fall for that bullshit that a victim deserves it. Look can you give me a ride to the station if you are headed that way?"

Linda frowned. "Yeah I am and yes I can. Why do you need to go to the station?"

I chuckled. "I want a to schedule a strip search, baby. What the fuck do you care Linda. Let's go I am beat and I really hate this fucking place. I have spent enough time here as it is."

She laughed and motioned me to follow behind her to her car. We began headed to the station when suddenly it struck her my possible reason to be there.

"Hey, Mother am I taking you to see Boyd by chance," she said appearing curious.

I shifted feeling a bit nervous about the question. "Uhm, yeah. He is my ride home."

She snorted. "Shit, Mother, I can take you home. You still staying at Maiden Mary's place?"

I shook my head "No, I live in Cumberland. I am just here for the weekends."

Linda looked startled. "Oh okay, but I still take you to Mary's right?"

I glared at her irritated at her nosiness. "No Linda. I am staying the weekend with Boyd if you must know. I am not headed to Mary's."

Her mouth flew open. "Seriously? You are living with him. Engaged, now living with Boyd. What the fuck Mother. Boyd? Why Boyd?"

I shrugged. "Why not Boyd?"

Linda growled. "Where the hell do I start. Do you have a pad of paper and a pen? Mother, he is not, you and him, yuck. Mother it is Boyd. You deserve better. What the holy hell do you see in him? Do you have any idea how fucking creepy he is? Are you taking your meds?"

Something inside me began to burn as she sat there making foul remarks about my Master. Never in my entire life had I ever felt such a need to defend the holder of Simon's Key from verbal attack of an outsider. Usually the Master had it coming. Maybe Master Boyd did, but only from me. He had never hurt anyone else in his life. Everyone acted like he was eating children left and right and had a few in barrels in the back yard for dinner later. I myself began to wonder what the assholes said about the violent schizophrenic who had a rep for living in dank cemeteries.

At least I deserved a bit of my bad reputation. Master Boyd did not.

"Linda, I am not going to lose my temper. I love you so much to say something I can never take back. I would suggest you think a moment and do the same. The last time you opened your mouth to me without thinking we both went on to regret it. Boyd is my fiancé, like it or not. It is not your business to judge him unless you too are his lover, or you have direct evidence to prove him a poor one for me. I will show you the respect you have earned from me by always being a good friend. You would be wise to do the same for me." I stared at her doing my best not to let the utter contempt at her appearing to try to bad mouth someone she claimed as a friend. She and Boyd worked together all the time.

Linda looked back at me with fire in her eyes. "Okay Mother, I was trying to stay out of it. You are right. If you and Boyd are really engaged and lovers then it is not my fucking business. However, I think a little red headed birdy told me once that you only sleep with someone who holds your collar. That means my dear co-worker may have decided to get himself a girlfriend at long last. One he wanted all this time. A girl that would not be able to turn his advances down even with his sorted history and nasty reputation if he knew he had her Key to turn her lock. It seems very interesting to me that after his sneaking around watching you for years like the weirdo he is, suddenly he shows up putting a ring on your finger. Boyd couldn't get the balls to even ask you out on a fucking date. I know because he told me so. I asked you hundreds of times and you turned me down. I know you didn't say no because you don't want me. It doesn't make sense. You said yes to Boyd but not to me? No fucking way. I see the way he acts around you and you around him. You cater to his every whim like he is God of the damned universe. Pussy ass Boyd who fears his own shadow and you act like his is your boss? Uh-uh, something is wrong with this picture, Psycho. Did that sneaky bastard do something very stupid? I know you would never lie to me. So out with it. Did Boyd somehow get his hands on your collar? Is that what is going on," she growled loudly.

I sat back feeling very anxious knowing damned well she had me dead to rights. Linda was always too clever. My acting job would have to be real fucking good or I would betray Simon's keyholder identity by sheer accident.

I looked at her calmly but smiling. "So that is what this is about? You are jealous that I chose Boyd. Well sorry Linda, but the man talked me into taking him for a spin. I found he was just the right ride with enough horsepower under the hood to get me right where I want to be going. Sheryl is my collar holder darling. Boyd is my fiancé. Unlike Ginger, Sheryl doesn't give two shits if I have a little strange on the side." I chuckled hoping this lie would work.

Lindas eyes went wide. "Sheryl? Ball breaker Sheryl holds your collar. Fuck me. Wait, she is a lesbian Psycho. She lets you date Boyd? If she said strange on the side well, I could understand picking him. They don't get any stranger." She seemed to be thinking my explanation made some sense but was not quite buying it yet.

I looked at the floor feigning sadness. "It is no secret Linda, Sheryl has breast cancer. Metastasized in fact. She has allowed me to marry because she loves me and wants to see me cared for after she is gone. No more sorry ass collar holders who thud the shit out of me, you know."

Linda looked at me in shock. "Oh fuck, I didn't, I had no idea. Poor thing. Yeah, she is a real angel to care for you like that. Look I can see you wanting to find someone to look after you now that you have explained it. But Mother, Boyd? Come on. A beauty like you could find someone less creepy." She snorted.

I shook my head. "Linda, did you forget I have schizophrenia? Did it not occur to you that someone like Boyd who doesn't have other choices in a mate may be just the right one for me? Don't you think it is a plus he still wanted me despite having very personal information about the seriousness of my issues? Not like a lot of fellows are lining up to take care of a drooling, pacing, insane piece of ass, is there? You can't marry me. So, at least with Boyd I have security and you must face the facts, he loves me beyond comprehension. You said he has wanted me for years. That is just the kind of loyalty I need now isn't it? His reputation of being creepy or weird, you forget who you are talking to. That is one fucking thing he doesn't own the patent to. And for the record, it is untrue about him." I looked out the window hoping she could not read the fakery in my eyes.

We pulled into the jail parking lot with Linda mulling over what I had said. "Okay, it makes sense, I will give you that. I just knew you would have told me if he had done something horrible like go for your collar. All right, you are right Mother. None of my business. I will ask you to forgive me. I didn't mean to be ugly. I was just worried is all. Boyd can be obsessive you know?"

I looked at her smiling. "Your heart is in the right place. However, I am fine and quite capable of managing myself. Thanks for always being there, Goddess."

She smiled while getting out of the car with me. "If only gay marriage were legal, I would so steal you away from that nut."

I winked at her. "If it were, I would totally run away with you tonight. Oh, what a honeymoon it would be."

She laughed out loud blushing. "Well I ask Boyd all the time to give me details and the greedy bastard won't spill a single secret about what it is like to sleep with you to me. Damn him."

I smiled as she slid her arm around my waist walking me into the station door. "He is granting you mercy. What he could tell you would melt your ears off and blast you into orbit. He and I have an arrangement. He doesn't kiss and tell, and neither do I." I chuckled at that only truth I had given her the entire conversation.

She groaned out in frustration. "God damned you both."

I laughed loudly. "Uhm, ain't that the fucking truth."

Cathy looked up from her desk at Linda and I. "Oh hello ladies. Psycho? What's up girl? Linda you have a couple of messages from Kirstin."

I looked at Linda. "Shame on you. And I thought I was the only girl who's heart you had stolen."

I chuckled then looked at Cathy who was staring at me hoping I would chat. I had refused all her attempts for many years since the day she had threatened to put me into a cell with a rapist. This was not going to be her lucky day either. I never forgive someone who hurts me when I did nothing to deserve it.

"Boyd here," I asked flatly looking on past her as if she was just a woman working there, not a friend.

Cathy frowned. "Yeah, he is in the office filing paperwork as usual. Hey Psycho, I stopped wearing underwear earlier this year." She began laughing.

I frowned then looked at Linda. "See you at temple darling. Right now, I need to make a call to the cops, I mean cop." I winked while she blushed totally ignoring Cathy's attempt to stir my tendency to retort to foul statements.

"Happy hunting, Psycho." Linda rushed off to her office to return her calls, while I headed to see Master Boyd.

I found my Master sitting at his desk writing down the information from the arrests of the gang rapists. His office station was the first of several and pointed toward the wall. Behind him sat six other small desks all belonging to other city and county police officers Keith, Mark, Will, Dennis, Chuck, Trenton and Randell.

This was the office that the afternoon and night shift cops usually used. Linda and other officers had a similar open space with desks across the hall. I noticed all the night shift officers were standing around a water cooler in the back of the large open room talking a laughing loudly. I noticed immediately the absences of Keith, Dennis and Randell.

Keith was likely guarding the prisoners while Dennis was slapping them around a bit. I assumed Master Boyd was stuck as usual doing all the filing. Dennis likely sent him to do the shit work so he could enjoy all the fun with Randell the weekend bull cop and Dennis's original partner.

It was lucky for me that the two commanding officers of this motley crew were away from their stations. Perfect for the implementing of a two-fold plan. I intended to repay my Master for his protection service and allow for the release of a bit of his steam before we discussed my on-call status later. It would be tricky, but I thought it could be done. If Master Boyd and I were really bonding in a true D/s relationship, then I would no doubt succeed.

It is typical for submissive to mirror the Dominant. That I had been doing deeply. It was apparent Simon approved his reign as our true Master and leader. Now it was time to see if my Master was starting to feel the natural pull of all Dominants to their subs in return. If the match was indeed right, he would find it difficult if not impossible to deny me his immediate attention if I begged his favor.

Testing his metal as my true Dominant in such a public forum would add the pressure of social ridicule. A nice variable to add a bit of stress to the experiment. If he gave in to my charms despite the teasing of co-workers, then it would prove once and for all that we were indeed in a strong partnership.

If he naturally fell into his role, I knew I would give up my last reservations about this once hated Keyholder. If the match were correct, Master Boyd would be more than worthy of my love, adoration and loyalty. If not, then I would find a way to get Simon's Key back as quickly as possible. I needed to end this yo-yo effect regarding how I felt about my Master. It was slowly driving me insane.

I made sure the rowdy group of loafing cops saw me coming toward my overly occupied Master. The voices and laughter ended the second that Will pointed out my stalking unit headed for the quiet, shy cop's desk. I could feel their bawdy eyes track me while I readied myself to pounce on my prey.

I heard Trenton say to his fellow gawkers. "Will you look at that? What the fuck is she doing here? Did you know she is engaged to Boyd? Is that a joke that I missed out on? Can't be true, is it? Boyd? Nah, it is bullshit. That boy couldn't tame a house cat much less please that wildcat right there."

Without hesitation I pushed my way onto Master Boyd's lap. I completely stunned him from his deep focus on the papers in front of him. He looked up appearing at first not to understand what his vision was telling him.

"Psycho? Baby, what, where and how did you get here?" He looked around the room nervously, suddenly noticing the crowd of watchers at the cooler.

I grinded my lap into his while purring, "I couldn't wait to see you lover. Don't you have a lunch break coming? It is getting late. Remember, you promised to show me that handcuff trick officer." I moaned out loud enough that anyone in the room could clearly make out my words.

Master Boyd looked at me confused. "Handcuff trick? Now? I mean here?" He again looked back at our now stunned audience.

I smiled seductively. "Take a break love. I need you right now. It is making me insane waiting. Please? Pretty please, you can be on top." I began to kiss him passionately using my tongue and biting his lips while pulling on his uniform shirt as if trying to tear it off.

I felt my Master stirring immediately into my gridding lap as his breathing became shallow and sweat began to form on his brow. He was melting in my hands, lap, mouth, okay all of me. He suddenly dropped his pen and grabbed my waist back with force returning my wanton kiss. His lust was overtaking his good senses. I realized in horror he was going to rip through his pants with his hard on soon thanks to my overdoing my seduction. His excitement was rising so fast I began to fear he was about to throw me on his desk forcing a coupling in blind desire.

I had not realized the full power of his inner addiction for carnal congress. The need to feel desired, wanted and lusted for had been pent up in him for far too long. I had noticed that if the wind blew the wrong way or he saw my ankle he would practically burst into climax most of the time. It had not occurred to me that he would be so damned helpless against it. He had told me, but I had not listened to him thinking he was being dramatic. I began to wish I had just rubbed his shoulders sweetly rather than put myself, and him, into such a very dangerous position of impulsive need.

He was beginning to pant and moan. If I didn't pull away soon, my experiment to see if he would give in to my favor would become a full-on porno moment in the middle of the jailhouse. Thankfully, Dennis walked in to get a cup of coffee just in time. His surprise to find his adopted son and town loon making out like hormonal teens at the desk caused quite a blast of irritation from the senior officer. He likely saved Master Boyd and me from a mistake we could never take back. I doubt he ever realized how close it got to be one hell of a story to tell the grandkids.

"What the hell. Boyd, Psycho, you two get out. Boyd, take a break son. Go walk that shit off. Psycho, get off of my officer and out of my office now. And what are you lazy sonofabitches doing? Shows over, get back to work," Dennis yelled out suddenly from the office doorway.

Master Boyd snapped out of his sexual enchantment upon hearing the gruff voice but to my astonishment didn't lose his interest in completing what I had accidentally started. Without a word he pushed back his chair. He grabbed me by the hand, pulled me off him and took off for the door running right past a shocked Dennis. My hand was held tightly in his as he hauled me behind him. I could barely keep up, he was moving so fast.

Fear gripped me when I realized we were headed for the parking lot. I thought for sure he was going to beat me to death for acting so overtly seductive in his place of employment. The teasing and possible reprimanding from Dennis would likely be severe. I tried to brace myself for whatever punishment I had coming. I shouldn't have done it. I was just so damned stupid. What was I thinking?

Cathy saw us practically sprinting by. "Boyd, where you headed hon? Boyd?"

He stopped at the door looked back at her glowering. "Lunch. I will be back in thirty minutes."

He opened the door dragging me behind him as Cathy yelled out, "Where are you getting lunch Boyd?"

He yelled back without turning around. "Mind your own damned business, Cathy."

Tears were starting to well up in my eyes as Boyd opened the passenger's side door then pushed me in slamming the door behind me. I looked in the rearview mirror seeing all he officers from the cooler spilling out to watch as Master Boyd jumped in started the car and tore off spinning tires and burning rubber. I closed my eyes in terror hoping my end would be swift.

"I need you so fucking bad baby. I am sorry but the woods it is. I can't wait till we get home," he moaned out as he sped for the edge of town.

I felt relief wash over me. Master Boyd wasn't going to kill me. He wanted to fuck me. It was obvious he had fallen for my request to be taken immediately. My Master was even willing to overlook Dennis's anger and his co-workers taunts to do as I demanded. While it may seem an easy thing to cause such eagerness in my Dominant, especially this one, Master Boyd was known for his shyness, calmness, manners and fear of being viewed as sexual due to the untrue rumors about him. All it took was my single plea to have my way at that very moment for him to ignore it all. As I watched his fervor continue unabated, I understood he would have obliged me without giving a fig who watched if I had said it was what I wanted.

The D/s relationship was indeed a match. Master Boyd was doing all he could to meet my wants and needs. He had allowed my request to finish Master Sheryl's reign and now he was dragging me into the woods to engage in the requested sexual union I had asked him for. I braced myself as he pulled over in the darkness. I was ready to return his many services to me that night. I knew it was going to hurt like hell, but he had earned it.

Master Boyd rushed to my door helping me out then carefully took my hand to aid me walking through the dark without falling. We walked in silence until we reached the same clearing from our last wooded violent mating call. I looked around recognizing the tree he had slammed me into the last time.

"How do you know this place, Master," I asked with much curiosity.

My Master chuckled. "I used to play here as a kid when church let out. I came here to think when I was a teenager. Now I am sharing it with you as our special place to be together." He took me into a loving embrace resuming our deep kissing.

I closed my eyes wishing I could just let him take me like this in his special place, but I knew my Master. His anger at Trenton would grow. Now that Dennis was going to slap his hand too, I couldn't take the chance. I pulled back from the kiss with as much strength as possible.

"I am sorry, Master. I changed my mind. Maybe later." I backed out of his embrace leaving him stunned.

"What? Psycho? You said you wanted to, what? I just got into trouble for this. I don't understand? Why are you doing this?" His confusion was evident, but I needed his anger instead.

I turned around and started heading back toward the car bracing myself once more for his attack. "Oh, you know, I guess it was just as passing thing."

He growled. "Psycho get back here now and kneel. We are doing this now. I don't want to wait till later, God damn it. You said now, well here we are."

I spun around smiling wickedly "No, I won't kneel Master. You can try to make me."

Master Boyd's eyes blazed with his crazy anger. "I have had enough of this. You never tell me no. I am your Master."

I giggled, taunting him. "Are You? Prove it, Boyd."

He came running at me like a madman grabbing me by my upper arms full of fury. I bite his arm causing him to let go of my right limb. With quickness I torn at his chest as he pushed me to my back on the ground using his weight to try to pin me. I rolled with him as we tore at each other cussing, clawing, ripping and slapping each other. He was not even getting close to using his full strength I noticed. The ploy was working. I had discovered he wanted the fight but had enough control to not injure too much if I didn't let it his anger fester too long.

I could see the thrill in his eyes when he finally overpowered, then subdued me tiring of his game. Quickly he forced me to my knees grabbing my shoulders to keep me still. As he tended to do, he then engaged in the coupling taking his position of Dominance from behind. I endured his rough, torturous thrusts as usual, this time noting if I cried out begging he would go a bit easier. His orgasm was swift and appeared to bring him a great deal of satisfaction based upon his moans of delight.

I had was grateful to have found a way to tolerate his violent urge without being ripped to pieces or beaten half to death in the process. It was still harsh, brutal and my begging him to stop during the act was very real. However, it was not as bad as a single night of thudding at the hands of Mistress Ginger, Master Julie's bench or Master Sheryl's caning. I decided as he panted, groaning still in ecstasy from his successful mount I could learn to live with it. I hoped maybe it would even get easier in time.

We both got off the forest floor to try our best to adjust our now torn and dirty clothing. Master Boyd began apologizing, appearing completely embarrassed that he had once again lost his temper and taken it out on me, or in me to be exact. I just chuckled and told him nothing was broken.

We kissed like lovers as he whispered promises to love me for all time. I held him assuring him that we would battle our demons together. He just had to have faith, and I would do the same in return. When we got into the car, he turned on the dome light so we could assess our damages. He checked me for injury finding only a few scratches and bruises. I looked over his unit finding a large scratch on his face, his uniform front pocket was torn nearly off, and he now had a slight limp from a well-placed kick to his upper right thigh during our mock sex battle. Both of us had leaves, ground in dirt stains and our hair (my wig) was sticking up full of damp Earth. My Master's watch told us our time had run out. Like it or not we had to head back to the station or he would get more than a mild warning.

When we pulled up the parking lot was full of Master Boyd's co-workers including Trenton. I didn't see Dennis or Randell to my relief. I knew, as did my Master, everyone was out there to see the show. I smiled at Master Boyd who had closed his eyes sighing, realizing he would have to walk in front of all of them disheveled from an obvious fist fight with his betrothed.

"It is okay Master. You are not alone anymore. Just follow my lead. I have your back." I kissed his scratched cheek.

Master Boyd looked at me appearing tired. "I will remember that when they put me back in jail. Send me cigarettes for my new boyfriend will you. That is a directive." He groaned.

I laughed. "You are not going to jail. You can't rape or beat me Master. I belong to you remember?"

His eyes went wide. "You are kidding right? What the hell did I just do then? Seem like rape and a beating to me."

I rolled my eyes. "Duh, yeah it was supposed to be. I love you Master. Whatever you need and want I will give it to you. All I want and need is your love and care in return."

He smiled lovingly. "You always had that Psycho. All you ever had to do is ask. I am your slave...forever. You wear that collar, but I am the one who can't live without your commands."

I nodded, "Yeah Master. That is how it works...when it is perfect. Now, let's not leave our adoring fans waiting. Showtime Master." I winked as I reached out and took his handcuffs out of the glovebox.

He watched in surprise when I cuffed one of my wrists then motioned him to get out of the car with me. We met behind the vehicle him limping and me with a single cuffed wrist. We kissed passionately then I slid my arm around his waist. Together we walked past the crowd of shocked and murmuring cops looking like two wounded soldiers helping each other to the medical supplies tent. Our hair sticking up, my Master's uniform ripped, both of us filthy. No one there doubted we had been engaging in one wild sexual escapade somewhere in the wild. Cathy came out the door as we started to go inside. She took one look at us and gasped.

"Oh my word. What happened to you two? You look like you have been hit by a train. Boyd why is Psycho cuffed." Cathy's eyes went even wide while she stared at my cuffed wrist wrapped tightly around my Master.

Master Boyd looked her dead in the eyes and said, "Use your fucking imagination Cathy. None of you seem to have much trouble coming up with stories that fit your fantasies when it comes to Psycho or me. Now excuse us, I have paperwork to get to and my fiancé needs a nap." We pushed past the gossip Queen Cathy headed for Master Boyd's locker so he could get his spare uniform.

Master Boyd changed quickly. He set me up for a nap on the cot usually reserved for cops pulling all double shifts. Dennis entered the small room to find him kissing and tucking me in.

"Boyd, you and Psycho need to come by the house on Sunday for supper with Carla and me. There are some things the three of us need to discuss, I think. Be there around five.

No arguments and no excuses." Dennis left briskly without any further comment.

I looked at Master Boyd a bit worried, "Uh oh that doesn't sound good."

My Master laughed, "Baby, it doesn't matter what he says or does. You and I are together. He can get over it or not. I am finally happy. No one is taking that away from me, not even Dennis."

He kissed me again then demanded I sleep for a bit. I closed my eyes as he left turning off the light on his way out. I laid there in the darkness praying the damned pager would allow me just a couple of minutes of…shit…it just went off again…

Chapter 65: Vigilante Justice
The D/s Power Couple
Master Boyd and Interim Master Sheryl

All around you every day there are plenty of examples of injustice. Most will not tolerate unfairness in this life. When someone hurts another, there should be a swift balance to provide vengeance to those injured, right? The question we must all ask ourselves is what is equal punishment for any crime? How can anyone but the victim ever know if the right person paid the price? In the end sometimes one must take the law into their own hands. Especially when justice goes blind and no one else is watching.

The D/s couple are in a truce. The white flag of surrender has been waived by the psychotic submissive. On her knees at long last, Psycho will kneel to her King. The deranged Dominant will accept nothing less than full control. It would appear the power struggle is over, but the war has only just begun.

The Key and the collar have joined forces hoping to end the darkness that spreads all around them. Spinning like an insane top, the two will hold on to each more tightly with each attack from outsiders. In their hearts is the ever-present terror that fuels the beasts within. Both are afraid to go back to the cell of walls with no windows. That fear will drive the duo into separate plans of defense. The trouble was their personal definitions of hell are completely incongruent with reality.

Dennis is a fine man. As father figure to the mating pair he is respected and feared above all others. His word is followed even above the Master's. He does not approve of the unholy union. His reasons are varied, but valid. Dennis will remind Master Boyd that Psycho is not the only one shattered. The Alpha is no stranger to madness. How can the crazed lead the cracked? Dennis's good advice will not be headed. He will blow up the wicked without consulting the evidence. This action will drive a deep wedge into the heart of his most beloved son.

Are you ready to go Monster hunting? That is glorious. Now for this chapter you will need to bring pitchforks, torches and a sense of outrage. Join the growing mob and chant with me, "kill the rapist, kill the rapist." Yes, now show no mercy. The bastard had it coming. We just know he did. Oh, don't listen to the victim. She is just high as usual.

"What do you mean you can't interview him because he is dead? I just saw him not more than about an hour ago. He was fit as a fiddle and more sober than a Baptist Preacher. Dennis and Randell where cuffing him to haul off to State for deportation. Dennis told me to go home. That he would handle the transfer of prisoners with his old buddy, as usual Dennis didn't trust me to do anything other than the fucking paperwork."
--**Master Boyd to Psycho when informed of the sudden death of Javier, September 1998**

I sat up in the darkness looking into the green eye of the pager. The number was from Jessieville. Another fifty miles away trip. I sighed but sat up to put back on my boots. I stretched my deeply fatigued muscles. I smacked the side of my own face trying to talk my brain into turning back on the lights of my unit. This was going to be an all nighter no doubt. I could forget the beautiful concept of sleep. It just wasn't in my cards this time.

I staggered to the door walking out into the quiet hallway of the police station. The strange image of being at the jail but not in a cell was making me feel like I was trapped in a weird dream. I walked to the phone hanging on the wall meant for unlucky prisoners to call friends or family begging bail aid. I picked up the receiver and called the number from the vibrating pest. The voice on the other end informed me of the need for an investigating officer in a case of abandonment of a small child found in a known drug house. Joy, I just couldn't wait to get there on that one, not.

I hung up the receiver and laid my forehead on the wall taking several shallow breaths. I had to wake up. There was no time for my biological needs when a little one was out there in danger. I reached deep inside to borrow some of that inner strength I always seemed to hoard from my consciousness. I pulled myself together and headed down the narrow walkway toward the only light I could see in the quiet building. My ears were already picking up the sounds of voices, some speaking all at one time. I hoped that Master Boyd would be among them.

I stopped shy of the door entry straining my ears to listen for the voice of my Dominant.

"Come on Boyd. Quit holding out on us. Where did you and Psycho go tonight? Don't even try to deny you were taking that little wild pony for a ride. Judging on the looks of you that girl is as crazy in the saddle as she is in everything else. Man, you have to share. We want details," said Trenton sounding desperate.

"Yeah, you know damned well we have all wondered for years what it would be like to bag Psycho. We would tell you all about it if it were one of us," I heard Mark join in the attempts to get my Master to discuss his intimate moments with me with the 'boys.'

I heard my Master growl back. "What I do or don't do with my fiancé is not anyone's business. You would all be smart to keep your filthy mouths shut about my girl. For that matter if I ever catch any of you looking at her again, I will beat the piss out of you."

I heard Trenton snort. "Oh fuck off, Boyd. Psycho and you ain't married yet. She could still wake up and realize she made a big mistake. How the hell did you even talk her into fooling around with you? I knew she was touched in the head but damn. We all know you have wanted that girl for years. How did your pussy ass manage to finally bag her. We all know what you are Boyd. There is no fucking way she jumped on you willingly. She isn't crying and trying to get away like we all expect any girl of yours would be. So, you did something to fuck with her head. What did you do? Did you catch her hallucinating and convince her you were a real man? Oh wait, I know, you fucked with her meds, right? Slipped her some Spanish fly instead of Thorazine. That is

297

what you did I bet." I heard all the officers begin to laugh at his cruel, but sadly somewhat correct, statement.

I heard a chair scoot across the floor loudly. "Fuck all of you. If anyone of you assholes wants to say another fucking word about me or my fiancé then you can come outside right now. We can just step into the road off the property and settle it like men. If not, then shut up. I won't stand for anymore of this disgusting talk about my future wife. She is more than any of you could ever hope to have. You are jealous she is with me. Fine! We can answer why she is with me by taking this outside. Want to find out if I am really a pussy? Who is ready to find out why Psycho wants me and not any of you," I heard Master Boyd yell out sounding furious.

I closed my eyes as my heart began to race. He was losing his temper. If anyone of those idiots decided to test him, Master Boyd would be the one in cuffs by morning. I felt a hand reach out and touch my shoulder. I turned, startled to be face to face with Dennis.

"Psycho, what are you doing sneaking around in the dark," said Dennis looking at me appearing concerned.

"Dennis, oh shit, thank the Gods. Please you must help Boyd. The guys have set off his temper. You need to stop him." I saw Dennis's eyes go wide and he pushed past me practically running into the office before I could even finish my sentence.

I stood there panting in terror as the old bull Dennis walked into the office just in the nick of time to end what was about to be an officers ball, errr, brawl.

"What the fuck do you boys get paid to do around here? Boyd, get that paperwork upstairs. The rest of you good for nothing loafing bastards get to your vehicles and get to fucking work. Break time is over. You don't get paid to gossip like a bunch of old hens. Judas Priest, go, all of you, now," yelled out Dennis like a pissed off drill sergeant.

I slinked back away from the doorway as the officers came piling out all grumbling angrily but doing what their commanding officer ordered. They all headed for the glass doors to pair up in their assigned squad cars to begin patrolling the sleeping towns. I waited quietly for my Master to come out too so I could catch his attention. I needed to be on my way to Jessieville fast as possible.

I heard Dennis stop Master Boyd. "Boyd, come here son. I want to know what was going on in here. Are the boys giving you shit again? We have talked about this. They don't mean nothing. You must just deal with it and keep your head down. Sooner or later they will stop making sport of you. Getting all fired up will only get you into more trouble. You don't want more trouble now do you," Dennis said soundly friendly, almost fatherly.

Master Boyd growled. "Sooner or later? Yeah, because eleven years is not enough time. I should wait maybe another twenty. Then maybe just maybe everyone will stop. I am done with sitting here and taking their shit, Dennis. I didn't rape Maddy. I didn't kill her either. Keeping my head down while they act like I am a child rapist is not working. I have had it."

Dennis cleared his throat. "Now Boyd, you did the time, so if you are innocent or not doesn't matter now does it? You're getting angry at these good ole boys. That worries me. Boyd, you have to face the facts if you hit one of them, they will send you back to the nuthouse over that mental problem of yours. This time they may keep you for good too. Ask that fiancé of yours. That ain't no way to go. Now take those reports upstairs and go home. I will see you two tomorrow at five. We can all sit down for a nice friendly chat then. Get some rest Boyd, you look like hell. That's an order. Now get out. Oh, and take Psycho with you. She has no business sneaking around the halls."

Master Boyd growled, "Yes sir," as he came storming out of the office.

"Boyd, over here," I yelled fearful I would not be able to catch the rushing cop.

He stopped dead turning to look at me with fire in his eyes. "Psycho? What the fuck are you doing up? You were ordered to sleep. You need rest God damn it." He started walking back in my direction still appearing very angry.

I began backing away feeling fear roll down my spine like an electrical snake. "Please, I just got paged. I have to go to Jessieville. I didn't mean to disobey you. It is my job. Forgive me." He caught up to me grabbing me by the upper arm dragging me down to the small room he had left me to sleep in.

He pushed me inside and closed the door turning on the light then slammed me into the wall pinning me with his weight. "I told you to sleep. I don't give a fuck if the pager went off. You are going to get sick if you don't sleep. How dare you ignore my directive," he growled getting angrier by the second.

I felt I would piss myself from total terror realizing he was nearly mad with his fury demon. "Please Master, it is my job. I must do my job or I will be fired just like you would. I beg your mercy please. I would never dare to question your authority without a forced cause. If it pleases you, then later, privately, you can do as you wish in retaliation for my disobedience. I must get to my call immediately. You have to believe me when I say you are my Master. My love, I will always do whatever you want me to do after I fulfill my duty to my job."

I felt the tears begin to well from sheer exhaustion mixed with abject terror of my Master's displeasure at me. I silently prayed to the mother Goddess that my pleas of full subjugation would call off his need to violently re-establish his Dominance over me.

The storm in his eyes began to dissipate while he listened to my submissive speak. "Okay baby, calm down. I understand. I shouldn't have lost my temper with you. You are right this is your job. I will take you to this call, and all the calls for the entire weekend. You are tired, sick and run down. I can't have you driving all over the State falling asleep at the wheel. Worse yet I won't have you being shot to death by some scum while you are protecting the kids. I can't stand losing you. You will mind me and sleep while I drive. Once this call is over we will sleep in shifts to make sure the job is done without either of us losing rest. I can see very clearly what old Sheryl is doing here even if you can't. She is trying to split us apart. Well that old cow is not going to do it. Her time is almost up. Then you will be doing what I say without excuse. You are mine Psycho, and soon you will be completely under my control. Nothing is going to stop me from having what was made for me by God's own hand. Now wipe your tears. Let's get these reports upstairs and get rolling." He backed off my unit unpinning me and took my hand gently while smiling.

I rubbed my wrists into my wet eyes as he told me to do sniffing back my tears. All the while I was trying not to shudder at his cryptic words. I was aware of his insane belief that I was made to be his mate by his God. Master Boyd believed that this deity only made one true love for each human being, a coupling pair. Somehow, through psychotic process or twisted up religious teachings in his youth, he had incorrectly assumed the one he lost his virginity to would be identified as his only one.

NOTE: *Even though I had not agreed to accept his gift of his sexual innocence, Master Boyd was fixated that it was indeed our consummation of an unbreakable union. He had told me during the rape in the white cell that it was our wedding night. No matter what I had done to try to convince him otherwise, in his cracked mind, we were* married in the eyes of GOD forever. He made it very clear we didn't need the pomp nor pageantry of a piece of paper, a ceremony or even a preacher. To Master Boyd our bond was ordained by the Creator himself.

I had finally figured out his pushing to get those signs of a legal contract were solely to announce to the world of men that I was his property and was not up for grabs anymore. He likely hoped it would stop the wagging tongues that questioned how he had managed to gain me as a lover in the first place.

A wife was a socially accepted badge of free choice in our society, since arranged marriages were not allowed in our country. If he could force me to become Missus Boyd Simmons, everyone would believe I did it willingly. He thought it would end the whispers that I was being forced, insane or tricked into being his girl. Most believed I would eventually wake up and realized my mistake at taking him as my lover.

Thanks to his delusion that we were married by God's law from the loss of his virginity, no other woman on Earth would be acceptable to my Master. He had explained to me in private discussions, during my two days of horror after the forced collaring, that he had invested his immortal soul through this one act of carnal desperation. He surmised that to lose his God given partner would result in a life of loneliness and damnation most cruel. I couldn't give him his virginity back, so he could not choose another and still be following God's rules of ordained sexual congress. He *believed you were only allowed to fuck your wife. To do so with anyone else was considered adultery, a sin most foul.*

If you committed adultery you were damned to hell for all eternity. That included even if she left you, died, or was otherwise unable. He believed this so strongly that he had actually withheld his desires waiting for over a decade to engage in the act of sex for the first time with the one he had identified as being Missus Right. Unfortunately, the object in his delusion would be Psycho, literally.

It had occurred to me over that year since the rape in the white cell I was dangerously stuck as a key figure in the psychotic symptom of Master Boyd's Obsessive Love Disorder (OLD). It was not his Intermittent Explosive Disorder (IED) I had to fear. That anger issue was completely controllable with weekly mildly violent trysts, medication and careful monitoring. His OLD on the other hand, that had gotten out of control and like my schizophrenia has no easy treatment. I had also, to my horror, discovered Master Boyd suffered from a severe and chronic case of Post Traumatic Stress Disorder with dissociative episodes as well. This very complex grouping of Axis I (severe mental disorder not personality defects) had created a very unstable, scary and potentially deadly concoction within this troubled man.

PTSD with dissociative episodes are flashbacks, feelings of unreality, memory loss for complex actions, and the feeling someone else is controlling you along with brief splits in the personality -all of which you have seen in him during his violent attacks. It was why I asked him if he even knew what he was doing when he came after me. His response was it is like I am dreaming, I try to stop but can't. I checked his records and found my suspicions about this complex mental disorder were correct. He had been diagnosed with it at age 15 while in the Snake Pit and again at eighteen in the Boys Prison. Basically, what we have in this D/s relationship is a well-documented violent psychotic that has collared a well-documented dangerous psychotic. The loony is attempting to guide the loony. Holy shit!.

My ability to tolerate violent attacks, lack of emotional depth, and disconnection from reality made me the perfect partner for Master Boyd. Not man, if any, females could deal with his nasty hair trigger, psychotic temper, need to cling, delusional thinking process, and constant demands for assurance that his bad behaviors would not result in abandonment. As his mirror and submissive he had found me capable of making the pain go away. This was the pain inside his mind.

Once he had tasted the feeling of relief, he acquired by submitting me to his will, there was no hope of his ever letting me get away from his clutches. I had become his drug, the cure for all his suffering. Nothing comes without a price. His peace of mind had cost me my every bit of my minimal freedom.

I already could see the writing on the wall. In time, he would want to narrow my choices even further, slowly whittling them all away, until at last I was in a prison cell with him being the only guard.

All I could do is hope that I could help him find a manageable treatment for his madness that didn't include me. Or I would need to find a safe escape before he locked me into his heart shaped box and never let go of the key.

My Master and I rushed to the closed court offices upstairs. He made me stay leaned on the wall while he went inside the court clerk's offices and placed the paperwork for the multiple arrests on Sherry's desk. She would come in during regular business hours to find Cindy's horror awaiting her before even getting her Monday morning work coffee.

I stood there watching him move like a stealthy panther, quiet, sure and with a look of deadly purpose. I felt my unit shuddering once again. I wanted badly to love this Master who appeared so perfect in his Dominant role, but his beast was coupling with my own. It was sure to breed a demonic inner madness unlike either of us had ever known. How could this unholy union ever work in our favor?

I really needed to talk to Simon about all this. I wondered if my dear friend would still be angry over our last little tiff. I called to him but knew he would not likely answer quickly. If he showed at all it would only be after he made sure I suffered a bit for my indiscretion of chastising him so unfairly.

Master Boyd came back to retrieve me from my holding up the hallway wall. He took my hand and moved rapidly toward his awaiting car. I gave him the address of the call and was ordered to close my eyes and sleep while he rushed us through the darkness to Jessieville. I fell asleep almost immediately, grateful he was enforcing a directive for a change.

I awoke when the car stopped. The drug house was still crawling with local cops. Master Boyd got out and stood quietly keeping watch while I took possession of a screaming one year old. The child had been in the abandoned building long enough for his diaper to be full of rotting feces and stagnant urine. I ripped off the foul covering and almost puked from the smell of decay.

I assessed the damage rapidly. His bottom was raw, scarred and infected. The baby required immediate medical help. I growled at the attending officers for having not notified the local emergency services, as I rushed into Master Boyd's car holding the now half naked child. Master Boyd handed me a blanket from his trunk, and I wrapped the little one as we speed to the ER. I looked at the now quieted little boy.

His big blue eyes were caked in goop from days of crying without use. His unit was poor from lack of food, and he was much smaller than he should have been indicating that most of his life had been that of extreme neglect. He smiled at me appearing to know somehow that finally someone cared. I reached down and wiped out his small soul portals. He giggled and tried to grab my hand appearing to enjoy the touch of another human very much. I smiled back and made a face. He giggled louder and kicked his tiny legs. Master Boyd looked at us engaged in our silly game.

"What kind of bitch would throw away such a gift. Shit, what a monster. I hope they catch her, lock her away in a diaper and let it rot on her ass," he snorted angrily.

I kept smiling at my little prince. "Now Master, this baby is better off without a mother such as he had. I will make sure he gets a good forever home. He is young, handsome, and some sad lady is out there tonight praying for the miracle that just happened. You'll see. He will be adopted in no time. This horror will never be a part of his memory. He is a lucky one, though he started at the finish line." I covered my eyes then pick-a-booed the enamored little man.

He clapped his hands in pure delight. His unit required medicine, but his spirit was strong. The ER was able to make his little booty feel better and save him from the monstrous infection that had been eating away at his nether parts. He would have a few scars to mark his sorry start in life, but otherwise the baby was healthy, thank the Gods.

The hospital admitted him for dehydration, infection, and long-term malnutrition. The kind doctors had sedated him to keep him calm. I made the call to authorities to officially take custody and place him in the State's care. I demanded that even if the mother could be located Termination of Parental Rights should begin immediately. The medical report indicated failure to thrive due to severe neglect. This child would have died if not found in another forty-eight hours. This was unacceptable.

After gaining permission to take the child as my own and end his sorry ass mother forever, I went to see my baby. There was no name for the child. No one knew anything about him. The nurses on call that night adored him, and he adored them all with greedy eagerness. He was starved for more than food and water, this little man needed love.

Everyone began to call the tiny child James. I stood there over his little sleepy unit. He was drugged and confused but he looked back at me. I could see a future of great joy in his eyes. One day, this little baby boy would be someone of worth thankfully saved from the grave that his unloving mother had left him to die in. I stroked his chubby cheek smiling as I told him he was going to meet his mommy very soon. Theresa Sorrall was the mother who would never ignore his cries for affection. She had been waiting a long time to give him all he deserved. I knew she was the one who had more than enough to make up for all he had lost.

The Sorralls had been a foster home for five years. Theresa was a lovely woman of thirty-eight who could bear no children of her own to her long-time love match Joseph. In their sadness they had opened their hearts and home to many a lost child. Always hoping, praying that one would decide to stay. Little baby James was their dream come true as they were to be his. The adoption would go through in record time. It was a match that healed three broken hearts and prove there is still some good left in this brutal world. I still smile when I remember it. I do not have many pleasant memories of my days as an investigator, but baby James is one of those rare gems.

NOTE ABOUT BABY JAMES: I *was not there when Theresa met her child for the first time. I was working on the other side of my realm. I was told by the nurses the moment the two laid eyes on each other one could almost hear the angels sing in Heaven. It was love at first sight.*

The Sorralls honored the hospital staff by officially naming him James Sorrall once he was their very own forever. They continued to keep their home open to children in need for another decade, allowing a haven for many a weary child traveler.

James caught up quickly once his health was back on track. He grew up strong and proud wanting to become a Park Naturalist in his own county. Theresa wrote to me for years of his many milestones and great grades. The last I heard of him he was in pre-college courses and had a girlfriend, a cheerleader no doubt. What can I say? Even at just a year old he could melt a lady's heart with that smile. He just had a way about him I suppose. I know he had me the moment I held his little wasted unit in my arms. He was very hard to let go. How his own mother could not have been enchanted by his charms is beyond me. I hope she rots in hell wherever she is and I mean that. I don't care how awful that makes me sound.

I often thanked the Goddess he had made it without any sign of distress caused by his neglectful birth and first year of life. The police never found his biological parents, and to be honest good. They were never to come forward. I always hoped that out there somewhere they were forced to watch the child they left to die, rise to a fine man loved by

his real parents. This year he will be twenty-four years old.
That little baby is now a man. One that was saved.

Master Boyd walked with me to his car after we made sure James was sleeping and stable. I was starting to pile up the paperwork. I had called the Sorralls with their blessed news. I barely was able to get her off the phone. I feared she was on her way to the hospital in her jammies to meet her baby that very night.

The feeling that this child would have a happy ending helped to beat back my encroaching fatigue, but I was very dizzy. The world kept spinning and from time to time I saw things dart about the rooms or parking lots. I could hear Looper getting louder, making understanding of human speech a bit more difficult. I usually could focus better on the real. That night I was starting to drift off into the realm between sleep and waking without closing my eyes.

I was about to get into the car when Master Boyd suddenly grabbed me harshly, which frightened me. In my confusion I cried out in fear that he was attacking.

"Psycho, Psycho baby, you just fainted. Speak to me. Sweetheart can you hear me?" I heard Master Boyd echoing in the darkness, but I couldn't tell from where.

"I am here Master, where are you," I said trying to understand the misshapen visions all around me as blasts of colors and light exploded across my visual field.

"Oh, this is bullshit. You don't even know where you are you are so tired. You are exhausted. Here, close your eyes baby, sleep. If that fucking pager goes off, I am throwing the motherfucker into the river. I got you, sleep now," I heard him say from far way.

I nodded. "As you wish Master." I closed my eyes and felt the sensation of falling into a hole pulling me down from deep within.

My Master was correct. I was exhausted, psychotic and quickly coming undone. I have no recall of getting home to Master Boyd's home or even getting into his bed. If that pager had gone off the rest of that night, I am sure he would have been true to his word and he would toss it into the river.

As luck would have it, not another call came in the entire Saturday or oddly that night. I did not awaken for a full twelve hours. Master Boyd allowed me to sleep unmolested and uninterrupted. He kept an eye on the pager when he woke up and he never left the house. He hung around all day fixing the broken mailbox and watching me for signs of continued life while I re-paid the sandman for my long absence from his loving embrace.

I awoke to find Master Boyd stroking my cheek lying next to me in his bed. I was initially startled, unsure what was going on. I jumped up confused but my Master calmed me quickly by reminding me where I was located. When I sleep, I tend to forget where I am. This is sadly still a problem to this very day. Sometimes the confusion can last up to fifteen minutes if someone is not around to remind me. Ask Master Jon. Yeah ain't schizophrenia grand?

"Psycho, baby we need to talk. First, I want you to get up, get a shower then meet me in the kitchen to eat something. We can talk over dinner. I have fixed us something, but that has got to change. Never mind, go get cleaned up. I would love to come help with that, but if I did, I would not be able to keep my cool, so you go now. See you in fifteen minutes. Don't bother to put your clothes back on after. You can eat with me naked. Doesn't hurt to look does it?" He smiled lustfully.

I nodded looking down with a sigh realizing his talk was not going to be pleasant if he was forgoing his rights to sexual service to stay focused on it.

He grabbed my chin. "Tell me you are happy to be with me. Tell me you love me. I need to hear it."

I looked back at his devil blue eyes. "I love you Master. I am happy to be here with you."

Master Boyd smiled then pulled me into a passionate kiss almost forgetting himself as he began to grope and moan in desire. Suddenly he pulled back and jumped off the bed. He rushed from the room yelling he expected my presence in the kitchen in fifteen minutes, so I had better hurry.

I got up and did as I was told well within the amount of time he had allowed. I wandered into his kitchen wearing only his black Boyd house shoes as was often his pleasure. He groaned when I walked in.

"Maybe I should have told you to wear clothes. I keep forgetting how damned beautiful your unit is. I lose my head every time I see it. Sit down, eat and listen. I don't want to hear a damned word come out of that sexy little mouth till I tell you to respond, understand me?" He continued to look me over with wantonness.

I nodded then sat down and began eating the meal sitting in front of me. I didn't bother with the utensils and was immediately chastised for it.

"Why do you do that? Use a fucking fork. I swear you eat like a damned animal Psycho. Stop that. You are not a fucking beast in the field." He slammed his fist on the table making me jump.

I picked up the fork and clumsily tried eating with it. The problem was that I was not used to eating with a fork, plate or even table. I had almost never done it all my life. That is the sad truth, ask Master Jon. I was bad about this when he collared me. My baby food came in jars or pouches. I just used my hands or turned them over and drank them. My mother Debbie had never allowed table privileges either when I was young. Eating for a submissive is always a rush without fanfare.

As a result, my table manners sucked big time. Hell, I never needed any. I had not bothered to learn the nuances of personally handling eatery tools. Even though I knew how to set them properly, including for fancy dinner parties, to serve a Master at a table.

Master Boyd snorted. "I am sick to death of this shit. You are never here to provide any wifely service to me. I can't provide any services to you because you are sixty fucking miles away. When you are home you are sick, tired, and worn the fuck out. I have had no time to teach you even proper fucking table manners. Sheryl is doing this shit on purpose. It is not enough that she works the hell out of you five days a week plus that funeral home job, then she sticks her nose into my time with my girl. When she puts you on call for the weekend she is stealing my time. I don't give a flying fuck if she is dying. This is not okay. I did not wait all my life for a part time fucking lover. I want my wife home. I think you need to quit that job Psycho. Not just because it is taking you away from me, but I see it slowly killing you. You don't sleep, eat, and the stress is horrible. Your weight is down by ten pounds. That is unacceptable. If I wanted to fuck a skeleton, I would go dig one up in Darlin. I am damned scared this bullshit is going to make you go psychotic or catatonic soon. I will lose you all over this stupid idea that you can work. Psycho, you are seriously mentally ill. Your psychiatrist says this job is bad for you. I love you baby. I won't stand by and watch you kill yourself. Why won't you please listen to me and quit before it is too late?"

I looked at the table wincing while he yelled out some of his words of warning to me. I felt queasy. I understood he wanted me to quit so he could keep me stuck in his house like a doll waiting for her Master to come home to play with her. I couldn't bear the thought. I had worked so hard to be valued in the community as useful and worthy.

Now that I had it, there was no one on Earth, not even Master Boyd, who was taking this away. I was no longer just a stupid loony who was only viewed as a piece of ass. I was tired of being conquered repeatedly and then passed on to the next predator in a never-ending line of scumbags. If he were to have his way, I may as well not have even bothered with college. You don't need a degree to suck cock or make dinner by five.

"Well? Are you listening to me? I want you to quit this job. I want you to come home for good and end this bullshit living with Sheryl. My wife belongs at home with me," he growled.

I nodded "I am listening Master. I beg your forgiveness but you promised I could finish Sheryl's reign without your interference. We had an agreement. I would beg you to keep your promises to me or I will not be held to keep any back to you." I kept my gaze down waiting for his anger demon to rear up because I was standing my ground against his desires.

Master Boyd sat back in his chair crossing his arms glaring at me hatefully. "Really? You are going to pull a threat, and that was a threat. Don't you deny it Psycho."

I shook my head "I would never dare to threaten you, Master. I am simply saying if you don't keep promises then you betray your collar. Then I can't trust you. Without trust there can't be any love, honesty or loyalty between us. You chose to break your bond by dishonoring your word, there is nothing I can do about it. You are the Master. I follow you wherever you go, whatever you do. Follow my leader. That is how this works Master," I yelled back at him feeling terribly angry he was trying to backdoor his vow that I could serve Master Sheryl till her death.

He sat there looking at me with his eyes colder than ice. "Is that so? Fine. I will keep my promise. Sheryl is moving away anyway. You will return to your children and me the second she is out the door in Cumberland the end of this month. You are to move in with me until we can get you set up. I would rather you and the children move in with me. But I will settle for just having my family close. Eventually, I will have my wedding ring on your finger and the kids will come home too. Until then, I forbid you returning to Darlin, or that shit Sayer boneyard. No more dirty, dangerous cemeteries. I mean it. When you are on-call weekends, I will be going with you until this stupid attempt at your working fails. No more traveling to these dangerous situations alone. Not my girl. Not anymore. Got that?"

I glared back at my Master in irritation. "While I am most grateful for the mercy my most glorious Master is offering to my unworthy person, I would beg that you reconsider your proposal to attend to my employment scheduling. You already work a forty-hour week and I would not wish to cause you more hardship. Your attendance during my on-call duties is an unnecessary waste of you precious time, Master. You are not getting paid for such a grueling task and would likely find the duties of no great interest. I will seek shelter immediately that will meet your extraordinary standards. It is not for me to dare to question your most excellent grasp of my uselessness in my ability to please you. Instead, I will offer my heartfelt gratitude that You bother to care for my reprehensible existence at all. I

317

throw my shameful self before you to beg your forgiveness for my most abominable shortcomings," I said in high protocol speak using the defense mechanism of reaction formation to hide my extreme anger at his attempts to control beyond his collar powers as my Master.

*(Reaction Formation: To act overdramatically honorable or caring to a situation that is causing unsaid intense anger. This defense mechanism is used to try to erase the underlying guilt or bad feelings elicited by the anger. Example: someone who hates their boss may be overly friendly, overly helpful and all around observably overly nice whenever that hated person is interacting with them. This behavior often comes off as appearing very fake. Another quite common example of this behavior is a man or woman who seeks out and attacks, verbally or physically, gay persons because they have homoerotic desires of their own and feel angry or guilty about them.

Master Boyd's look darkened at my obvious attempt to goat him. "Psycho I am going to warn you this one time to not test me. If you are trying to pull the wool over my eyes by trying to use Sheryl to escape my collar you had better rethink that plan. I am not going to chase you around anymore. I am not going to wait another decade to have what is mine. Sheryl could linger for another five or seven years for all we know. If you are up to something then cut it out. I have watched you since you were just a kid. I know just how tricky, clever and downright sneaky you actually are. You are not going to fool me. I know damned well you are just pretending to love me so I don't hurt you. I am willing to overlook it for now. I will play as nice long as you don't give me a reason to get mean. Just let me remind you, if I ever catch you trying to get away, telling anyone about us, or outright lying to me, well I will make sure it never happens again. That is one promise you can count on." He reached out and grabbed my left wrist pulling my arm roughly toward his mouth to kiss his ring.

I felt a mouse run over my grave. "Master, I fear I am confused by your threats. It was my understanding you knew I had come to love you despite our difficult start. I am not clear on what has caused this sudden shift in your faith in our true D/s relationship?" I did my best to try to curb my Master's dark side that I suddenly realized was sitting across the table staring at me with suspiciousness.

The evil Boyd smiled at me bitterly. "Oh, yeah sure you love me, Psycho. You love not being in pain that is all if I stopped hitting you, stopped forcing you to your knees and believed your bullshit about adoring me. Well baby, that door wouldn't swing into that beautiful ass before you'd be gone fast as a jackrabbit and never come back. You stay with me because you know what I would do to you if you tried to leave me. No other reason. So cut the crap. Like you always say, I may be crazy but I am not stupid. I don't expect you to ever really love me. You didn't want me. You ran from me. You hate me and I know it." He jerked my arm pulling me harshly forward so that my face was nearly smacking into the table.

I took a deep breath to calm my nerves. "I apologize for being so cruel to you, Master. I was wrong about you. I admit I did hate you in the beginning. Over time I have come to love you for the great person you really are. Hearts can change Master. Some people fall into hate for the one they once loved every day. Why is it you can't believe it is possible to fall out of hate and into love just as easily? How can I prove to you that I do want to make this D/s coupling work? Please Master, I beg your favor." I held steady keeping my gaze down praying to the Goddess the beast Master Boyd would go back to sleep and bring back my kind and gentle Keyholder.

He paused while still holding my arm tightly. "Okay, you will move in with me. Let me come with you when you get called out on weekends. Start providing services on a regular basis and start showing me more affection in public like you did tonight at the station. It felt good to have you want me so much you couldn't wait until we got home. I want more of that."

I nodded. "As you wish Master. I told you I will deny you nothing except for what you promised to me. Sheryl finishes her reign and I must keep my job until she becomes Area Manager. I will move in with you but my children stay at Mary's until we are married. They are not subject to the rules of the Key and collar Master. It is improper to even involve them in our discussions."

He growled. "Those should have been my children. Timmy stole my chance to be a father. Now I will never get to know the joy of raising my own blood sons. That sonofabitch took advantage of you and me by proxy. If you had wanted a child why didn't you call on me. I had offered you my heart even that far back, Psycho. Instead you bedded down with a sorry ass Voss. I would have been an honest father for you but you didn't want me." He pulled my arm harder making my shoulder socket burn and grind from the stress.

I gritted my teeth fighting back the memory of considering calling on Master Boyd to father my daughter. I had indeed almost called him to ask him to help make that baby. I had always thought I made a mistake choosing Timmy's seed over my Master's but now I had decided I had indeed picked the lesser of two evils after all. At least Timmy stayed the fuck out of my life. If either of those kids had been Boyd's, holy shit. I would never have made it this far.

Taking a deep breath again I looked at him tearing up. "I have to be honest Master, I didn't believe I was good enough for you. I was not pure and not even loved enough to have a home. You were so handsome and brilliant, far beyond my reach. I thought you were just showing pity for me. I didn't want to taint your life with my madness or foul history. I thought you deserved better than I could ever hope to be."

I was this time being very honest. I had no idea all that time of Master Boyd's reputation, his hurts or his lack of choices in a mate. Had I known these things I may have indeed made the biggest mistake of my life by choosing him as a lover as far back as when I was seventeen years old. Thankfully, I didn't know. I viewed him as everything he definitely was not.

Master Boyd let go of my arm. "Oh Psycho, you couldn't have been more wrong. I loved you from the second I saw you that day in the woods. I would have died for you. You are all I have ever wanted. Baby, I am so sorry you didn't understand that. I should have been more open and honest. It is not your fault. You didn't know. You can't read minds. Now I find out we could have been together all this time. I am so stupid. Well, I won't lose any more time with you. We are together and there is no stopping us anymore." He got up and pulled me out of the chair hugging me with much tenderness. Speaking of tenderness, my shoulder, ouch.

I nodded. "Yes Master, we are together now. Please just let go of the past as best as you can. I know I have."

He grabbed my chin to look in my wet eyes. "Do you really mean that Psycho? You really are letting all the stupid shit I did go? You really love me and are not just acting like you do?"

I nodded. "Master I cannot prove it overnight any more than you can. Please have faith in me. You must learn to trust so I can trust you back. I do love you. You have earned it. I am trying my best to earn yours in return. Everyone hates us or fears us in these towns. You and I we are the same. If you will hold me up, I will lift you in return. We must stop fighting. That no longer matters because we have each other. You are the Master just like you wanted to be. I am yours and you are mine. If that is not love, then I don't know what love is." I smiled at him sweetly noticing the storm was gone in his blue skies. Not a typo there. I meant skies for his eyes.

Master Boyd leaned down and kissed me deeply. We returned to his bedroom and made love most aggressively enjoying each other's employment of the carnal art till very early in the morning. I no longer fought with him even when he requested darker sexual desires. My Master always made sure to return my sacrifices by making sure my own needs were met. He had learned the lessons of damage from enforcing of cruelty from Gothic Barbie well. Master Boyd always was empathetic during these all nighter sexual sessions by taking all proper precautions necessary to keep down any chance of significant damage that could be caused by hours of friction or stretching. He was mindful to assure as much comfort and safety as possible for me, so he did not end up breaking his plaything.

He made extra special efforts to assure any unusual sexual practices he wanted were carefully prepared for in advance of his taking them. While I still did not care for it, at least he was no longer ripping me apart. Masters get what they want, how they want it and that is just the way it goes. I could dislike it till the cows came home, it didn't change the fact that that is my life and too bad for me.

The next morning I had no choice but to head back to Cumberland to do the mountain of paperwork and court reporting from my Friday night escapades. Master Boyd was worn to a frazzle from his sexathon so he decided to sleep until his regular shift began that night. Dennis had asked us to Sunday dinner but that had been cancelled early that morning through a phone call from his wife Carla. She didn't say why the couple wanted to take a rain check, but I didn't ask my Master.

Reality was I was happy to be off the hook. Whatever Dennis wanted to chat about couldn't be something in either my Master or best interests. I recalled that he had warned me to stay away from Master Boyd on a few occasions. I was certain he was less than happy to see, despite his warnings, his two troublemakers had become a mating pair. If Master Boyd had his way, for life. Yikes!

I went by to visit my children and Seine for a bit. Maiden Mary was thrilled to hear I would be moving back home within the next two weeks. The kids and Seine jumped for joy as well at the news. I didn't say a word about my own heartbreak at not having the much-needed freedom from Master Boyd's tight control. There was nothing I could do about it. Master Sheryl was moving away and my five days a week sanctuary was going with her. All I could do is hope my constant running from county to county would keep me away from home often. My workdays were already more than ten hours long at least three days a week and sometimes twenty-four when the case calls were heavy.

I was driving through Wheatly when I decided to make a quick stop by the hospital to visit with Cindy Slater. I assumed she was likely still heavily sedated, but I just thought I would feel better knowing she was still safe and on her way to recovery. I pulled into the parking lot and noted the squad car parked out front. It appeared Cindy was a popular gal that fine Sunday. Everyone had decided to stop by to say hello.

I walked through the lobby headed for her room when I heard the voice of Dennis call out my name. I turned around to see him coming out of the men's room having just barely caught me before I disappeared into the patient's hallway wing.

"Yeah, Dennis, what are you up to? Breaking up bullies in the boy's room?" I snickered at my stupid joke.

Dennis chortled. "Okay, okay, enough. Can I speak to you privately for a moment if you are not too busy that is? I wouldn't want to keep you from work. It can wait if need be. I was hoping to catch you later today, but Randell and I are transporting Javier to state late this afternoon so that got called off." He rambled on appearing uncharacteristically nervous around me.

His strange behavior piqued my curiosity. "Sure Dennis, I have a second. Want to go outside maybe near my car? I believe if we are careful no one will be privy to our discussion there. What is this about?"

Dennis looked around to make sure no one heard him. "It is about Boyd. Yeah let's go outside and get some fresh air. You know it sure is odd talking to you in the lobby of the hospital instead of talking while you were strapped to a bed in one of the rooms." He chuckled as I rolled my eyes and started heading back outside for this most unexpected discussion.

Once we were safe at the Intrepid, Dennis looked around for eavesdroppers then spit on the ground appearing satisfied. "Alright, I am not going to beat about the bush, Psycho. Something about you and Boyd ain't adding up. I know damned well he has been sweet on you for years, and you knew it too. I told you to not fool around with him, and you asked me to call him off you. Now here you stand wearing my boy's ring and there are rumors about the two of you scraping in the parking lot then coming back all moon eyed for each other. I was going to stay out of it figuring it would fizzle out. But then it suddenly struck me you are not with the Bruiser woman anymore. So, I did some checking around. No one seems to be claiming you in town anymore except Boyd and I know that boy. He would do just about anything to have you for his own. Boyd he, well, he has problems. I don't really want to get into that right now. I guess what I am asking you outright is did Boyd do something he shouldn't have to get you as his own? Don't lie to me girl. You and him together all of a sudden isn't making any sense. Did he take that damned collar of yours?" Dennis stared right into my eyes looking to see if he could read my unit language.

I had not expected Dennis to consider the possibility since up until this moment he had appeared happy about Master Boyd and me being engaged. Dennis sure did have a fine poker face. I had not even suspected that he was suspicious about the sudden explosive love affair. I briefly considered confessing with the hopes that Dennis could somehow aid me to get Master Boyd to release me.

However, my long years of loyalty to my Keyholder, and strong delusional process stayed my tongue. I had never betrayed the collar and I was sure as hell not going to start now. Even if Master Boyd was an issue, I would get out of it sooner or later on my own. I was sure of it.

I looked up chuckling. "Oh shit Dennis, is that what this is about? Damn. Boyd holding my collar. Now that is a joke. That kitten couldn't make me do a fucking thing. I have a Keyholder up in Cumberland…you know her Sheryl Fressman?"

Dennis's eyes went wide. "Uhm, yeah I know her. Quite a firebrand. We've had our run ins over the years. So, if I called her, she would claim you for her own?" He wasn't buying it.

I smiled. "Let me get you her number Dennis. You can call her right now. She is the collar owner right now." I started to dig in my purse for a scrap of paper.

Dennis spit on the ground then began to rub his handlebar moustache. "Nah, that is okay Psycho. If you say she is the one I believe you. I will give you a bit of a warning though. Don't you ever discount Boyd as a kitten. If you are planning to marry my boy there are some things you need to know about him. Pushing his buttons sure ain't smart. Boyd has got a monster temper missy. I can't promise your safety if he were to be rubbed the wrong way. He also has some trouble with letting go when he comes up with an idea no matter how crazy it is. I assume he has told you about that business with that hill girl when he was knee high to a grasshopper?" He looked at me seeming genuinely concerned.

I nodded. "Yeah Dennis I know about Maddy. I know about the Snake Pit and I am very aware of his temper. I would wonder did you warn him about my violent history too?" I smiled while winking.

He chuckled. "Well you got me there, Psycho. I suppose it makes more sense than I care to admit. Both of you are madder than marsh hares. That is what scares me I suppose. Something isn't right with you two getting hitched. I feel it in my gut. It can't be good for either one of you. But your both adults. I can't stop you. I will ask you to remember I am around if that boy gets out of hand. You call me if needed. I know how to get Boyd to calm his ass down."

I laughed. "So do I Dennis. We have known each other a long time. Have a little faith in me will you? There isn't much I can't handle."

He frowned. "That is exactly what worries me. Psycho just be careful with Boyd. Now I will let you get back to work. We can talk more later. I have to go to the jail with Randell and haul that piece of shit Javier to turn over to State. They are deporting him tonight back to Mexico."

I grimaced. "Boyd said he will just be back on the next bus back. He won't stand trial for what he and the others did to Cindy, will he? That is a fucking shame. Poor Cindy won't get any justice. Guess no one cares about the girls they think are just whores." I looked at the ground.

Dennis smiled wickedly. "Oh this town does care about its ladies, even those girls of the night. You leave it to me. Cindy will get her justice this time. I will make sure of it. Have a great day, Psycho." He turned and went back to his squad car.

I watched him and Randell take off headed back to the jail. I returned to my task of visiting my little lost girl, Cindy.

Cindy was awake and bright eyed to my astonishment. She had come back from her place of regression and smiled as I walked in to visit. Her mother Eva was reading a romance novel to the bruised teen. Her face looked tired but relieved.

"Well what have we here. Ah, I apologize ladies. I didn't realize this is where the runway models hung out. I am looking for the Slater girls." I smiled appearing friendly.

Cindy snorted. "Gosh Psycho, stop it. I look a mess." She began to frantically primp her frizzy red locks.

I laughed. "Girl if this is you a mess, I couldn't stand it if you were perfect. I would just slink away like the toad I am knowing damned well I had no chance to be seen by anyone." I winked at her while she giggled.

Eva smile lovingly. She knew that Cindy was extremely prideful of her looks. I was making a girl who had just been treated like a pile of horseshit feel pretty for a moment. Each rape victim is different. You must know who she is before you open your dumb mouth and hurt someone already kicked into the dirt as low as they can be. Some want to be held. Some want to hide. Some want to feel pretty again. Some want to die. The key to helping a woman find her way back from the dark place a forced sexual act takes her is to find a way to give her back what was really taken, her dignity. For Cindy it was to know that those men didn't steal her beauty. She was still the most gorgeous girl in the world and to me she was. Only twenty-four hours after that horror she could smile. Now that is strength. I bow before her with mad respect. You go girl.

I asked Eva if Cindy and I might speak privately. The weary mother agreed and gave me a quick hug warning me that her girl was still quite fragile. She begged me to be easy. I smiled while nodding to let her know Cindy was safe with me. I would never harm that little girl, not even to save myself.

Once we were alone, I looked at the pretty red head. "I want to talk about what happened, darling? Feel strong enough? No hurry. You take your time. We could just bullshit about the weather if that is more your speed."

Cindy teared up a bit. "Nah, I am okay now Psycho. I need to tell you something. The cops won't listen to me. Maybe you can help?" She looked at me with a pleading eye.

I nodded. "Shoot darling. I am all ears. I can't promise I can do anything, but I can promise to try my damnest."

She smiled. "Yeah I know you will. Okay, Javier didn't do it Psycho. He is innocent. We were making out and working on these eight balls he bought. You know just hanging and taking it easy. Well, these four guys bust into the house. They had guns. They said Javier owed them money and they was going to kill him. Oh, Psycho I was so scared. Anyway, one of them asks him if I was his girl. He said I was. They told Javier they were going to take out what he owed by fucking me and then killing him slow. So, they dragged him to the closet, tied him up and locked him inside.

They took me, and well you know what they did. I thought they killed Javier. But I heard he was still alive. I heard he got out of his ropes and someone unlocked the door. He ran because he was scared the cops were the druggy dudes Psycho. He didn't do this, I swear it. Please tell those police Javier is innocent." She started to cry silently.

I looked at the floor. "Cindy are you sure this is not just because you love Javier? I mean are you certain he didn't sell you to those guys and that maybe he fooled you while planning to keep the cash for himself? Look I am not saying you are not a smart girl but Javier, he is a thug sweetie. Those fellows can mess up a girls mind." I winced hoping that Cindy wouldn't clam up now that I had pointed out a possible flaw in her story.

She shook her head. "Psycho, he was crying in that closet. I could hear him begging them to kill him and let me go. Please go ask the neighbors. I swear they had to hear him in there. Talk to Javier. He will tell you. Javier may be a skunk but he didn't do this, you have to believe me."

I looked at the grieving teen, "Okay Cindy. I will go ask around for your sake. You must promise me if I find out he did pull a bait and switch on you that you will accept it? I also want you to go without argument to the Girls Colony for forty-five days inpatient treatment. I think you and I both know it is time to get off the street. You have so much more to offer than that pretty face. Cindy. You deserve to be free. Are you always going to let that asshole keep his control over you? Are you ready to take back your power, girlfriend? Have you had enough of the pain or should I just cut you lose right now to go find your death on some filthy ass mattress for a couple of bucks?" I glared at her sternly.

She wrinkled up her face nodding. "Yeah, I am ready. I don't want that life anymore. You are right. I am tired of hurting, tired of the fear. I want my life back. I can't stand to see my momma crying. She thinks this is all her fault. It isn't. I did this to me. I got what I deserved."

I growled, "Stop that. No, you didn't Cindy. Look at me. You deserve to be treated with respect, love and kindness. No one has the right to hurt you. Not like that, not in any form. You did nothing wrong. I want you to remember this whenever you think this was your fault. You were tied down. Why was that? Because they were bullies. They had to subdue you or you would have killed them all. Honey, people like that hurt people because they think they can steal their power. But Cindy, your power was never taken. You never gave up the fight. They didn't win, baby girl. You remember that." I smiled at her with a knowing this is what she needed to hear.

She looked up stunned. "You are right, Psycho. I would have killed them all. They did have to tie me up. Bunch of pussies is all they were. I didn't think of that. Yeah, I am ready to kick my drugs and ready to see my momma smiling again. I want her to be proud of me like she used to be before I got all mixed up." She frowned.

I stood up and took her hand. "Cindy, I have news for you. Your mother is still proud of you. She is here. She was looking for you when you were missing. You are her greatest treasure and she wouldn't stop looking for that when it was stolen from her. What you need to do now is find that pride she has for you in yourself. Stop hating Cindy for things that were never her fault. Make peace and take back your future while you still have time to do it. I will be back on Tuesday to take you to Wells. I have them prepping a room just for you. Ah, you lucky girl. You are going to love it there. The food sucks, but Margaret makes up for it with her smile. If you need anything call the office and have them get to me. Rest. I am going to talk to Javier."

I started to head out when I heard Cindy say, "I bet your momma is sure proud of you, Psycho."

I laughed as I walked out of the room. "I sure as hell hope not. See you Tuesday."

I went to the jailhouse to request a visit with Javier. I was told Dennis and Randell had already transported him off to State only half an hour earlier. Cathy laughed and said I had just missed Master Boyd who had been sent back home when he was told his assistance wasn't required for this trip. Cathy began one of her many attempts to get me to banter when I head Dennis call in over the radio.

"Cathy, this is Dennis. We have a situation out here. The prisoner just went into cardiac arrest. We are going to need medical personnel. Out on route 28, pronto," his voice wafted through the airwaves.

Cathy grabbed the speaker. "Dennis is the prisoner conscious?"

Dennis called back. "Negative Cathy, he prisoner is now deceased. Get a fucking ambulance out here will you. I don't want his dead body stinking up the back seat. It is hotter than blazes out here. Tell them I want this trash gone pronto."

Cathy 10-4'd Dennis then called out the ambulance giving them the location of the squad car that now carried a dead Javier in the back cage. I looked at Cathy glumly. "You said they been gone just over thirty minutes huh?"

She nodded. "Well forty-five or so actually. Why?

I nodded. "Just wondering. Javier is twenty-one. Awful young for a heart attack, don't you think."

Cathy snorted. "No, that bastard loved his methamphetamine. Likely, his heart gave out from all those years of using that nasty shit."

I smiled while headed out the door. "Or from that heavy dose he just took while traveling down 28. Guess you had all better step up your strip search techniques around here."

Cathy yelled after me, "Psycho, that is stupid. How could he have gotten enough drugs in him going down the road to stop his heart with Dennis and Randell sitting right there watching."

I yelled back as the door shut, "Exactly Cathy. See you around."

I decided not to head back to the office in Cumberland just yet. I thought maybe Master Boyd could answer a few questions about the condition of Javier and what may have been found in that closet now that my alleged offender had been silenced, errrr, couldn't speak for himself anymore.

Do you think that Javier just had a heart attack or is there something else more sinister here?

To be continued in Book Nine of the
"27 Masters" series entitled
"Bugs in the Wall, Turkeys in the Ditch"

About the Author: Alexandria May Ausman

Alexandria May Ausman in her 16th year was diagnosed with Schizophrenia. She was quickly abandoned by her foster parents. While still only a teen, she was forced to battle this devastating illness alone.

Alexandria has struggled with lack of a support system, numerous psychotic episodes, exploitation, homelessness, and an uncaring mental health system.

Alexandria raised two healthy children. After obtaining her bachelor's degree in psychology she worked as a child abuse investigator and became a diagnostic psychologist while acquiring her Master's in psychology. Alexandria never forgot the experience of 'slipping through the cracks.' Her life's goal is to help people suffering abuse and/or mental illness have access to necessary services. By accident, she became a model of 'gothic attire' and the World Goth Queen.

She began writing a fictionalized account of her life experiences after a catastrophic return of psychotic symptoms. Today, Alexandria is retired, and homebound due to crippling symptoms of schizophrenia. She currently lives in Tallahassee, Florida, with her loving husband and loyal support dogs.